LISA SILVERTHORNE

TIMELESS

8 TIME TRAVEL ROMANCES

Timeless

8 TIME TRAVEL ROMANCES

LISA SILVERTHORNE

Table of Contents

Novels by Lisa Silverthorne

Standalones:

ISABEL'S TEARS

LANDFALL

PACIFIC BLUE TATTOO

BEAUTY: CAPTURED AND FRAMED

A Game of Lost Souls series:

THE CINDERELLA HOUR

THE PRINCE CHARMING HOUR

THE EVER AFTER HOUR

THE FALLEN HEARTS SEASON

THE RISING SPIRITS SEASON

THE ETERNAL SOULS SEASON

THE ROYAL WEDDING HOUR

THE HEAVENLY HONEYMOON HOUR

THE DIVINE NEWLYWEDS SHOW

THE CELESTIAL COUPLES SHOW

THE ENOCHIAN APOCALYPSE SHOW

The Spiral series:

BETWEEN

REPRISE

AVENGE

The Resurrectionist Papers

GRAVE RECKONING

Short Story Collections

THE SOUND OF ANGELS

THE MAGIC OF ORDINARY THINGS

Introduction

Borrowed time. Lost time. Out of time.
A turn of the clock hands. A twist of fate.
Will it be enough?
To save eight happily ever afters from the mists of time?

Time travel and romance, two concepts that always get my writer's heart pumping. It's one of the first things I pick up as a reader, too. Revisiting lost moments in time. Missed connections. Love that never was because of a tiny turn of the clock dial.

In the pages of this collection, turn the clock hands and discover those missed connections, those rekindled chance meetings, and those second chances to find the one person—across time—that makes your heart race and your soul ache. Love that has blossomed for lifetimes. Romance in the unlikeliest places. And soul mates separated by the twist of hands on a clock face.

Eight couples search for their happily ever afters through the mists of time and memory in **Timeless**.

A missed first date, a secret ritual on an odd holiday, a Victorian house hiding secrets, second chances with the clock stuck at three minutes until midnight, a Victorian portrait with a story to tell, a mysterious disappearance, tools out of time that lead to an Egyptian tomb, and finally…a Victorian artist and rare conjunction of time and space. Will our eight couples find their way back to the ones they love? Or does time win another day?

So, brew your favorite cup of tea, settle back in your favorite chair, and journey through time with me. Searching for love among its folds and creases. Eight, time travel romances that include three brand-new stories.

Lisa Silverthorne
July 22, 2023
Las Vegas, Nevada

Love's Leap

I didn't know people celebrated Leap Year. I thought it was just a way to keep the calendar on track. Until I met Leap Day revelers at Washington State's Roche Harbor on San Juan Island. It was just after my girlfriend, Sarah dumped me for another guy. That night at Roche Harbor changed my life forever.

Just before midnight on February 29th, I took a walk around the century-old hotel, winter being a slow season. Crisp, cold night so quiet and still as the distant sound of boats undulating against the docks carried above the wash of waves against the rocky shore. The sky was so dark and vivid with stars, old brick walkway rasping against my boots. I could almost hear the whisper of time in those century-old bricks.

Everything felt so electric and alive, charged—like I could reach out through time and touch the world from a century ago.

The wind coming off the harbor was cold, smelling of brine, scent of roasting salmon wafting from the nearby restaurant. The chill cut through my parka, blue sweater, and jeans, wind slicing through my dark hair and blowing it off my face as I walked around the white picket garden fence. The gardens were fallow this time of year.

Somehow, the hibernating garden with its brown stubs of rose bushes, skeletal maple trees, and bare clematis vines older than my grandparents comforted me. Made me feel like I just needed to walk through the pain to the other side. If I could find it. Sarah said that even when I was there, I wasn't. She wanted someone who ached to be with her—something I'd never felt before. After that, all I wanted to do was lay in bed and sleep, but an ER doctor didn't have that luxury. After a couple of weeks, I decided to take vacation time, leave my Seattle apartment, and take the ferry up to the San Juan Islands. Get my head on straight.

For my patients, if no one else.

Black wrought iron streetlamps illuminated the brick walkway in front of Hotel de Haro with eerie brilliance. The stark white, century-old hotel took on an almost dream-like feel in the misty yellow lamplight.

I heard whispers in the indigo darkness just beyond the streetlamps. Followed by laughter. And glow sticks in yellow and blue.

Not sure why, but I walked toward them. I felt safe.

At six feet tall, I was a little lanky, but I didn't look like an easy mark. Dressed casually, I didn't look like someone carrying wads of cash, either. Student loans still got most of my income these days.

A woman and two men stood shadowed on the brick walkway. They were in costumes. The woman with brown hair dyed blue on the ends wore an indigo hoop skirt. A tall man, had to be six foot four, with dark hair and a beard, was dressed as a wild west sheriff. He wore a tan leather vest with a gold star badge that read sheriff, black string tie, white shirt, dark pants, and cowboy boots. The shorter, stocky man, clean-shaven, wore a Union Civil War uniform.

They all got quiet as I stopped beside them.

"Is there a costume party tonight?" I asked.

The resort had activities, but I hadn't seen anything about a costume party.

They looked at each other and shrugged. The woman smiled at me and motioned me toward her. I took a step or two closer and she spoke in a quiet voice.

"We're about to celebrate Leap Year," she said.

I frowned, glancing at the two men who looked embarrassed,

avoiding my gaze.

"How do you celebrate Leap Year?" I asked, trying to keep my voice down.

Her mouth fell open. "You mean, you don't know?" She poked the tall sheriff. "He doesn't know."

The three of them laughed, the tension breaking a little. A little. I was still confused. The two men didn't speak, but the woman held up an old book. Its pages were yellowed, spine of the red leather book cracked. White lettering, a little faded, read, "A History of the Antebellum Era, 1812-1861."

The sheriff held out an old yellowed newspaper from Tombstone, Arizona about the fight at O.K. Corral. And the man dressed as a Union soldier held up an old tintype with white lettering that read, Battle at Gettysburg, July 3, 1863.

I shook my head. "Is this a book club or something?"

All three laughed at me again and I started to feel uncomfortable.

"Well, I'll leave you to it then," I said. "Have a good evening."

"Wait!" the woman cried, holding up her hand, smiling at me.

She reached into a tote bag behind her and pulled out more old books. She scanned their titles and handed me one of them.

Under the thin yellow lamplight, the blue cloth book looked worn, yellowed pages thick and edges crisp. The title in gold lettering read, *Greyfell* by Archibald Bell.

I squinted at the book and then glanced back at the woman.

"What's this for?" I asked.

"It's a first edition," she said, motioning at the book. "Printed in 1848 in London, England. It's a pseudonym for a female writer." She smiled at me again, a shyness coming over her. "You seem like a romantic. Who's lost someone."

Her instincts were good, but I didn't understand why she handed me this book. It made no sense. I'd read it in an undergrad lit class. The author, Aria Blythe, was a gifted young writer who published two ground-breaking novels but died young of tuberculosis. At twenty-eight, she barely saw her first book's publication before succumbing to the disease.

I held up the book and smiled politely. "What makes you say that?"

"Because people usually come here for two reasons," said the woman. "To get married or to get over heartache. Sometimes, it's both. Come, celebrate Leap Day with us and give it a go. It's only one day, right?"

I had no idea how anyone celebrated Leap Day, especially with really old books and newspapers, but I was lonely and filled with heartache.

Why not celebrate instead of mourn?

I nodded at her finally. "Okay, I've never celebrated Leap Day before, so I'll join you. Like you said. It's just one day, right?"

She laughed, a nervous sound, as the sheriff handed me some blue glow sticks.

"Do I need a costume?" I asked.

The Civil War soldier shook his head, dark curls settling around his face. "Not the first time."

"This place teems with magic," said the woman, "and with all its history and Ley lines, it's the perfect place to celebrate. Our way anyway."

"Ten seconds to midnight," said the sheriff.

"What do I do?" I asked.

"Just hold onto that book," she said and closed her eyes, clutching her book to her chest. "Don't lose the book. Keep it close or your celebration will end early."

"Five seconds…"

I nodded, gripping the book. I slid the glow sticks into my pocket and listened to the sheriff count off the last seconds.

"Have a good leap," the woman said to me. "See you in March!"

"What leap? And what do you mean, March?"

A tremor of fear shot through me.

When the sheriff hit zero, the resort and brick walkway began to fade around me. I tried to shout, but I was falling.

Cold, wet grass clung to my face, my jeans damp against the sharp, cold wind rushing past. The air smelled crisp and clean, the grass sweet with heather and clover. The ground was hard and bumpy, tall grass whipping against my face, but I couldn't open my eyes because everything spun around me. I laid my forehead against the cold ground, my head throbbing.

Something poked my black parka. A stick?

A giggle lilted against the wind, a soft soprano sound that hung in the air like delicate chimes.

"Is it a what or a who, sister?"

The other voice sounded lower. Flatter.

Another melodic giggle echoed in the wind, sweet and warm with life. Enchanting.

The sound ached through me and I desperately wanted to see who had uttered it. Had she just spoken in a British accent? Where the hell was I? This wasn't Roche Harbor.

"Definitely, a *who*, sister," said the captivating soprano voice.

Filled with wonder and intrigue. Sunlight.

At last, the spinning stopped. I opened my eyes, head still hurting, and stared up into the oval face of a thin young woman, alabaster pale, with blue eyes that shone violet in the thin sunlight penetrating the grey sky and mist. All around us, tall grasses fanned across rolling, endless plains.

She smiled at me, holding a stick, and I lost my ability to speak. I could only stare into her beautiful violet eyes, haunted by her playful smile. And her soothing crystalline voice.

"What manner of man lies so exposed in the Yorkshire moors at dawn?" asked the almost stern voice behind the woman with the violet eyes. "Is it from drink? A drunkard, perhaps?"

The violet-eyed woman, her hair in light brown ringlets around her face, smiled and bent toward me, smelling like the roses and lilacs from my mother's garden. She wore a black wool coat over a long tan dress that had a ballooned skirt, almost like the woman at the resort, not quite so wide. She smiled at me as I lifted my chin, but then her expression changed, delicate shadowed lines across her porcelain face. It was concern.

The shadows beneath her eyes gave her a pale cast. It brought out the doctor in me. She looked bony. Frail. Ill.

"No, sister," she said, her gaze still on me. "I think perhaps he has been waylaid or had some other misfortune. His face is far too fair, his eyes far too kind."

She reached out with long, delicate fingers to touch my face. Her touch burned through me, so gentle and concerned.

"And such a nasty bump on the head," she said, still bending toward me. "Can you walk, gentle sir?"

Gentle sir? Where the hell was I?

"Yes, I think so."

I struggled to sit up and then stand.

She giggled again, a hand covering her mouth as the giggle changed to a deep cough that shook her entire body.

"Why are you laughing?" I asked.

Behind her stood another pale young woman, but not so frail, in a dark green dress with the same style of wide skirt. She had dark hair and hard blue eyes, looking older and stern.

And fearful.

The younger woman pointed at my parka.

"That ridiculous overcoat," she said with a laugh that ended in another cough. "It's—ghastly."

"But it's warm," I said with a laugh.

Her mouth fell open and she bent down, plucking something out of the grass. One of the blue glow sticks had fallen out of my pocket. Her eyes widened, staring at it like she'd seen a shooting star.

"What is this—this candle that is not lit and does not burn, but gives off light? And no heat!"

She turned it over in her bare hands, eyes wide, her long, delicate fingers tracing over the smooth surface.

"It's called a glow stick," I said in a quiet voice.

"It is like magic," the violet-eyed woman said, holding it up to her face.

"Keep it if you like," I said, smiling at her childlike wonder.

God, she was charming. A word I'd never used before, but it suited her.

"He is an American," said the other woman, like it was a disease.

The violet-eyed young woman curtsied and watched me with

bright eyes and a shy smile.

"Well met, my new American friend. I am Miss Aria Blythe and this is my older sister, Miss Emma Blythe."

"This is most improper, sister," said Emma, glaring at me like I was something she'd scraped off her shoe. "We have no chaperone and he does not even have a proper hat. And what would Sir Hayden say if he were to call upon you this day, sister?"

"Sir Hayden may think whatever he likes," Aria snapped, her gaze fiery. "Despite what Father wants, I will not be betrothed to that man. He despises the pen and I will not put mine down. Not for him. Not for anyone."

"Sister!"

Aria crossed her arms against her black wool coat. "You heard me. Sister."

I knew nothing about Victorian manners or this Sir Hayden, so I just bowed and hoped I wouldn't make Americans look even worse to Aria's sister.

Then Aria extended her hand to me.

"Aria, no!" Her sister cried, but Aria ignored her.

Surprised, I hesitated, but then gently gripped her bare hand and shook it.

The connection felt electric and all I could do was stare into her violet eyes as she smiled at me. Like I was an old and dear friend she hadn't seen in months.

"I'm Doctor Braxtan Chambers and believe me, the pleasure is all mine, Miss Blythe. And I think the pen is mightier than the sword, too."

"A doctor who appreciates literature! You surprise me, sir."

She let go of my hand, but her gaze fell to the book in my hand. Her oval face lit with excitement.

"Sister! He carries Greyfell!"

I held it up. It was brand new! Blue cloth cover was pristine, gold lettering sharp, ivory pages unmarred. No threadbare edges, no yellowed pages. I could only stare at it as I opened it to the copyright page.

A first printing. February 29, 1848.

Another leap year! Was that how this worked? Leaping from one leap year to another? It still made no sense to me.

A cold wind from the moors rushed over me, chilling me to the bone, making my head pound harder. Had I really leaped into the past by carrying this book to its leap-day publication? I couldn't process this. It was unscientific and technologically impossible to just leap backward in time holding an old book and standing in a place of *supposed magic* like Roche Harbor's gardens. I didn't believe in magic—or much of anything right now—but here I stood in Victorian England.

I glanced up at the grey sky, listening for the buzz of a plane or *whup whup* of a helicopter. It was just birdsong. And the whistle of wind. No sound of a car engine or tires hissing across asphalt. Not a single mechanical sound in this whole unsettling quiet.

Was I really standing in 1848 England? On February 29th?

"Have you read it? What did you think of the book? Did you like it?" Aria asked, firing questions at me, watching me with intensity, eyes wide as she stepped closer.

Then it clicked in my throbbing head. This was *the* Aria Blythe who wrote this book using the pen name Archibald Bell. I had no idea how vibrant and beautiful she was. Or how sick she'd been with consumption while writing her second—and last—novel.

I'd treated patients in the Philippines with latent and active tuberculosis infections when I volunteered with Doctors Without Borders, enough to recognize the signs of an active infection. I'd even taken the vaccine. In 1848, consumption was still rampant, wiping out whole families. Decimating towns and villages. They called it the White Death because of the pale cast of its victims and Robber of Youth because it killed so many young people in their prime.

People like Aria Blythe. It made my heart ache.

"A masterful first novel," I announced as I slid the book into my coat pocket. "I look forward to reading Mr. Bell's next book. He has an extraordinary grasp of the plight of women today, wouldn't you say? Miss Blythe."

A grin lit her face and her eyes burned with life, eclipsing the dark circles and pale cast of her skin. Already, she had some mottling on her skin, characteristic of collapsed capillaries.

"Yes, I would quite agree," she said, "Doctor Chambers."

I stepped closer, trying to ignore the pain in my head.

"I think that people will still be reading this book in a century or so."

Her eyes widened. "You think so? Like Byron? And Keats? And Shelley?"

"I do," I said, unable to look away from her face, her passion intoxicating.

My vision was fuzzy, but I blinked it away.

"Please, call me Braxtan."

Those expressive violet eyes burned through me until I could barely speak.

"Please call me Aria," she said, her gaze locked with mine.

"Aria!" Her sister, Emma, stepped between us. "You, sir, are much too familiar with my sister!" She shook her gloved hand at me. "Please keep your distance."

"I meant no disrespect," I said, holding up my hands and taking a step back.

"Emma, please," said Aria, still watching me. "It is all right. I do not mind."

"You know nothing about this man," Emma snapped. "This—American." She almost spat out the word. "He could have cholera, Aria—or worse. And you are not well."

The pounding in my head intensified. I reached up to my forehead, the knot throbbing as the tall grass began to rise, the moors spinning around me. Aria's concerned gaze was the last thing I carried into unconsciousness.

Something cold pressed against my head. A fire crackled and popped nearby. I opened one eye, seeing the blazing fire dance across firewood in a stone hearth and the walnut posts of a bed. A heavy walnut armoire stood against a burgundy wall beside a matching chest of drawers. A wash basin and bowl edged gold and covered in blue roses stood on top of the chest of drawers.

"There you are," said the bright, melodic voice.

My heart jolted as I turned my throbbing head to the right.

Aria sat in a wooden chair beside the bed, a wet cloth in her hand. My parka and clothes were draped over a chair, my boots underneath it. The blue book peeked out of the pocket and I sighed in relief.

Someone had dressed me in a long, white linen shirt.

"Where am I?" I asked in a softer voice than I'd expected as she pressed the cold cloth against the knot on my forehead.

I tried to sit up. Nausea shot through me. Defeated, I laid my head back against a cool feather pillow, the white cotton bed linens soft and smelling like soap and rainwater.

"My father and a stable hand collected you in a wagon and we brought you to the house." She leaned over me, her eyes watery, pupils dilated. "How do you feel?"

Weak and nauseated. I laid my hand on hers, squeezing.

"Much better. Thank you for your kindness. And I can't wait for your next novel."

She gasped and drew back her hand. "How did you know?"

I touched two fingers to my mouth. "Your secret's safe with me," I whispered.

The thump of heavy footsteps against hardwood drew my attention.

Aria sat up straight in the chair as a man with bushy grey hair and rough features entered the room. He wore a pressed white shirt, black coat, and black pants. Beside him stood a taller black-haired man, wearing a dark suit and long coat. The taller man glared at Aria and then at me as I forced myself to sit up.

Had to be this Sir Hayden that Aria mentioned.

He looked like a tool with his long horse face, beady brown eyes, and mutton-chop sideburns. I glanced over at Aria, at the apprehension in her eyes as she pushed herself back into the chair, as if trying to get away from this man. It was obvious that she despised him.

"Miss Blythe," he snapped a bow to her but turned his angry dark gaze on me. "You must be exhausted," he said, snapping on leather gloves. "Caring for this drunken American lout. Allow me to take him to London Hospital." He chuckled. "Or perhaps the Foundling Hospital would take this—American."

I started to speak, tired of being insulted, but Aria stood up from the chair.

"You assume much, Sir Hayden. This American was injured. He is no drunkard. He is a doctor, if you must know, and he required our care. Which was the moral thing to do, sir."

Hayden's gaze darkened, his mouth pressing into a flat, angry line.

"Aria! Watch your tone." the other man snapped. Her father, I realized. "Sir Hayden has come to call upon you. He still seeks an answer to his proposal."

Aria put her hands on her hips, tan dress flouncing around her, fabric swishing. Her face flushed despite her pale, sickly cast.

"His offer is appreciated, but I must decline his advances."

"Aria!" Her father shouted.

Hayden moved toward Aria, towering over her slight frame. She held her ground despite the fear in her eyes. He pulled back his hand to strike her.

It was too much for me.

I threw myself out of the bed in front of her and grabbed his arm in mid-swing. I shoved Hayden backward.

"If you even graze her with your pinky, I'll bury you," I said, barely holding onto my rage. I wanted to rip his damned throat out. "Get out of the lady's face. Now."

He gritted his teeth and pointed a finger at me. "You American filth! You dare touch a nobleman? I'll see you in chains!"

I felt Aria grab hold of my waist with both hands. Hiding behind me.

"In your dreams!" I laughed. "Nothing noble about hitting a lady, asshole. And last time I looked, we, American filth kicked your noble asses. Hard. All the way back across the pond. So, keep your royal elitist bullshit to yourself and leave Aria alone. She's not property. She's a bright light full of talent, something you'll never understand, Hayden. Now, get out."

Hayden glared at me and snapped off his glove. He slapped my cheek with it.

"Apologize or duel, your choice," said Hayden, putting his glove back on. "American."

"Rot in hell," I snapped.

"Then we duel," he said with a leering grin. "Pistols. Behind the Blythe house. In two hours." He turned away and walked toward the doorway, but paused. "I must warn you…I never miss."

"You done with the bravado yet? Because I'm not impressed. But I'll be there."

Hayden stormed down the hallway and slammed the door.

Aria turned me around and grabbed hold of my chin. "He is a marksman, Braxtan! A deadly shot. You must not face him. He will kill you!"

I laid my hand against her cheek and leaned toward her.

"And if you're forced to marry that monster, he will kill you. I can't let that happen. If that means facing him in a duel, then that's what I'll do."

Aria's father moved toward me. He laid a gentle hand on my arm and I turned to face him. There was concern on his face, his gaze softening.

"Son, I appreciate you standing up for my headstrong daughter, but that man has a lot of power and sway. He can and will make our lives miserable long after you have returned home to America."

My gut twisted. I had no idea how long my stay in Victorian England would last. If it only lasted until March 1st, then her father had a point. Hayden could do anything to her after I'd gone.

"I guess I'd better aim for his heart," I said to him. "If he had one. I'll aim for a headshot then. His ego."

Aria stepped beside her father, her eyes glassy, a cough rattling through her chest.

"I barely know you, Braxtan Chambers, and yet, here you stand, ready to risk your life to protect me. Why?"

That was a damned good question.

There was something so vibrant and alive about Aria Blythe. Something I never realized I'd lost until I saw it in her eyes out in the Yorkshire moors. Sarah was right. Somewhere between college and med school and the ER, I'd lost that passion. That part of my soul that was willing to fight my way to a goal or a life that was more than an existence. More than a series of routines that went on day after day until I became an automaton trying to please everyone but me.

Until this moment.

And here in front of me was this beautiful, passionate soul pouring every last moment, every remaining breath into sharing her heart with the world one last time. In her second novel. And both would still be read a century and a half later. A bright light quickly burnt out, but her passion would burn white-hot on the page and touch generations of people.

I took her hand in mine. "Aria, you are the most alive soul I have ever met. Your passion, your light burns so hot and I just can't let that tool destroy you. You've made me see exactly what I've been missing all these years. My passion. My drive. And the hope of sharing that with someone like you. I am infatuated with you, Aria Blythe, and I'd do anything to protect you."

She stared into my eyes as if she could see into my soul. I didn't pull away this time.

"There is something special about you, Braxtan Chambers," she said in a soft voice, gripping my hand. "Something I want to discover about you in great detail."

Aria's father tugged on my sleeve. "Get dressed, young man," he said and pointed toward the dim hallway, flicker of oil lamps dancing against the bright hearth fire. "If you are hellbent on facing Sir Hayden and championing my Aria, then I had better teach you to shoot a dueling pistol."

After I'd dressed in my jeans, sweater, and black parka, Aria's father, Parlan Blythe, took me out behind the brown brick, saltbox house and taught me how to aim and shoot a flintlock pistol, something I'd never touched before. And I wondered if people died in these leaps. If I'd known what those revelers meant by celebrating Leap Day, I would have asked more questions.

Maybe I'm just asleep in my hotel room, dreaming all of this after too much scotch?

Aria and Emma, woolen coats on, walked outside as a black carriage pulled up to the house. Aria looked pale and worried, chewing on her bottom lip. Her eyes looked weak, fever-bright. She held her hand over her mouth and coughed hard.

Hayden strutted around the edge of the house in a long black coat, white shirt, black pants, and tall black riding boots. Two men walked behind him. The light-haired man wore a brown overcoat and trousers and carried a polished mahogany case. The other man, with warm brown hair, wore a long tan coat and brown trousers.

"You showed," said Hayden with a chuckle. "I thought perhaps you had turned tail and toddled off to a ship bound for the Americas."

I took a step toward him. "Not in this lifetime. I'm not afraid of you, Hayden, so shut up and get on with it."

"I am impressed, American," he said, still leaning on that word like it was garbage. "I will almost regret killing you. Almost."

He snapped his fingers and the light-haired man stepped over to him and opened the case. Hayden reached into the red velvet lining and pulled out a polished wood and silver flintlock pistol. The light-haired man swiveled around and turned the case toward me.

I took the remaining flintlock.

Hayden turned his back to me. "Walk thirteen paces and turn. When the handkerchief drops, fire. Go."

Whelp, so much for my Hippocratic oath.

I walked ahead thirteen paces and turned my body sideways. Raising the pistol. Aiming at Hayden—and his big fat ego. I wouldn't give him an easy shot.

My stomach twisted into knots as I waited for the man in the tan overcoat to drop the handkerchief.

The man lifted a white handkerchief over his head. Waved it once Twice.

And dropped it.

I pressed the trigger and fired.

It kicked like a mule, the bang deafening, smoke rising. Smell of gunpowder stung my nose as something slammed into my left side. Knocking me to my knees.

"Braxtan!" Aria cried.

Hayden grinned, his pistol smoking. The red stain on his shirt startled him as he reached up to his right shoulder, the black fabric smoking.

She rushed to me.

Hayden's entourage rushed toward him as he hunched forward, clutching his shoulder.

She threw her arms around me, searching for the pistol wound. She pushed my parka off my shoulders and reached toward my sweater. Finding a large bruise.

I reached into the left pocket of my parka and pulled out the book. With a lead ball embedded in the center of the book's back cover.

"Your book just saved my life, Aria," I said with a laugh, watching her grin.

"I am so relieved," she cried, pulling me close, holding onto me as she began to tremble. "I was terrified he would kill you."

I brushed a light brown curl out of her eyes and laid my hand against her face. Wanting desperately to kiss her.

She began to cough. Hard wracking coughs. I held her, rubbing her back until they subsided and she let me go.

I stood up, holding out the pistol.

"So, do we go again or what, Hayden?" I asked, trying to ignore my physician's instinct to go and treat his wound.

"I—concede," Hayden groaned.

I let the pistol drop to my side. I handed it off to the man in the tan long-coat and trotted over to Hayden.

"Let me see," I said, pushing his coat off his shoulder as he dropped to his knees, falling against the other man who anchored Hayden against him.

I pulled back his white shirt. The lead ball was embedded into the right shoulder, missing bone. And fortunately for him, it missed both brachial and subclavian arteries. He wasn't going to bleed out or need a bone set, but there was probably some nerve damage.

"Get him inside," I said. "I need to scrub up and find something to take out that lead."

It was evening by the time I had boiled water in the Blythe family's large plaster-walled kitchen painted a soft blue. It smelled like onions and ammonia. The black cast-iron stove was built into the wall with a large black stovepipe. I poured the boiling kettle water into a metal pan to soak a sharp knife and tweezer-like tongs.

Beside the stove stood a cabinet made of oak like the floors, a big metal pan on top. For washing dishes, I realized. I filled it with hot water. When it cooled, I washed my hands with soap, scrubbing hard. I carried the sterilized knife into the burgundy-walled drawing room where Hayden lay on a green velvet sofa.

It took only minutes to remove the lead ball and clean the wound. Then I bandaged his shoulder with clean strips of cotton and sent him into the care of his men.

When the carriage rattled away, Aria rushed at me, throwing her arms around me.

"You have freed me, Braxtan Chambers!" she cried, hugging me hard.

I put my arms around her and held her tight, wanting to protect her. What was the matter with me? I was falling for this woman.

"And you have saved me," I said in a hoarse whisper.

She slid her arms back, staring at me with watery, quizzical eyes.

"Saved you?" she asked in a quiet voice.

"You've made me feel again. Cutting through layers of numbness I didn't even know existed." I sighed, bowing my head. "Finding my heart again."

She reached up and stroked her hand against my face. The heat of her skin burned through me.

"You are so kind, Braxtan. So direct. Propriety be damned."

Another wracking cough vibrated through her thin, pale frame. She doubled over and I caught her before she collapsed. Her chest heaved as she struggled for breath. The mottling on her skin was brighter now in the dim light of the oil lamps.

"Aria, talk to me," I said, trying to gauge her awareness.

I pressed two fingers to her wrist, checking her pulse. Thready and rapid.

"Aria," I repeated, searching for her radial pulse between wrist and thumb. So faint. I pressed the back of my hand against her forehead. She was burning hot.

She moaned, blood at the corner of her mouth. She was becoming septic.

"Braxtan," she called. "I cannot see you…where are you?"

She needed antibiotics. Isoniazid or rifampin. Soon. Or she would die. But how? There was no such thing in 1848—anywhere! Dammit!

The book.

That woman at Roche Harbor told me to keep the book close. If I moved away from it, would it return me to the resort? With Aria in my arms? Or did I have to wait hours until midnight? For March 1st?

Aria wouldn't last that long. But I had to try.

I slid the book out of my pocket, lead ball still embedded against the back cover. I threw it as hard as I could down the hallway.

It thunked hard against the hardwood floor as I wrapped my arms tighter around Aria.

I stared at the drawing room with its curved and elaborate green velvet couches and marble-top tables, oil lamps guttering. Giving the room an almost dream-like quality.

It began to turn, the light and the furniture swirling into a dark vortex. Spinning into darkness.

And I was falling.

It felt like forever until I opened my eyes.

I was sprawled across the dark bricks of Roche Harbor. Alone.

Aria!

My eyes stung with moisture. I tried to turn my head, but it sent shooting pain through my neck and side, nausea rising until I laid my head back down.

That's when I felt vibrations against the bricks. Footfalls. Moving toward me.

I forced my eyes open.

"Aria?" I called.

A man dropped down beside me. Blue jacket said the paramedic.

"Stay with me now and we'll get you to the Anacortes hospital."

"Aria?" I called. "Aria!"

"Take it easy," he said as I felt someone else beside me. "We're going to slide this transport board underneath you now."

From somewhere off in the distance, I heard a *whup, whup* sound. A helicopter. Landing nearby.

But their voices were fading as I felt myself blacking out again.

I came to in an emergency room in Anacortes. Glass rooms with blue curtains lined the blue walls. Being on the patient side of the E.R. felt so strange to me. The bright light burned my eyes, but all I could think about was Aria Blythe. Back in her time. Lying on the drawing-room floor. Dying. My heart ached now and I felt sick inside.

Why couldn't I have saved her? Why!

I wanted to scream and punch the walls, but I could barely lift my head.

A short blond nurse in burgundy scrubs walked into the glass cube that smelled like germicide and dried blood. She carried a silver clipboard in her left arm.

"How do you feel, Doctor Chambers?"

"Like my head exploded. Can you cut me loose now?"

She laughed. "Soon. When we get your lab results back and I know you're not going to pass out again. Doctors make the worst patients."

She was right about that, but all I could think about was Aria. My chest hurt. My heart ached. I sighed as the nurse started to leave the room.

She stopped, turning around.

"Oh—your friend's going to be fine, too," she said.

I frowned. "What friend?"

"The young woman with you. We've got her in isolation. She's stable."

Aria!

I threw myself out of the bed, the aqua hospital gown hanging on me.

"Take me to her. Please!"

She grabbed a wheelchair and I sat down. She wheeled me out of ER and into a crowded back hallway to an elevator, up two floors to a door with a card-swipe. She swiped through onto the isolation ward. She handed me a surgical mask and I slid it on as she wheeled me into a pale green observation room.

Aria lay in the bed, wide-eyed, staring at the IVs in her arm, at the room, and the strange faces she didn't recognize.

"Braxtan!" she called when she saw me.

I pulled myself out of the wheelchair and dropped down beside her on the bed.

Aria struggled to sit up, so deathly pale, and put her frail arms around me.

"Aria!" I cried, my voice breaking. "I thought I'd lost you."

I held her close, feeling my eyes well up. With tears. I bit my lip, trying to hold them in, but couldn't.

She shook her head, reaching up to cup my face. "I was lost. Until I found you in the moors. On Leap Day."

Through my mask, I kissed her. It was the best I could do until she was well.

"And it was the best leap of my life, Aria," I said.

I held her in my arms, knowing there were lots of hurdles ahead. Healing her illness. Teaching her about the modern world. Supporting her writing. And there would be other leap years when she got homesick for her sister and father and I would show her the way across time. To her home again.

But one thing I knew for certain. In her arms, I was at last home.

Christmas, Interrupted

Something didn't feel right about the new apartment. From the first day Mallory Winter moved into the hundred-year-old house, she felt uncomfortable and anxious, like something was pushing her or she was late for something. It was only her second week back home in Friday Harbor, but she still felt uneasy. And, at times, like an intruder.

The white gingerbread house looked like a fairy tale with its white picket fence, stepping stones, and English roses. After three years of living on the mainland, she was glad to come home to San Juan Island. The furnished, upstairs apartment seemed perfect with its full kitchen, two bedrooms, and big bathroom. At first.

It had been a rough year. First, the breakup with Ben and then months of friends trying to fix her up. Blind dates, a friend of a friend, her best friend's cousin's best friend—she'd lost count of all the failed dates. She tried, she really did, but none of them clicked. One didn't even show up. And none had the spark she craved.

Then her sisters moved away to find jobs—Portland, Seattle, and Spokane, leaving her alone in the area (both parents were gone now). Even she'd moved to the mainland for a job. And got laid off. Right now, she felt a little lost and a lot lonely. December was officially the worst month ever.

Mallory sank back on the brown leather couch, her mind racing. She needed to find a new job. She glanced around the still unfamiliar apartment, wondering if the previous tenant had lost their job, too. It looked like someone had just walked out and left their life behind.

Dust outlined empty spots on the walls where pictures had hung. Rings imprinted the beige area rug where furniture had been. Pens and papers were scattered across the Moroccan-style desk, along with a year-old grocery flyer and a DVD of *It's a Wonderful Life* (one of her favorite movies). A six-pack of Pyramid ale and two Coke cans had been left in the refrigerator and a can of shaving gel, a bottle of aftershave, and a disposable razor were left in the medicine cabinet. A grey flannel shirt had been left hanging behind the bathroom door.

The apartment had a quirky, old beach cottage feel to it, with its antique chairs and hand-painted tables in cool blues and pale greens. The art deco lamps of nymph-like women holding frosted globes of light were charming against the clusters of glass floats and lanterns strung across the soft blue walls. She hadn't expected glow-in-the-dark paint on the ceilings that splashed stars and galaxies across the darkness.

The space almost felt magical, except sometimes, out of the corner of her eye, she saw movement. A shadow. A shimmer. A brush of cold air. Like someone had just walked past. Several times, she'd smelled the faint scents of cedar and sandalwood, like someone had just slapped on the aftershave in the bathroom.

Something rustled behind her. She turned.

Two newspapers lay on the desk, pages fluttering as a burst of cold air ached through the room. The chill hurt, turning her arms to goose flesh as she stared at the newspaper. She'd bought one this morning, but it was still in her backpack.

Shivering, Mallory saw the blue curtains billowing. The window was open.

Her UGGs squeaked across the honey-colored hardwood as she closed the window. She hurried past the leather sofa and hand-painted coffee table to the desk, fingertips like ice, and picked up the newspaper. The *Seattle Times*.

The headline read *Friday Harbor Man Fatally Shot*. The *San Juan*

Islander lay beneath it, front page headline glaring back at her, *Local Woman Arrested in Christmas Day Slaying*. The photo of a gorgeous young man stared back at her.

Her heart dropped—Rowan Brophy.

The caption read, *Twenty-seven-year-old local, Rowan Brophy, was shot to death on Second Street around 6:30 P.M. on December 25, 2012.*

Her eyes welled with tears. No wonder he hadn't shown up for coffee last December.

She had such a crush on him in high school. Last year, a friend reconnected them. They'd exchanged texts, agreeing to meet. She just thought he stood her up. She had no idea he'd been murdered.

Her stomach twisted into a knot, hands shaking as she read the details. She couldn't stop staring at Rowan's photo. Large, wide-set blue eyes that looked right into her soul. Sandy blond hair and sweet smile that went right through her. He'd always been so funny and so kind in school, quick to help anyone with anything—homework, moving, a ride home after too much beer. It was so unfair.

She read both articles, sickened when she saw classmate, Lindsey Tull's mug shot. The woman stalked him for nearly a year, leaving dozens of messages every day on his phone, showing up at his shop, at his house, and outside his store. The restraining order had only kept her at a distance.

Two gunshots thundered through the apartment. All the lights flashed.

Mallory screamed, dropping to the floor.

Footsteps pounded up the stairs and someone knocked on the door.

Heart racing, Mallory got to her feet. She straightened her lavender sweater and opened the door.

Her landlord, Strother Kittering, stood in the doorway, brow furrowed, thin white hair disheveled. He was tall and stocky with wide-set, clear blue eyes. He and his wife, Stella, lived below.

"Mallory?" he asked, glancing past her into the apartment. "Are you all right? I heard you scream."

She nodded, still out of breath. "Didn't you hear those loud bangs?" she asked.

He shook his head, frowning at her.

"Must have been a car backfiring or something."

Had she somehow imagined it? This apartment was starting to unnerve her.

One of the newspapers tumbled across the hardwood, wrapping around Strother's leg. He picked it up, his face turning white.

"Where'd you get this?" he demanded.

Mallory pointed behind her. "It was on the desk. The previous tenant must have left it."

He shook his head, his lips turning pale. "That's impossible."

"Why do you say that?" Mallory asked.

His eyes turned watery. "My grandson was the last tenant. He was murdered in front of his shop last Christmas."

Mallory gasped and took the paper out of Strother's hand.

"You're Rowan's grandfather?"

Strother nodded.

Rowan was gone and here she was living in the place he called home. Sitting on the sofa he probably made plans on, dreamed of things on, lived his life. So many remnants of unfinished things he'd left behind and couldn't finish. She felt sick.

"I'm so sorry," she said. "Please, come in."

Strother stepped inside and walked through the apartment. He seemed lost in thought as he touched some of the furniture.

"Going through his things was hard. We weren't very thorough in clearing everything out, I'm afraid. Probably left behind some important things. Stella still can't come up here."

"We went to high school together. We were supposed to meet for coffee last year after Christmas. I didn't know until now that he'd been murdered. I'm so sorry. We lost such a good man."

Strother smiled, a tear sliding down his cheek. "Everybody loved Rowan. He was the kindest, sweetest guy. He did everything around this place for Stella and me. Helped people all over the island. There were over a thousand people at his funeral last year."

He pointed at the hand-painted chest with beach scenes.

"Rowan painted that. He was quite an artist."

It was Mallory's favorite piece in the apartment. "I loved walking past his shop. His displays always brightened my day."

"That shop was his pride and joy," Strother said with a nod. "It was his way of bringing a little more magic to the island. He was always filling the shop's windows with little treasures. Rowan was such a light in this town. Killing him was like shooting down the sun."

Mallory felt a breeze brush across her face, like fingers against her cheek, a hint of sandalwood warming the room.

There's still time, a voice whispered in her ear.

She glanced at Mr. Kittering, but he didn't react.

"We haven't got much to remember him by. Not even that cat."

"Cat?"

Strother bowed his head. "Rowan and that cat of his were inseparable. Found the four-week-old kitten in the middle of a rainstorm and bottle-fed it until it could eat solid food. Vet said it was a purebred Maine Coon. Marshall ran off the night Rowan was shot. Stella and I searched for months, but finally gave up."

"Too bad no one ever found him."

The old man wiped away tears. "God, I miss that boy. He was like a son to me and Stella. She cries every day. Rowan never hurt a soul and he had his whole life ahead of him."

Mallory put her arm around Strother and hugged him. "I'm honored you'd let me live here."

He kissed Mallory on top of the head. "Rowan always said you were something special, Mallory. I see that now. Wish you'd been with him instead of that crazy woman. Why'd she have to kill him?"

Mallory winced. Crazy had no rules and it only heard its own voice. "I'd give anything to go back and change it," she said.

She'd been crushing on him for so long. She couldn't believe it when he'd texted her about meeting for coffee. Now, he was gone.

"Didn't mean to go on so long," said Strother. He moved back to the door and Mallory followed. "Just wanted to make sure you were all right. If you need anything, just call."

"I will, Mr. Kittering. Thank you."

Strother started out the door but paused a moment then turned around.

"Mallory, have you come across a small crystal clock? Shaped like a snowflake? It's a family heirloom. I looked all over, but couldn't find it.

It's been in the family for generations. Stella gave it to Rowan a week before—he died. To help him find his true love."

"What?" Mallory asked, smirking.

A magic snowflake clock? She didn't believe in magic.

Strother shrugged. "Stella says it has a strange power to it. It draws true love to the owner. We met because of that clock. Stella says relationships are like snowflakes. No two loves are alike. When two matching hearts find each other, they can start an avalanche. Sounds silly, doesn't it? Just takes a turn of those clock hands during Christmas and the snowflake will glow in the presence of true love." He let out a heavy sigh. "Rowan never got the chance to find his."

"I'll keep an eye out for it."

"Thank you, it might bring Stella some comfort," said Strother, closing the door.

Mallory headed to the bathroom, taking a quick shower and drying her hair. She ate some leftover chicken fried rice and streamed her favorite television shows on her laptop until her eyes were closing. She slipped on a yellow nightshirt and turned out the lights, the shimmering stars and galaxies on the ceiling lulling her into a restless sleep.

Around two A.M., she awoke to the sound of clicking against the hardwood. Somewhere nearby, a bell tinkled.

She sat up, glancing around the room. Clock on the nightstand burned red numbers into the darkness, everything so deathly still.

Click, click, click. Jingle.

Her breath quickened, the sound closer.

Click, click. Jingle, jingle. Thump!

Mallory froze, her heart pounding as a dark shape appeared in the bedroom doorway.

Two glowing orbs stared back at her. She couldn't move, her breath ragged and aching through her chest as her heart slammed against her rib cage.

Whump! Jingle.

Something hit the bed and Mallory screamed, fumbling for a light.

A large, cat-shaped object sat on the bed, staring at her with green eyes the size of nickels. It had huge pointed ears, tufts of cream-colored fur streaming out like a lynx. It was the biggest cat she'd ever seen! It had long white whiskers, a pink nose, and black stripes against a thick grey coat. A worn green collar was fastened around its neck, a tiny bell and something bright hanging from it. It was small and gleamed with a strange light. The snowflake clock!

The cat looked thin despite its long, shaggy coat that was cold and wet. It poked her with a big paw and then rubbed against her shoulder.

"I hope you're not planning to eat me," she said, the fear dissipating.

She let out a sharp breath and cupped the silver tag that hung beneath the snowflake clock. The cat meowed, poking her again. Mallory turned the tag toward the light. Marshall. Beneath it was a phone number.

"Rowan's cat!" she cried.

She hugged the huge cat and he rubbed his face against her cheek, purring like a buzz saw. He was beautiful. And the biggest cat she'd ever seen!

He tapped her with his paw.

"You must be hungry, huh?"

He headbutted her, lifting his chin and she stared at the snowflake clock again. She tried to unwind it from a tangle of string but finally used some nail clippers to free it.

The faceted snowflake clock was small, only about three inches across. It gleamed with a strange, inner blue light, looking like a fallen star that had frozen solid. The clock hands were loose.

Save me, a voice whispered in her ear.

Near the window, the air shimmered, a wispy coil of white smoke floating through the room.

She froze when it took on a ghostly human shape, like a man.

There's still time, Mallory.

A hand stroked her hair, fingers brushing her cheek. Then the apparition disappeared into the closet.

Mallory couldn't move. Was that Rowan's ghost? Or maybe she just needed to lay off the caffeine?

The cat meowed again, the bell on its collar jingling.

"Let's get you some food," she said and bolted out of the bedroom, turning on every light in the apartment.

She took the cat into the kitchen and grabbed the deli turkey. Tomorrow, she'd buy some dry food and a litter box. It was the least she could do for poor Rowan.

Mallory spent the day looking for a job and running errands, coming home exhausted. After supper (chicken teriyaki she shared with Marshall), she made the cat a bed in the closet using a cardboard box and some fleece throws. She feared seeing the apparition again, but everything was quiet as she pulled on navy sleep pants and an aqua T-shirt. She popped Rowan's DVD into her laptop and crawled into bed. As she turned out the lamp on the nightstand, she bumped the snowflake clock. It flickered blue.

The cat bed lasted about ten minutes before the big Maine Coon jumped in bed with her and stretched out, taking half the bed.

"I bet you wonder where Rowan is, don't you, big guy?" she said, stroking his head as *It's a Wonderful Life* played, George Bailey telling Mary he'd lasso the moon for her.

She thought about George saving his brother from falling through ice and stopping a druggist from dispensing a poison prescription. Why couldn't she have been there to save Rowan?

Marshall meowed, purring like a cement mixer as he walked across her pillow onto the nightstand. He grabbed the string on the snowflake clock and dragged it onto the bed.

"You want to play, big guy?"

He turned in a circle and pawed at the glowing clock. Then he sat down in front of her, staring with those unblinking, soul-deep green eyes as if willing her to do something.

"Is this some kind of Maine Coon mind trick?" she asked.

He meowed.

She picked up the clock, pulsing blue like frozen fire, staring at its delicate structure. Why hadn't it been smashed to bits? He'd been running loose for nearly a year with this thing on his collar. It was amazing it was still intact.

Save me, whispered a voice in her ear.

"Rowan?" she called, pausing the movie.

She felt foolish. She was hearing things.

There's still time.

Marshall turned to stare as the white mist coalesced into a man. He stood at the foot of the bed, reaching out to her.

She wasn't scared this time. "Rowan?" she called, reaching toward him.

He moved toward the closet and Marshall bounded toward him.

Mallory jumped up, her stocking feet sliding on the hardwood as she followed the smoky figure to the closet. She slid into the dark closet, snowflake clock still in her hand as the smoke vanished.

Remembering Strother's story, she felt for the clock hands.

What could it hurt?

With a flick of her fingers, she spun the hands backward.

She turned, tripping over the cat, and fell headfirst into the closet.

Everything went dark. She struggled to her feet, turning around to find the closet door shut. She struggled to turn the knob, but it seemed stuck. Several more times, she pushed until the door creaked open. Marshall shot out of the closet.

"There you are!" a male voice shouted.

Mallory froze. Who was out there?

"I was afraid I was gonna have to crawl in there after you."

Crouching in the dark, Mallory peered through the opening, feeling confused and scared. Had someone broken into the apartment?

A sandy-haired man with haunting blue eyes stood there in jeans and no shirt as he pulled on a grey T-shirt. He was lean and tall. He had a strong chin shadowed with sexy stubble and laugh lines that curved across his cheeks. The scents of cedar and sandalwood drifted toward her as the man turned around and picked up Marshall.

Rowan Brophy!

He was so beautiful. The photo in the paper hadn't done him justice. But how was he standing here? She had to be dreaming this!

"You gonna help me at the store today or break stuff like yesterday, big guy? We need to finish that Christmas display. It's almost Christmas Eve."

He scratched the cat's ears and set him on the bed. Then he grabbed a flannel shirt and pulled it over his T-shirt. He slid on brown hiking boots and hurried out of the room as the phone rang. Marshall trotted after him.

Mallory crept out of the closet, pausing at the bedroom door as an answering machine picked up the call. She glanced at the snowflake clock. Its hands moved slowly forward.

This was crazy! She had to be dreaming. But it was so real.

Rowan stood by the desk, his back to her.

"Rowan—pick up the phone, baby. Please?"

He backed away from the desk.

"Why do you keep pushing me away? I thought I meant something to you! We're soul mates!" A pause. "I'm tired of talking to this goddamned machine! Pick up! Please, call me back, so we can talk about us. Don't you understand? We have to be together on Christmas. Please! I miss you. Don't make me beg." A pause. "You'll regret pushing me away. I promise you will."

Rowan cursed under his breath. He was shaking, hands over his face. He leaned his head against the wall and sighed, so deeply and with such hopelessness that she wanted to go to him.

"God, I hope she doesn't find this place," he muttered.

He grabbed a navy blue parka off the desk chair, picked up the cat, and left the apartment. Outside, Mallory heard an engine start and a vehicle drive away. To her surprise, it was light outside. What time was it?

The phone rang again. The answering machine picked up. Lindsey Tull again.

"You think I don't know you're seeing other people? Think you could hide at Bella Luna's with your friends? I saw you with Emily Raintree. And I know Hildy Geller set you up with Mallory Winter. Don't you want to know how I found out you were cheating on me, Rowan? I see everything you do. Everywhere you go." A long pause. "You're lucky I'm so forgiving. I'll make you come back to me. You'll see. I won't let you ruin Christmas. If you do, you'll be sorry, Rowan Brophy. Very, very sorry."

The line went dead.

Mallory remembered Lindsey's frequent drama in high school, her weekly grasps for attention, a.k.a. suicide threats, made-up boyfriends and relationships, and chronicled visits to the emergency room. Mallory kept her distance.

The phone rang again. A hang-up. The machine's counter read eighteen messages. She gasped at the date: Thursday, December 20, 2012.

Rowan only had five days to live.

She stared at the snowflake clock in her hand. Had this thing somehow brought her to Rowan? Helped her travel a year into the past?

Could she actually save him?

As long as he was still alive, there was a chance. She'd borrow some clothes from her friend, Hildy, and head into town to find Rowan.

Rowan Brophy's gift shop, Island Dreams, stocked the most magical treasures on the island. He was finishing his annual Christmas display: *A Mermaid Christmas*. Draped with sheer blue organza, teal silk, and twinkling lights, the window glittered with dichroic glass shells and starfish. Pastel seahorses, plush sea turtles, and green seaweed hung from fishing line, a small fan making them undulate across mermaid statues, dolls, and prints. He'd placed plush narwhals and orcas in the center. Washington State loved its orcas. In the center stood a white coral Christmas tree he'd fashioned out of wire and bleached coral. He'd wrapped it with colored lights, tiny glass ornaments, earrings, and necklaces.

He couldn't concentrate this season. His stomach was in knots, his dreams fitful, fearing Lindsey Tull would show up. For nearly a year, the woman had harassed and stalked him almost daily. He jumped whenever the phone rang, dreading her daily barrage of messages. He'd changed his number twice. His stomach dropped into his feet whenever he saw blonde hair. Everywhere he went, she showed up. Watching him at a distance.

They'd only gone out twice when she told him she loved him, describing their kids and planning their Christmas Day wedding. She demanded he meet her parents and fill out wedding registries. She'd scared the hell out of him. He told her that he didn't want to see her again.

Enraged, she'd thrown a drink in his face, accused him of cheating on her, and stormed out of the restaurant. The next day, she blew up his answering machine, leaving thirty-seven messages, begging, crying, accusing, and threatening. And stalking. Sitting outside his shop, following him everywhere. She was destroying his life.

Most of the time, he stayed home, afraid of what might happen. He couldn't sleep, could barely eat or concentrate. The police said they couldn't do anything unless she broke the law. For the longest time, he was afraid to file a restraining order. Until last month. But he feared what would happen next and had contemplated selling the store and moving.

The bell chimed, the door opening behind him.

He lurched up from the window, his heart in his throat.

A young woman with a shy smile stepped inside the shop. She had thick sable hair and intense grey eyes. She wore black yoga pants and a black North Face fleece, black purse over her shoulder. God, he loved a woman in yoga pants!

Ten years peeled back and his heart melted. Mallory Winter.

Her shapely long legs filled out those pants like a pro. He even forgave those ugly damned snow boots.

"Mallory Winter," he replied.

She nodded as he stepped forward.

"I wasn't sure you'd recognize me."

He laughed. He'd know her anywhere. "You look like you just stepped out of the yearbook, Mall. It's great to see you."

Had the universe just started turning backward? Was his horrible luck beginning to reverse itself? This woman took his breath away and thanks to Hildy Geller, he was taking her out next week.

"You haven't changed a bit, Rowan. It's great to see you."

Mallory squeezed his hand. The moment her fingers touched his, an electric rush of energy flooded his body. The powerful surge of emotions almost knocked him to his knees. She gasped, glancing at her hand and then his face, a momentary look of surprise changing to a grin. She'd felt it, too. He'd never felt such an intense attraction to anyone before. God, it was intoxicating. He could barely breathe.

Finally, he let go of her hand. "Can't wait to have you show me around Anacortes," he said with a smile.

"Oh," she said, her cheeks reddening. She looked disoriented. "Right, Anacortes."

His heart dropped. She'd come by to cancel out on him.

"Hope you don't mind that I stopped by your shop, but I thought maybe, if you had time, we could get together this week for coffee. If you're busy, I understand—"

"No, no," he said, moving toward her, relief washing over him. "I've definitely got time this week." He couldn't help but smile. She seemed sweet and considerate. He glanced at his watch. Almost noon. "What about this afternoon? Three o'clock. The bakery off Mullis?"

Mallory returned his smile, running her hand through that thick, dark hair. Her intense grey eyes seemed lit from within and they made his heart race every time she smiled at him.

"Three o'clock it is," she replied, those grey eyes bright.

High school memories flooded back and he remembered passing the long-legged sophomore in the hall every day just before lunch. She always looked a little shy, standing there in Doc Martens and ripped low-rise jeans (that embraced every curve) as she'd smile at him over her books. By her junior year, she'd graduated to miniskirts and midriffs (at basketball games and the spring festival). He'd been too scared to ask her out though, since she was constantly surrounded by half the guys in school. He thought he'd grown out of that crush, but seeing her brought it back full force. He'd even been dreaming about her.

At twenty-seven, she'd barely aged. He couldn't believe she wasn't taken. When Hildy urged him to text her, he thought it was a joke. After so many bad dates—and that psycho, Lindsey Tull—he'd considered either the Peace Corps or the priesthood.

Maybe things were starting to turn around? He'd get his grandma to watch the store—and Marshall—this afternoon. He was taking out Mallory Winter, the woman of his dreams.

"I'll meet you there," said Mallory, moving toward the front door.

Rowan waved as she walked out.

He could barely hold the phone as he called his grandmother.

Mallory sat near the ferry terminal, smartphone in hand, collecting every bit of information she could on Lindsey Tull. The salt air mixed with the cool scent of pine. Front Street faced the harbor where moored boats bobbed in the Salish Sea's deep teal waters and the ferry docked. The sleek white and green ferry offloaded passengers, cars pouring onto Front Street and up Spring Street where dozens of unique shops and local restaurants lined both sides.

Lindsey made it easy. She'd posted so much personal information on Facebook and her abandoned Myspace page. Address. Phone number. Where she worked (Granny's Attic antique shop). Mallory found even more by searching Google images, finding pictures of her car, restaurants she frequented, and where she shopped. And a creepy photo blog that should have been titled *Way Too Much Information*.

Her blog was filled with posts about Rowan and how this Christmas would be the best ever. It was plastered with photos of Rowan in restaurants, with friends, and on the street. Captions beneath the pictures read *my adorable fiancé, my beloved, my soul mate,* and *father of my future children.*

Most disturbing was the latest entry, pictures of her stalking Rowan all the way to work, from truck to parking lot to the shop, all taken from a distance. She'd badly edited the photos, putting herself beside him in every shot. She wrote about how they'd had a fight and he'd hung up on her.

She ended the post by saying she'd make it up to him with dinner. The post ended with her writing that she expected him to propose on Christmas Day.

Mallory squinted at the post's timestamp: *Thursday, December 20, 2012, 1:14 P.M.*

The time on her phone was 1:24 P.M.

She shuddered. Ten minutes ago.

Mallory walked toward Rowan's shop, searching for his stalker.

Tourists walked up and down the streets lit with Christmas lights. They wore heavy jackets, fanny packs, and cameras around their necks, walking two and three deep, carrying sacks and coffee cups. Lindsey blended in with them.

She saw a bleach blonde with too much makeup sitting on a bench across the street from Rowan's shop. She had a camera with a huge telephoto lens in one hand, smartphone in the other. She wore a white stadium coat, her hard brown eyes looking wild as she snapped photos, shutter clicking continuously, lens pointed at Rowan's store window. At five-eight, Mallory always felt like she'd towered over her in school. She seemed oblivious to anyone around her.

Mallory sat on a bench, pretending to read a real estate guide, as she kept a close but distant watch on Lindsey Tull.

The woman's gaze never left the shop and never wavered as people passed her on the sidewalk. She had a trance-like expression on her face as she alternated from camera to smartphone, snapping pictures and texting.

After thirty minutes, Lindsey walked away, crossing Spring Street. Mallory followed at a distance.

It was a ten-minute walk to Sunshine Alley where Lindsey went into Granny's Attic. Mallory waited a few minutes and then entered the store.

The long shop was cavernous, furniture stacked like a flea market sale. The air smelled musty and dry as Mallory walked down the main aisle. One side was filled with tables and chairs and the other arranged with sideboards, dressers, bed frames, and sofas. Stacks of old Depression, carnival, and milk glass dishes and knick-knacks lined the back wall. An antique cash register sat on a display case where Lindsey stood beside a sixty-something woman with curly, reddish brown hair.

"How was lunch?" the older woman asked as Lindsey wrapped a milk glass vase in tissue paper.

"Good. Sorry, I was late. The place was packed and it took forever to get my food. I'll make up the time on Tuesday."

"That's Christmas Eve."

Lindsey grinned, handing the bag to a customer. "I know. Rowan's taking me to the Duck Soup Inn. To propose."

Mallory cringed, wanting to gag. This woman was delusional. And dangerous.

Customers left the store, the bell jangling. The older woman raised thin eyebrows, bright hazel eyes looking confused.

"Weren't you married before on Christmas Day?" the woman asked

Lindsey's eyes narrowed, a look of almost hatred burning on her heart-shaped face. "Where'd you hear that?" she said with a growl, fury churning in her eyes.

"Your mother and I have been friends since you were in diapers, young lady."

"Yes," she snapped. "Until last Christmas when left me for some whore." She grinned. "I got the house and half his paycheck in the divorce. He never loved me like Rowan does."

Mallory wandered out the door.

Lindsey was married once on Christmas. That explained the fixation with Christmas. And the cheating husband explained the crazy.

If any of that's true.

The alarm on her phone chimed. Fifteen minutes until coffee with Rowan. She hurried up the street toward the bakery.

Rowan was waiting when she entered. He seemed more relaxed. They stood in line, ordering separately, and then slid into a wooden booth against the wall. They removed their coats. In the light, he looked tired, his bright blue eyes shadowed.

"I can't believe I'm actually here with you," said Rowan, resting his elbows on the table, grey flannel shirt sleeves rolled up.

"Why's that?" Mallory asked.

He bowed his head a moment, looking a little shy, sandy hair windblown. "I've wanted to ask you out since high school."

Mallory's mouth fell open. "Are you serious?"

He looked up, nodding. Those laugh lines curved across his cheeks, giving him a boyish look that melted her.

"In school, I waited two years for you to ask me out, but you never did. Why?"

He looked shell-shocked, the smile fading. "You mean you'd have gone out with me?"

She laid her hand on his forearm. "Of course! I was too scared to ask you, you being a year ahead."

He shook his head, rubbing his face. "We're a couple of cowards, aren't we?"

Mallory laughed as he put his hand on hers, stroking her fingers. Attraction burned through her like a bonfire, warmth spreading from her heart to her head and down her ribs into her toes like a thick quilt settling around her shoulders. He squeezed her hand and she entwined her fingers in his.

She could get used to this.

The woman at the counter brought over their food. Mallory grinned. Both cups of coffee had whipped cream and both pastries were blueberry-peach crumbles. They'd ordered the same thing.

"I like a little coffee with my milk and chocolate," he said, laughing. "Not the manliest of drinks."

"We ordered the same thing," said Mallory.

"Wow, that's never happened before," he said, staring at her. His eyes lit, enveloping her in warmth.

She felt a vibration at her hip and reached into her fleece pullover's pocket, but her phone wasn't vibrating. It was the snowflake clock. Her pocket glowed soft lavender now.

"Okay, favorite band," Mallory asked, picking up her coffee cup.

"Pearl Jam," said Rowan.

"Zeppelin," said Mallory.

"A classics woman," Rowan replied. "I like that." He took a sip of coffee. "Favorite movie?"

"Tie. *It's a Wonderful Life* and *Lord of the Rings*," Mallory replied.

"Which one?" Rowan asked.

"*Return of the King*," they both said in unison.

"That's my third favorite movie," said Rowan, picking up his fork. "Mine are *It's a Wonderful Life* and *The Shawshank Redemption*."

Mallory frowned, crossing her arms. "No fair, Shawshank's in my top five. Cats or Dogs?"

"Cats," he said.

"Same." Mallory laughed and took a bite of her pastry.

A huge grin spilled across his face. He leaned closer. "Favorite holiday?"

"Christmas," they both replied.

"Art or Science?" Rowan asked, his forehead almost touching hers.

Mallory pointed a finger at him, chuckling. "Trick question. Art *and* science."

He nodded. "You got me!"

He took another sip of coffee, whipped cream smearing his chin. Mallory reached out and gently wiped it away. He cradled her hand, staring into her eyes and she felt herself tumble into the clear blue depths of his eyes, not wanting to look away. All those pent-up high school feelings rushed back, the attraction so strong.

She couldn't help herself. She leaned forward and brushed a kiss across his lips. Surprise filled his eyes for a moment. He kissed back.

They talked about high school, movies, and life approaching thirty until nearly six o'clock. She walked with him back to the store and he told her how he found his cat, Marshall. Halfway there, he slid his hand into hers, fingers entwining. He felt so familiar, so comfortable. She smelled a trace of his aftershave, hints of sandalwood complementing her vanilla body spray. The snowflake clock vibrated in her front pocket, reminding her why she was here.

Just before they reached Second Street, Rowan mumbled a curse and jerked her into the nearby alley. He pressed his back against the bricks, chest heaving, brow beaded in sweat as he motioned her quiet and held his breath.

Mallory understood as a flash of white-blonde hair streaked past the alley entrance.

Lindsey.

Mallory watched her round the corner and disappear. Had she been watching Rowan's shop? Or them just now?

Rowan grabbed her hand and pulled her across the street into the drugstore. By the time they reached the back door, he was shaking.

"What's wrong?" Mallory asked.

"I'll explain, I promise," he said as he glanced outside and across the parking lot.

He pulled her outside, both of them running across the parking lot and around the back of his shop. He unlocked the back door and they bolted inside, locking it behind them.

She desperately wanted to tell him that she'd come to save him as he paced the small store room. Homemade wooden shelves packed with cardboard boxes and sacks lined all four walls. Two long tables stood in the center of the room, one with spools of ribbons in various colors, another with stacks of colored tissue paper. A coffee mug with pens, markers, box cutters, scissors, and a stapler set on the other table. The room smelled like wet paper and bayberry from a nearby box of candles.

Still shaking, Rowan paced the room, hands on his hips.

"Tell me what's happening," said Mallory.

"I wish I'd found you a year ago, Mall," he said, exasperation in his voice, a haunted look in his eyes. "That's when I had two dates with a crazy woman. Now, she thinks we're getting married and I'm going to father her kids. She follows me day and night, leaves tons of messages on my phone—even sits outside my apartment." He sighed, running his fingers through his hair. "I've moved twice already."

"Have you called the police?" Mallory asked.

He nodded, his frantic pacing slowing. "I already filed a restraining order." Desperation crept into his eyes. "I'm afraid she's going to do something, Mall."

Mallory couldn't stand the vulnerable look on his face, the hint of fear hovering there. She put her arms around him and he held onto her.

"Who is it?" she asked, knowing already.

"Lindsey Tull."

"The blonde you hid from?" she asked, knowing it was.

"Yeah. Sorry for scaring you to death back there. Didn't want her to see you and come after you, too. She's already scared away two women."

Mallory let him go. "Well, she won't scare me away."

"You don't understand. She's dangerous. She's been arrested twice. Once for attacking her ex-husband. Once for attacking his new wife. But both times, they dropped the charges."

Rowan's grandma, Stella Kittering stepped into the back room wearing black pants and a fuchsia blouse, thick silver hair in a ponytail. "I thought I heard you back here, Rowan. I just locked up." She smiled at Mallory. "Mallory, isn't it? Your high school crush, right?"

Rowan's face turned bright red and he nodded, staring at his boots.

"Good to see you, Mrs. Kittering," Mallory replied.

Stella glanced from Rowan to Mallory. "How was your date?"

"It was terrific," said Mallory, smiling at Rowan. "Can't wait to go out again."

He reached out and took her hand, squeezing. "I'd love to take you to supper, Mall. This weekend, next week—you pick the day and I'll be there, no matter what."

Her heart ached. On Wednesday, he'd be dead. Unless she could stop it.

"As soon as we take care of this problem," said Mallory.

Stella's face darkened. "That Tull woman?"

Mallory felt something brush against her leg. She looked down, seeing Marshall against her calf. He trilled a meow and put his paws on her knee, begging her to pick him up.

"Hi there, big guy," she said, hefting the huge, purring cat into her arms. "He's beautiful, Rowan." She hugged him and set him down. "I have an idea about how to stop this."

Rowan shook his head. "Nobody can stop this."

"The police won't arrest her unless she breaks the law. So what if we turn the tables on her? Push her into acting—violating the restraining order."

Stella looked frightened. She put her arms around Rowan's waist. "How?" Stella asked.

"Let's put a sign in the store window," said Mallory, "announcing that the store will close early on Christmas Eve due to a private celebration of your engagement to...to me. She shows up, violates the restraining order, and they arrest her."

"No," Rowan snapped. "I'm not involving you in this mess, Mall. And I don't want her coming after you."

"Hildy's husband's a cop. He'll help."

Rowan relaxed a little.

"Strother knows the Sheriff well," said Stella. "I'll call home and have Strother invite him and Rick Geller over for supper tonight to discuss this."

Mallory winked at Rowan. "Think you could pretend to be engaged to me for five days?"

He pulled her into his arms. "It'll be a struggle, but I'll manage."

"All right," said Mallory, leaning against Rowan. "Let's move. We only have five days."

Mallory went to the gingerbread house on Spring Street for supper. It seemed so strange. She already lived here. She hoped that, by the time this ended, so would Rowan.

Shortly, Sheriff Clark and Deputy Rick Geller, both in street clothes, arrived for pot roast and Cabernet.

Rowan met Mallory at the door, looking handsome in his blue dress shirt and khaki pants. He took her hand, smelling like cedar and sandalwood, and led her into a formal dining room with built-in sideboards, white wainscoting, burgundy striped wallpaper, and an antique mahogany dining table.

Stella wore the same outfit, her husband, Strother in a yellow sweater and tan pants. The mood over dinner was light, Sheriff Clark and Strother telling stories. Rick, tall and lanky with short black hair, joked about high school with Mallory and Rowan.

After peach pie and ice cream, they settled onto mint green couches in the parlor, listening to Mallory's plan.

"This is very dangerous, young lady," said Sheriff Clark, his belly straining against his white dress shirt and dark pants. He wore glasses, his thin brown hair combed over. "Restraining orders don't stop bullets. This woman has a history of violence. Someone could die."

Mallory winced, the memory of Rowan's obituary still vivid.

"If we wait for her to snap, Rowan could die. Why not force an overload where we can control it? With officers as backup?"

Rick nodded. "Why Christmas Eve, Mall?"

Mallory felt time twist around her. Everything went back to Christmas Day. By changing the date and location of Lindsey's attack, Mallory hoped to alter the event. And stop Rowan from dying.

"According to public record," said Sheriff Clark, "Lindsey Tull was married before, on Christmas Day. And divorced five years ago."

The room fell quiet.

Mallory reached into her pocket for the snowflake clock. It was gone! She searched both pockets and her purse, but it wasn't there.

What happened now?

"Now, officially, I can't sanction this and I can't assign officers," said Sheriff Clark. "But as a friend of the family, I'd be happy to attend your engagement party, Rowan."

"With his deputy," said Rick.

"Thank you," said Rowan. "I'll put up a sign tomorrow."

Stella entered the room, carrying the snowflake clock. Mallory relaxed.

"Rowan? Mallory? Come here, please."

Rowan rose from the couch, Mallory beside him, following Stella into a sunny yellow kitchen with painted blue cabinets. It smelled warm with onions and garlic as Stella pressed the clock into Rowan's hands.

"This is a family heirloom," said Stella. "Its magic helped four generations find true love, including your Mom. Now, it's your turn, Rowan."

The moment the clock touched Rowan's palm, it glimmered a soft red, the hands spinning.

Rowan laughed. "Magic? Really, Grandma?"

"During Christmas, the clock glows in the presence of true love."

She put Mallory's hand on top of Rowan's. The moment their hands touched, the clock gleamed purple. The hands stopped, ticking slowly forward now.

Rowan smiled at Mallory. "It's glowing."

Stella grinned. "Like snowflakes, no two loves are alike. When fire and earth collide, like two hearts, they entwine forever—like crystal."

Was there magic in this clock or was it just a game?

All Mallory knew for sure was that she'd been crazy about Rowan since high school. She looked up and he was staring at her.

"We need an engagement ring," said Rowan.

"Here," said Stella. "Use mine. I'll put a bit of tape on the band. It's a little big for Mallory."

Rowan grinned. "Will you marry me, Mall?"

"Not even on one knee," Mallory snapped, rolling her eyes.

He sighed, dropping to one knee. He slid the ring onto Mallory's left ring finger. "Will you marry me for five days, Mall?"

"I will."

He stood up and put his arms around her. His kiss was like a lightning strike coursing through every nerve and blood vessel. He let her go and she gasped, overwhelmed by the heat and force.

"I hope this works," said Rowan, glancing at the clock.

"Me, too," Mallory whispered, gripping his hand.

The next day, Rowan put a sign on the door, closing the shop at 4 P.M. on Christmas Eve and mentioning the private engagement party for Rowan Brophy and his fiancée, Mallory.

All weekend, he and Mallory were inseparable, kissing and holding hands in public, shopping, and eating out. The news spread fast through the island town. Sunday night, when Mallory and Rowan walked back to his apartment, Rowan found all four of his truck tires slashed.

Inside, Lindsey left forty-eight messages on his answering machine. All of them were screaming, hate-filled rants, threatening him and Mallory. But the last message was the most chilling.

"Merry Christmas, Rowan," she whispered and hung up.

Rowan was shaking as he sat down on the sofa. Mallory went into the kitchen and grabbed two beers out of the fridge, opening them. Two cans of Coke leaned against a six-pack of Pyramid ale.

She shuddered, remembering them still in the fridge a year later. Fear washed over her now. She couldn't lose Rowan. Somewhere over the past few days, she'd fallen in love with him.

She handed Rowan an ale. He took a long pull off the bottle as Mallory settled beside him. He snuggled against her, arms around her.

"I'm so glad you're here, Mall," he whispered, pressing feather kisses across her neck and mouth, sipping her lips.

"I'm so glad I walked into your shop this week," said Mall.

"I put in *It's a Wonderful Life*," he said between kisses. "Let's lasso the moon."

"And the stars," said Mallory as the movie's opening credits appeared.

The next morning, Christmas Eve, Mallory awoke on the couch in Rowan's arms, her face against his chest. Marshall was curled up between them. She caressed Rowan's face, sexy with beard shadow, and brushed a lock of hair off his forehead. The snowflake clock lay beside him, still glowing purple.

His eyes rolled open and he smiled through half-closed lids.

"Mornin', Mall." He kissed her softly on the lips.

"Good morning," she said, "Merry Christmas."

He stiffened, his face turning pale.

"Sorry," she said, remembering last night's creepy message from Lindsey.

He sat up, shooing the cat onto the floor. "It's okay," he said, rubbing his face. "What time is it?"

"Nine," Mallory replied, stretching.

"I've got to open the shop," he said, sounding distant and distracted. He glanced at the answering machine. No new messages.

The calm before the storm.

"I need a shower," said Mallory.

"Okay, see you soon," he said, pulling her into his arms for a kiss.

Mallory left the apartment to make preparations at Hildy's place.

It was almost one o'clock when Mallory entered the shop, carrying mochas and pastries. Marshall lay on the counter beside Rowan who rang up items for a huge line of customers. The red sign announcing the engagement party in big, bold letters was still on the door.

Rowan's head snapped up when the bell chimed. His welcoming grin softened her uneasiness as she stepped behind the counter, setting down a coffee and a pastry for him. He wore a thick green sweater, jeans, and those familiar hiking boots.

Mallory saw the snowflake clock tied onto Marshall's green collar.

"Hi, Mall," Rowan said, leaning up for a kiss.

"The fiancée?" Mrs. Ridgeway asked, smiling. She lived up the street from the Kitterings.

Rowan nodded. "That's my woman."

Mallory stood behind him, rubbing his shoulders with the ring on display. He patted her hand.

"I'm not letting you out of my sight," she whispered in his ear.

"Same," he replied.

Mallory handed out candy canes and wrapped purchases while Rowan rang them up. She pulled out her smartphone, checking the time. Three forty-eight. Almost closing time. Then she checked Lindsey's blog.

Every photo of Rowan had been digitally spattered red with blood. Lindsey's post was short, saying it was her last for a while because she was about to confront her cheating fiancé. The last line read, *Merry Christmas.*

The door chime jangled. Sheriff Clark walked in wearing jeans and a heavy black sweater. He moved toward Mallory, carrying a brown grocery bag.

"Do you have it?" Mallory asked.

He nodded. "Rick's right behind me."

"Look at this," said Mallory, handing him the phone.

Sheriff Clark stared wide-eyed at the pictures as Rick walked in the door. Rowan rang up the last customer.

"Rowan, a word in back please," said Sheriff Clark.

Rowan followed him into the back room as Mallory turned the open sign over and locked the door.

"I've got an unmarked car outside, just in case, Mall," he said.

"Thanks, Rick," said Mallory.

In a few minutes, the Sheriff and Rowan returned, Rowan adjusting his sweater.

And the wait began.

By seven o'clock, it was dark, lights sparkling outside as it began to snow. Big, heavy flakes. Mallory watched them fall, looking so beautiful against twinkling Christmas lights. She glanced past Rowan's coral Christmas tree, searching for a sign of Lindsey Tull. But everything was still and quiet.

At eight o'clock, Sheriff Clark called it.

Everyone put on their coats and filed out of the store together. Mallory stepped out ahead of Rowan who turned to lock the door.

A shadow flitted past the edge of Mallory's vision.

She turned at the flash of white.

Lindsey Tull stepped out of the darkness, leveling a silver handgun at Rowan's head.

"No!" Mallory shouted.

She lunged at Lindsey, tackling her as she pulled the trigger. The air popped, sounding like a child's toy. The air smelled burnt and hot as Rowan fell back, dropping to his knees.

Shouts and then sirens erupted, shadows rushing past as Mallory beat Lindsey's arm against the pavement until she dropped the gun. Sheriff Clark and Rick were on her now.

Tears surged down Mallory's face as she crawled across the snow-covered pavement toward Rowan slumped against the door, clutching his chest.

Mallory called out to him, reaching, but the world was moving away from him. Somewhere, a clock was ticking.

She shouted as the distance increased, pulling her away.

Mallory awoke in the closet. With the snowflake clock in her hand, glowing blue.

She fumbled out of the tangle of clothes. Her laptop sat on the bed, *It's a Wonderful Life* still paused.

Her heart sank. She'd failed.

The clock's strange magic had given her a once-in-a-lifetime chance to save Rowan and she'd failed. Lindsey Tull still shot him.

Marshall bounded into the bedroom, startling her. He sat down, a huge red and green bow around his neck. And a sign. She squinted at it.

I'm a cat and cats don't beg, but for catnip, I agreed to carry this sign. Somewhere between the mocha, the blueberry-peach crumble, and the snowflake clock, my buddy fell in love with you. Now, there's a question that needs an answer.

Shaking, Mallory ran out of the bedroom.

Rowan stood in the hallway, grinning.

She ran to him and threw herself into his arms. "Rowan! Oh God, Rowan! You're alive!"

He laughed, enfolding her in his arms. "Of course, I'm alive!"

It's a Wonderful Life was paused on the television. In the corner stood a seven-foot Douglas Fir dripping with gold and silver ornaments and sparkling with snowflakes and colored lights, a dozen or so wrapped presents underneath. The snowflake clock gleamed purple at the top of the tree.

"You're crying! You have a bad dream?" His gaze softened as he wiped the tears off her face.

She nodded. "About last Christmas. You died."

He held her tighter. "It was just a bad dream, Mall. That's all over now."

"Remind me what happened," she asked.

He frowned, looking confused. "Thanks to your quick tackle and convincing Sheriff Clark I needed a bulletproof vest, Lindsey only broke three of my ribs. She'll be gone a long time. Have I told you today that I love you?"

"Tell me again," she said.

"I love you, Mallory. You saw my sign, right? I have a question." He dropped down on one knee. "Will you spend the rest of forever with me?" He slid a big, square diamond ring onto her left ring finger.

Mallory could barely speak. "Yes, every single moment of it. I love you, Rowan."

He took her in his arms and kissed her.

"Merry Christmas at last, Rowan," said Mallory, laying her head on his chest, then whispered, "It's about time."

Music to Her Ears

"Sleep well, Miss Eleanor," said the weary-eyed orderly. He reached for the Velcro bed straps. "Your daughter and her husband will be in early. They've got something to discuss with you."

Eleanor Canada Newell, paper-white skin clinging to her furrowed face and puckered lips, shook her head at the straps, her delft blue eyes desperate. She gazed from the straps to the music box on the nightstand.

The orderly sighed and crossed his arms. "This is for your own good, Miss Eleanor. I don't want to come in here and find you lying on the floor again. Last time, it took four weeks for those fractures to heal."

"Please, Harvey. Let me sleep in peace tonight," she said, a whisper of the South in her voice. "Just for tonight." She already knew what news her daughter, Brenda, brought.

Harvey talked strict, but he'd been sweet to her since she'd arrived here, sneaking her butter cookies and hot tea in the evenings. He gazed down at the over-starched sheets.

"All right," he said, wagging a finger at her. "But just for tonight."

He opened the door, the scalding hallway lights cutting through the cool darkness of her room, but she called gently to him.

"Harvey, could you wind my music box before you go?"

She pointed a skeletal finger toward the rosewood and glass music box on the nightstand.

He paused on the threshold, silhouetted by the harsh light, and glanced back at her.

"Can't you go one night without playing that box? You've played it every night since you been here."

Three months she'd been here—after a fall in her kitchen. They told her she could go home as soon as she had healed. He didn't know how much that music box meant to her, especially now.

When she didn't answer, he groaned and ran his hand across his spiky blond bangs. Finally, he reached for the music box.

"Thank you."

"Don't know what's so special about this thing."

"My husband, God rest his soul, won it for me on prom night, the night he proposed."

He smiled. "Good night, Miss Eleanor. Tomorrow's going to be a busy day."

The music box's crisp chime plinked out *In the Good Ol' Summer Time* as Harvey slipped out of the room. Eleanor closed her eyes, savoring the timeworn melody. The cool darkness and the notes intertwined with her breathing until the veils of her memory parted.

The clop of horse and carriage replaced the clinking of dishes from the hallway. The starched sheet became a white pinafore draping her frame. Slowly, she swung her fragile body off the bed, her feet touching the cold, dusty linoleum. With unsteady limbs, she reached for the music box. It vibrated in her hands as she carried it toward the closed door. Fighting against her aching body, she bent down and set the music box in front of the door.

She reached beneath the lid and plucked a tarnished corsage pin from the pink velvet interior. She smiled. From her prom corsage. The faux pearl on top of the pin had yellowed, but it was still ramrod straight. She attached it to the lace collar of her nightgown.

The song's summery chorus filled her soul until the bricks of Seaside's misty Promenade hardened beneath her feet. The turn-of-the-century sparkled in the music box's beveled glass top and she reached her quivering hands through the glass toward it.

The weight of the decades stripped away from her until the salt-tanged air was cool against her smooth, taut skin. Pain left her spine and knees. She reached back, grateful to find her thick braid of sable hair pinned beneath her white hat. The corsage pin glowed with a white-gold sheen. The rush of waves mixed with the sounds of the music box.

A few hundred feet down the Promenade, lamplighters lit gas lamps. One by one, the lamps winked on in the misty twilight. Girls in white prom dresses adorned with pastel ribbons strolled past, smiling gentlemen with slicked-back hair and white coats on their arms. Colored parasols to ward off the sea mist sprouted up and down the Promenade, shielding wide-brimmed, floral hats tied with scarves over Gibson Girl hair. Twitter of voices echoed down the walkway. She smiled. Prom night 1916.

From the dance hall terrace, violins lamented a waltz haunted by the soft echo of a piano. Shadows danced in the gas-lit twilight. The prom was in full swing.

There on the turnaround stood a man in a pressed white coat and a boater hat. He leaned against one of the walkway posts, the flicker of lamplight across his face. He smiled at her and tipped his hat, hiding his sandy-colored hair.

"Miss Eleanor," he cooed.

"Arthur Newell," she said, the South stronger in her voice now. "Have you been waiting long?"

"Not long," he said, his face handsome and freshly shaven. He smiled and his brown eyes warmed her.

She sat down on a wooden bench. He followed, sitting beside her. Seagulls fluttered nearby and she watched them land on the Promenade, pecking at flecks of peanut shells and sugarplums scattered around a trash receptacle. Behind her, Shaker chimes from the prom night carnival brightened the maudlin waltz, drowning out the music box that still echoed in her ears. Laughter and bells punctuated the rush of the sea. She even remembered the prom's theme now: Summer Magic. Beyond the terrace, there were tea cookies and cakes, old friends, and carnival games.

"Do you want to play some of the carnival games tonight," Arthur asked. "Or how about a carriage ride down the coast?"

He glanced at a young couple who sat down on a bench across the turnaround. The girl twirled her pink parasol and giggled, covering her mouth with a white-gloved hand. Pink roses wrapped around her wrist.

"One night is never enough time, is it?"

"No, Arthur," Eleanor answered and reached for his hands. She held them against her lips and kissed them. "Tonight, will you just hold me and tell me you love me?"

He laughed, the sound of summer and daisies in his voice.

"Silly girl, I always tell you that just before I propose to you. Remember?"

He put his arms around her waist, rustling her pinafore and she snuggled closer to him. Like the flow and ebb of an ocean wave, the Shaker chimes crescendoed and fell silent.

"I thought you might be tired of it and would want something else tonight," Arthur said with a sigh. "You've heard me say I love you every night for three months now."

"And I never tire of it, love," she answered, closing her eyes.

He leaned over and pinned a gardenia corsage to her dress, just as he had done that prom night in 1916. The sweet smell of his bay rum and the heady scent of gardenias made her feel eighteen and giddy again. Like the sugary taste of tea cookies at her first high tea. Or the spring social where she wore her first pair of silk, elbow-length gloves. Or the glitter of an engagement ring on her finger. She opened her eyes when she felt Arthur slide the ring onto her finger.

The marquis diamond made her cheeks burn with delight. She held her hand out until the flicker of gas lamps caught the ring. Finally, she leaned over and kissed Arthur on the lips. He pulled her closer.

"I wasn't sure if you were tired of the ring. I tried to make it different this time, but that carnival fortune-teller told me that part was etched into the chimes. No way to change it."

She pulled back from him. "Don't change a thing, Arthur. I want everything as it was on prom night, the night you won the music box. Remember?"

He took off his boater hat and scratched his head.

"My memory's not so good anymore, Ellie."

"I'm not surprised, love," she said, "considering you passed on three months ago. I feel bad that I keep calling you back to me like this, but the nursing home is so lonely. Besides, I miss you terribly."

He took her into his arms again and she reached up, running her fingers across his smooth jawline. The white daisy in his lapel felt dewy against her fingers.

"I missed you, too. I didn't know you'd even kept that old box until I smelled the salt air and the peanuts roasting. When I saw the gas lamps guttering, I knew you'd kept it— that the old Gypsy had been telling the truth."

She pulled him up from the bench and hooked her arm in his.

"Walk with me, Arthur. Walk through 1916 again with me."

He plucked the daisy from his lapel and handed it to her, bowing. She smiled and pressed it to her nose, knowing daisies had no scent, but it smelled of 1916. Everything smelled of horse-drawn carriages, sugarplums, and fresh lemonade. Of pinafores, pin-striped suits, and boater hats. For a few more hours, it would all smell of 1916 until sunrise brought back the smell of mothballs, oatmeal, and bleach mixed with urine.

"I have a surprise for you," said Eleanor.

She dashed down the Promenade, pausing underneath a gas lamp. The cool sea mist caressed her face and she wanted to shake her long hair loose.

He chased after her, laughing. Taking hold of the lamp pole, he whirled around and around it, always pausing to gaze at her as he moved past. She watched him turn in time with the waltz music, tracing the age lines that would appear on his youthful face with the years. The bullet wound in his left leg from World War I, the scar across his hand from breaking the window in their first house. The curve of his spine from years at a desk job he despised. There was no sign yet of the boredom that set in after his retirement, no sign of the cancer that would kill him. The flame that had first drawn her burned hot and alive in him tonight, like the dancing flames of the gas lamps.

"What is it, Ellie?"

"I was just remembering," she said, her Southern accent growing wistful as the sea mist thickened. "I think I've fixed it so we can stay here forever."

His eyes widened. He stopped turning and moved toward her, taking her by the shoulders.

"How?"

"Remember how that gypsy told us to be careful with the music box? Even a crack or a bent pin could ruin the magic."

He nodded. "She said if you or I broke it, we could never come back."

"What if someone else breaks it? While we're here?"

"I don't know, Ellie. We never asked her that. What are you saying?"

She smiled. "I've fixed it so it will break before dawn. Harvey does his rounds about five A.M. When he opens the door, he'll hit the music box. When it breaks, we'll be together—here—forever."

His expression turned sad, almost frightened.

"What if you're sent back and can never return and I'm stuck here forever—without you."

She gasped and grabbed his arms.

"I don't know."

She hadn't even considered that possibility.

"Back there, I was so sure it would work, but now, looking into your eyes, Arthur, I wish I hadn't. I'd rather spend the nights I have left with you than without you."

From the dance hall terrace, the Shaker chimes sent their tinny chords across the Promenade, the violin's sad notes trembling above them. It sounded like a pipe organ, the merry strains comforting. There, at that prom night carnival, she and Arthur had won the music box with its magical tune, just as the fortune-teller had promised. Eleanor had kept it safe in her hope chest for when she or Arthur would need it. Arthur's frightened gaze unnerved her and she couldn't look away, afraid that if she blinked he would dissolve in front of her like cotton candy in rain.

"Let's talk to the Gypsy woman," she said. "She can tell us what will happen before sunrise."

"What good will that do now?"

"Come on," she said, tugging on his sleeve. "Let's find the fortune-teller. We should be at the carnival anyway."

Nodding reluctantly, he took her hand and she pulled him toward the prom night carnival.

Firecrackers and sparklers crackled like popping corn through the Seaside street as carnival performers in their brilliant silks juggled brightly colored balls. Some did handstands and backflips, others coaxed terriers to jump through hoops. Carnival games lined the street that led toward the beach. A couple rushed by, pink taffy stringing from their hands. Other couples lingered in front of the game booths, gazing at the prizes.

Down at the end of the booths, farthest from the Promenade, stood Madame Ralenka's fortune-telling tent. A heavy swath of amethyst velvet covered the entrance and a man in a skimmer hat stood in front. His over-waxed mustache matched the slickness of his dark hair. He pointed his cane at Arthur's chest and smiled wryly.

"How'd you like to see your destiny, young man?" He waved the cane through the air. "Madame Ralenka knows all. Find out the strength of her powers."

Arthur cast a quick glance at Eleanor who nodded slightly. He gave the man a nod. Slowly, the man reached out and lifted the velvet curtain. With reticent steps, Arthur ducked under the velvet, Eleanor behind him.

Inside, a round table draped with ruby and amethyst satin stood in the center of the tent. The air looked as misty as the Promenade, except for the crystal ball in the center of the table. Gold charms and bells draped around the woman's wrists and neck and she jangled as she motioned toward the crystal ball. Her coarse, ebony hair hung wild around her dark face and made-up eyes.

"Come. Sit with me,""she said, her Romanian accent thick. "I show you your destinies."

Eleanor sat down in the chair closest to the crystal ball, just as she had in 1916. The Gypsy woman studied her for a few moments and then stared at Arthur.

"I seen you before, no?"

"Yes," Eleanor answered. "On a long-ago prom night like this one, you told us about the music box. Do you remember?"

The woman smiled. "Yes, the box. I tell you if you win it on prom night, you and husband never be apart."

"Yes, but you told us to be very careful," said Arthur, leaning forward.

"Box is very old. From an old Romanian sorceress in the old country. The magic was woven between you when you first won music box. If you or she break box, you never return to the night you win it."

Eleanor gripped the edges of her skirt. "What if someone else breaks the music box, while Arthur and I are here?"

The Gypsy shook her head. "Then magic will be lost."

"Will we be trapped here forever?"

"No. The magic bond between you is fragile. If it break, no one can return here."

"This can't be!" Eleanor shrieked, leaping up from her chair. "Is there any way to go back before the sun rises?"

"Is not possible. The magic was woven at night, so only works at night." The woman reached out to Eleanor and touched the daisy in her hand. "Is pretty."

"I bought it from a little dark-haired girl selling them on the Promenade, before you arrived, Ellie."

"A fragile thing, like the box," said the Gypsy. "My daughter sells these by the sea. You pin on to be safe. That is all I can say."

Slowly, Eleanor rose from the chair and holding onto Arthur, she walked out into the night.

———————

Eleanor sat on a bench in Arthur's arms and cried into her handkerchief as she waited for the sun to rise. The music had faded from the terrace along with the Shaker chimes. Slowly, the horizon lightened to grey, and then the lamplighters arrived to turn out the lamps. She could hear the whir and snap as the lamps, one by one, were snuffed out.

"I don't want to say goodbye, Arthur," said Eleanor in a tear-strained voice. "I want to be with you forever."

He held her tighter, resting his chin against her cheek.

"And I you, Ellie." He sat up and made her look at him. "We had each other three months longer than most people got."

The tears rushed down her cheeks. "But it isn't enough. Especially now. I can't leave you like this!"

"I loved you, Eleanor," he said, making her look at him. "Remember that. Especially the woman who stayed at my bedside and held my hand as my life slipped from this world. That woman, I love as much, maybe more than fiery, eighteen-year-old Eleanor Canada who captured my heart back in 1916."

An off-key chord chimed through the silent town of Seaside and Eleanor shivered, the wind coming off the ocean suddenly cold.

"Arthur Newell, I fell in love with you the day I met you and even when I lost you, I never stopped loving you. You will be with me always. Hold my hand now."

Arthur rose from the bench and held out his hand.

"Dance with me, Eleanor."

Nodding, Eleanor stood. Arthur slid an arm around her waist and gripped her right hand in his. Dancing to the sound of the waves and the dowsing of the gas lamps, Eleanor and Arthur waltzed down the Promenade.

Glass shattered. Arthur held her hand tighter and she gripped his hand as the sea mist settled thick on the Promenade, obscuring the gas lamps and benches. Arthur's steps quickened and they twirled faster. Wood splintered. Eleanor laid her head against Arthur's shoulder and wept.

Seaside disappeared in the mist, Arthur, prom night, and the

Promenade fading into the predawn greyness as the veil of Eleanor's memory fell over 1916. It was then that she felt him let go of her hands.

Eleanor awoke to Harvey's rough hands placing her back in her bed. Bits of wood and glass littered the floor, a custodian sweeping them into a metal dustpan. Tears funneled down her wrinkled face and plopped onto stiff white sheets.

"Miss Eleanor, you gave me quite a scare!" cried Harvey, out of breath. "I'm sorry about your music box. I didn't see it by the door."

She wanted to apologize, but couldn't find the words. Arthur was gone and so was the music box. Her selfishness had taken it all away. She reached up to wipe away her tears and felt a softness against her face. Pulling her hand away, she saw Arthur's daisy peeking through her fingers. She kissed the flower and cradled it against her cheek.

"Are you in pain anywhere?"

Her chest ached, but she shook her head.

"Mom?" Brenda called from the doorway and stepped over to the bed. "What's the matter? Are you all right?"

Harvey smiled at her as he moved toward the door.

"She fell out of bed again, but it looks like she was lucky this time. No breaks or fractures. We'll get her down to the doctor this afternoon though, just to be safe."

Harvey hurried into the hallway, leaving Eleanor alone with her daughter and son-in-law.

"Good morning, honey," said Eleanor. "How are you?"

Brenda, looking much older than Eleanor remembered, leaned down and kissed her on the cheek. Her blonde hair was streaked with grey, the lines thick around her mouth and eyes. She looked frightened. Eleanor looked past Brenda, at her burly, silent husband leaning against the wall. Husband number two. She hoped this would be Brenda's last one, a man who treated her right.

"I'm fine. Now, what's this important news you have for me."

Eleanor knew she would never leave this nursing home. She knew what Brenda would tell her.

"Mom, we found a buyer for your house. I need your signature on these papers to sell it. But I need it today."

Tears welled in Brenda's eyes. Eleanor reached out to her and Brenda took her hand.

"I didn't want it to be this way, Mom, I didn't! I wanted you to come live with me, but the doctor says that isn't possible now."

Eleanor smiled and patted Brenda's hand. Over the years, arthritis had nearly crippled Eleanor. Her brittle bones could crack by turning over wrong in bed.

"It's all right, dear. I knew. It's okay now. Sell the house. Without Arthur, it just wasn't a home anymore."

"But I'll come visit you every day," said Brenda, wiping away her tears. "I promise I will."

"I know you will, honey."

Eleanor stroked the daisy with her fingers. Brenda meant well, but she had no understanding of how it felt in here. Poor thing had her own troubles and Eleanor didn't want to add to them.

After Eleanor signed the house papers, she ate her breakfast and listened to Brenda talk about Eleanor's grandchildren. How well they were doing in school. Finally, Brenda rose from the chair and hugged her.

"I'll be back to see you tomorrow night, Mom. I love you."

Eleanor squeezed Brenda's hand. "I love you too, dear."

As soon as the door closed, Eleanor knew she had to try one last time to return to 1916. Fighting down her panic, Eleanor pressed the daisy to her heart and began to hum. A cart squeaked by her door. Someone coughed. Concentrating, she scrunched her eyes closed and hummed louder, but prom night 1916 was beyond her reach.

Sobs trembled through her frail body as she kissed the daisy. The little flower was so fragile. Then she remembered the fortuneteller had said something about the daisy's frailness. That Eleanor should keep it safe. She smiled. Like she had told her to keep the music box safe all those years ago.

Laying her hand against her lapel, she found the yellowed corsage pin. Gently, she pinned it through the daisy's stem and against her nightgown. She hummed louder. The corsage pin began to gleam. Closing her eyes, Eleanor clutched the daisy.

The veils of her memory parted. Above the Shaker chimes piping *In the Good Ol' Summer Time* across the Promenade, Arthur called her name. Eleanor went to him. Waves whispered against the sand, autumn sharp in the cool air as Arthur took her in his arms.

Laughing, he twirled her around and around. Eleanor tossed her hat into the air and at last, she shook her sable braid free.

One by one, the gas lamps went dark and as first light touched the Promenade, Eleanor and Arthur danced.

The next morning, Brenda and Harvey found Eleanor cold and grey on the floor beside her bed, a fresh daisy pinned to her nightgown. Harvey comforted Brenda as best he could, telling her that Eleanor hadn't been in pain, that her heart had just given out.

But Eleanor knew otherwise. Her heart hadn't given out. It had given in.

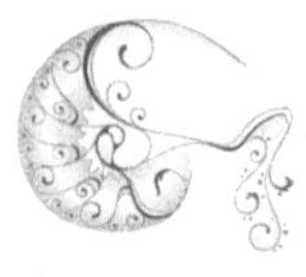

Ripples of the Pharaoh's Curse

Everleigh Maine was more interested in the mystery surrounding dashing archaeologist Harry Lawrence's death than the centennial anniversary of the opening of Tutankhamun's Tomb.

The last thing the world had to remember him by was the black leather tool wrap containing his dig tools, inherited by her English grandfather and left to her because of her passion for archaeology and history. And all things Harry Lawrence. Grampa Al once said he lived on through her because she'd kept his memory alive in the world.

The box from London, sent by her Nan, arrived in Nevada today. Ever couldn't wait to open it.

An amateur archaeologist, she had worked on digs in Utah and Nevada. With Harry Lawrence's fabled tools in hand, she would honor his memory by using them at an upcoming dig in California.

Dressed in khaki shorts, lavender tank top, and brown field boots, Ever sat cross-legged on the cool terracotta tile floor of her Las Vegas apartment and leaned against her tan sofa, scent of fresh-cut lavender heady from the vase on her kitchen counter.

With box cutter in hand, she cut through the packing tape and peeled open the box flaps.

She pressed her tortoiseshell glasses against the bridge of her nose and smoothed the rivulets of long chocolate brown hair that hung free of her loose messy bun as she reached into the box, underneath folds of old newspapers.

Her best friend had talked her into these frames, saying they accentuated her slate-blue eyes, and then tried to get her onto all those stupid dating sites. Where she fit in like an old rotary phone.

Modern dating frustrated her. These apps and online services made her feel cursed—like she'd never find a man that got her. At twenty-eight, Ever tired of swiping left or right on her phone for dates with guys that didn't share her passion for—anything. Especially history and antiquities. She longed to meet someone interested in more than just a hookup. Someone that burned to discover the past's legendary mysteries and share them with the world.

Like famed British archaeologist Harry Lawrence.

She removed another layer of newspaper from the box, setting it on the floor.

Ever envied the dashing young scientist who had traveled the world, unearthed some of the most enduring treasures, and helped preserve some of the most important finds in history. Like Tutankhamun's tomb. What would it have been like to step into an Egyptian tomb untouched by human hands for thousands of years?

To be the first to enter Tut's tomb and peer inside at the vast treasures waiting to be discovered.

The thought gave her chills.

Harry Lawrence had been there. Touched relics from Ancient Greece. Rome. Ancient Mesopotamia. He'd been among the first to enter King Tutankhamun's tomb.

But something happened at the dig site that night. In Egypt's Valley of the Kings. After they'd opened Tut's tomb amidst a flood of reporters, Harry Lawrence was dead. And no one ever discovered why.

There was no autopsy. No cause of death listed. Harry's body had been hurriedly returned to England and cremated.

But the papers had a field day with his death. Another soul claimed by the Pharaoh's curse, said *The London Times*. Several American papers claimed that Harry Lawrence had ignored the hieroglyphic warnings above Tut's inner sanctum and died for his carelessness.

The supernatural angle sold lots of papers back then. And it kept Harry Lawrence's memory in the public eye for decades. Until the world forgot him, his tools changing hands and collecting dust. Until they landed here in Las Vegas.

In her eager hands.

Ever removed the last layer of newsprint and peered inside.

An aged black leather roll of archaeological tools nestled in a bed of shredded paper. In each of the weathered pockets several brushes poked out, the top of an old magnifying glass, various sized pegs to mark artifact locations, a weathered grey tangle of string, and—his trowel.

With reverence, she carefully lifted the tool wrap out of the box and unrolled it in front of her. And ran her fingers across the exposed tools.

Brushes that had revealed amphorae beneath the dirt, sarcophagi, and early Roman glass. Armor. Statues. And maybe even remnants of the seven wonders of the ancient world.

She grinned. Harry Lawrence had held these tools. Excavated antiquities and revealed mysteries that she'd only dreamed of discovering

But the trowel. She hesitated touching it. It was an almost sacred tool of archaeologists. A foundational part of digs since the beginning.

Ever studied the wooden handle, smoothed with time and use, its glossy sheen almost glowing. Despite the wear on the small, flat diamond-shaped metal blade, it had been well-kept. Then she saw Harry Lawrence's name burned into the trowel's wooden handle.

What would it have been like to have lived during the time of so many discoveries? Major historical relics? Doing fieldwork beside legends that only sought to preserve artifacts, not profit from them? So many others had stolen these priceless antiquities and sold them.

She leaned closer to the tools.

"What happened to you, Harry Lawrence?" she muttered, wishing his tools could speak across time and tell her what happened that night in the Valley of Kings.

Light glinted off the trowel which had an almost otherworldly glow to it.

With shaking hands, she reached toward it, dying to hold it in her hands. Feel its heft. Its weight. The gentle scrape of the blade against soil.

She lifted the handle and gripped it in her fist, feeling the whisper of time surround her.

As the light—and the trowel—began to fade.

The trowel fell out of her hand as she felt herself sinking into a rush of images that churned into a maelstrom of light and shadow and silence.

Until shadows hung over her, obscuring the bright sunlight as a flood of voices chattered. The sand beneath her burned as more shadows—people—blocked the sun. And the voices around her spoke…Arabic?

"I think she's come around."

Someone fanned her with a palm frond as a man knelt beside her, gently brushing hair out of her face.

"Miss? Are you all right? Miss!" The bright baritone voice with a smooth British accent slid across her ears like silk.

"Making the ladies swoon already, Harry?" asked a rough but jovial male voice, older, also British but less refined.

Harry? She gasped, her eyes widening. Harry Lawrence?

That was impossible…wasn't it?

The sun was desert-bright, high in the sky as it baked the hard-packed pyramid-like mounds of dirt and rock surrounding a deep, square hole in the earth. Egyptian pyramids towered around the dig site. A wall of stacked stones obscured the excavated hole. Distant bray of a donkey squawked above the hiss and scrape of shovels moving dirt and the tangle of more voices speaking Arabic.

Workers in long white cotton robes wore turbans and helped carry rocks and dirt past dozens of white tents surrounding the dig site.

But the man that hung over her wore a devilish smile beneath his thick mane of blond hair. He wore a loose white cotton shirt, shorts, and laced dusty brown boots. His sandy hair was windblown and clung to his handsome oval face, light green eyes reflecting an intrigued smile. At her.

"Miss, are you all right?" he asked as he reached out and brushed dust off her face.

His skin was bronzed by the sun and he looked like someone had just told him an amusing story, his smile burning in those soft green eyes.

Harry Lawrence, renowned archaeologist and adventurer that had been the international face of exploration and discovery since 1913.

"Harry Lawrence?" she said and sat up.

His smile broadened, but he kept his sun-warmed hands firmly on her forearms.

"In the flesh, my dear," he said. "But tell me, who are you and what's an American doing on the other side of the world? At this dig site?" He looked her over a moment. "And I do applaud you Yanks for the shockingly attractive American fieldwork attire. Giving women the vote has done wonders and this—" He held out his hands. "It's made my day."

Ever had no idea how she got here, but his words—and attention—made her blush.

She groaned. She was dressed like Lara Croft in shorts, a tank top, and boots. Not a *proper* 1920s woman.

Might as well own it.

But she had no idea how to explain her presence here. She had no idea how she got here.

A dozen thoughts rushed through her head.

"I'm uh, a reporter and amateur archaeologist," she said quickly, watching his eyes widen. "From—The Los Angeles Daily News." She reached out and laid her hand on Harry's arm. "I've come a long way to interview you, Mr. Lawrence."

"Rubbish!" said the older Brit behind him with greying hair and a thick, coarse mustache. "Bloody American reporter comes all this way and doesn't give sod all about Tutankhamun's tomb. Wants to interview this rotter instead."

Harry laughed as he gripped Ever's hand and helped her to her feet. His touch was fiery and she felt a connection to him.

And the whisper of time.

"See, Bertie, old chap," Harry said, glancing over his shoulder. "Told you I was famous across the pond, too."

"Daft luck, if you ask me." The older man called Bertie, dressed in a tan tweed suit and white dress shirt, walked away shaking his head.

Ever struggled against the rock and sand, wobbling and still dizzy from her trip a hundred years across time to Egypt. Harry's grip on her hand tightened and he studied her a moment, the hint of a smile crinkling around his eyes.

That stretched into a growing awkward silence.

"Easy now," he said finally. "Can't have you fainting again. Even in March, the Egyptian sun can drain your energy dry. Let's get you some hydration and out of this heat, shall we?"

She nodded.

His stubbled jaw gave him a ruggedly handsome look that enhanced his calm demeanor and sure swagger. Laugh lines curved around his cheeks, a hint of sadness in his green eyes. He had Cary Grant's charm, Pierce Brosnan's poise, and Brad Pitt's looks wrapped into a rugged Indiana Jones façade that made her lightheaded.

He was everything she'd imagined. Vibrant and full of life. A bright white light that dimmed the Egyptian sun. And made her heart pound faster.

Harry led her inside the shade of the nearest tent and sat her down on a wooden crate that doubled as a chair. He handed her a canteen and she drank the cool, sweet water.

"I thought perhaps you were here for today's tomb opening," he said as he sat down on the crate beside her, propping one leg on the other, hands in his lap, studying her like one of his Egyptian artifacts.

She gasped. They were opening Tut's tomb today!

Her gaze flicked back to him, admiring his handsome face and electric green eyes that made every thought in her head disappear. But his vibrancy made her sad.

Harry Lawrence only had hours to live.

The silence built between them. She had to respond.

"No," she said finally. "My editor sent someone else to cover that event."

He clicked his tongue and shook his head.

"Blighter hasn't gotten it through his head yet that women got the vote. That you can work and explore and be regular human beings just like men. Who knew?"

She smiled, wanting to run her fingers through his golden blond hair.

"I know, right? Joke's on him. If he'd let me write the article, it would have cost him half as much. If you're going to be a sexist ass, at least make it work for you."

His laughter filled the tent. But his expression turned serious as he fixed her with his gaze. Like she was the only person in his universe.

It gave her chills.

"I don't believe you gave your name, Miss—"

"Maine," said Ever, her gaze not leaving his face. "Everleigh Maine, but everyone calls me Ever."

"Ever," he said in a soft, almost dramatic voice, the silky baritone notes vibrating against her chest. "As in happily ever after?"

A twinkle sparkled in those heavenly green eyes.

For her?

She nodded. "I love a good happy ending, don't you, Mr. Lawrence?"

He leaned closer and she felt the heat of his proximity, hotter than the Egyptian sun at noon, hotter than the sea of sand surrounding the Valley of Kings.

"Please—call me, Harry," he said. "And yes, I do love it when everything pulls together for a jolly good ending. I prefer to leave the tragedy to Shakespeare. Or the bloody Greeks. Masters of tragedy."

Ever grinned. "What was your favorite dig, Harry?" she asked, wanting to reach out and hold his hand.

Protect him from what would soon creep across the night and harm him.

The corners of his eyes crinkled, pupils dilating, gaze enveloping. Sending shivers through her. He held out his arms, chuckling.

"Why, the one I'm on, of course! Every dig is my favorite."

"No favorites?" she countered.

"Ever, I live in the moment because I will never again experience stepping foot in a boy king's tomb that has been sealed since before the time of Christ."

His gaze burned with life and she felt his energy and excitement about the world in every single word.

"I've excavated temples in Greece," he continued. "Discovered a centurion's helmet in Italy. Viking runes in Norway. Touched the most storied artifacts of my time. Every dig is a celebration. Every find, the achievement of a lifetime." He laid his hand against his heart. "My life is straight out of legend and I'm a lucky bloke—for however long it lasts."

His words moved her in ways she couldn't even process. That was the life she wanted, but she hated knowing what was about to happen to him. He didn't know that it was all about to end.

And she had no clue how to change that.

Or stop it.

"Nothing you would change?" she pressed.

He laughed. "Not a moment. Not a single experience. Including this one."

A man strolled past the tent opening with a woman on his arm. Ever recognized her as Lady Lillian Howe. The man with pomaded black hair and a bushy mustache was lead archaeologist Frank Carson.

Harry's gaze got far away as he stared at Lady Lillian dressed in a loose-fitting shift-style lavender dress, long double strand of pearls, ivory heels, and wide-brimmed wool hat that matched her dress.

A past relationship? Or did Harry long for a relationship of his own? All accounts of his life never mentioned a woman or marriage. At nineteen, he'd married his work and never looked back.

Until now.

"Anything you'd add to it?" Ever asked, pushing back against his contradictory response.

Harry's gaze returned to her, all smiles and good looks as he shook his head. But his eyes told a different story. He had regrets. They shadowed his eyes as he watched Lady Lillian and Frank Carson together.

Those electric green eyes twinkled, filling with charm again. His face was an attractive mask that hid something darker. Something that ached in his expression for a moment or two.

"Oh, come on, Mr. Lawrence," she said. "Harry. I see that look in your eyes. There's something missing from your life. What would you add?"

He cast one last look out the tent and fixed her with his intense gaze.

"A partner," he said finally and stared down at his hands. "It is difficult to connect with someone when you're a week or more away by ship though." He chuckled. "And all you talk about is the past."

So, the globetrotting archaeologist did have a regret.

"How do you plan to turn this tragedy into a happily ever after, Harry?" she asked.

"You're quite good at this, Ever," he said. "You go right for a vein."

"My readers are very interested in your love life, Harry," she said. "You're something of a celebrity back home."

She was interested. She wanted to know everything she could about him. And just maybe that knowledge would keep him from dying.

He sat up straighter, that charming smile diminishing the shadow of regret from his face. Those laugh lines returned, curving across his cheeks.

"A celebrity, am I?" he said, his hand pressed against his chest. "I wish my love life was something to celebrate. I'll have to let you and your readers know as soon as I dig up this relic."

He was dodging the question again.

"Straight answer, Harry," she said, her voice rising. "Is there a girl back home in Manchester?"

He looked intrigued again. "How did you know I was from Manchester, Ever Maine?"

She tapped her index finger to her right temple. "Did my homework."

A young Egyptian boy with tousled dark hair rushed into the tent, chest heaving.

"Sir, sir!" He called and waved his arm toward the tent flap. "Come!"

Harry's smile fled as he got to his feet and moved toward the young boy.

"Forgive me, but they need me onsite. We're preparing to open the sealed tomb."

"Now?" Ever cried as she stood up. "Before the press arrives?"

He laid a finger to his lips and shushed her.

When she frowned, he moved toward her and laid his hands gently against her bare shoulders.

Even in Egypt's desert heat, his touch sizzled across her skin. Like a hot car seat in summer. Like Fourth of July fireworks in Vegas.

She couldn't help herself. She reached up and laid her hand on top of his and squeezed.

"Frank does what Frank wants," he whispered. "Regardless of what anyone else thinks. I only want to see inside the tomb before these chaps empty it of its valuables. To glimpse a scene out of the Book of the Dead before the march of time erases it forever. Or man's greed."

His words gave her chills. He cared about the find, not the prestige or the money. He had integrity. Passion.

And it was intoxicating.

"I hope you find the woman of your dreams, Harry."

She meant that, hoping against hope that he would survive the night.

For several moments that felt like an eternity, Harry stared into her eyes.

"I think I just did," he whispered, leaning toward her face until his mouth was deliciously close to hers.

She wanted to slide her fingers into his sandy, windblown locks and pull his mouth against hers. She shifted her body toward him until her lips were a breath away.

"Come, sir!" The boy shouted, tugging hard on Harry's shirt. "Come!"

Sighing, Harry rubbed her arms a moment, glancing at his feet.

"I'll be back soon," he said and met her gaze. "Wait for me?"

"As long as it takes," she said.

Harry rushed out of the tent, the lanky boy fluttering around him like a moth as he disappeared around the rock wall. Into the dark hole beyond it.

By late afternoon, a dozen men from *The London Times* had arrived to capture the exclusive story and photos of the opening of King Tut's tomb. Ever stayed in the tent until the event was well underway and then slipped over to the wall to watch.

Harry stood alongside Lord Howe and Frank Carson and others whose names Ever didn't know.

The blue burst of flashbulbs popped off as newspaper reporters, dressed in tweed suits and hats, huddled in whatever shade they could find while Lord Howe and Frank Carson spoke at length, Lady Lillian seated between them. Finally, the reporters got to Harry and asked him several questions that Ever couldn't hear.

His outgoing demeanor set everyone at ease and his humor made the reporters laugh several times. They photographed him from many angles and then everything got quiet, awaiting the moment when the tomb was opened.

Ever watched Harry from the wall as he pried the remainder of the seal open with his trowel, revealing a flood of cool, ancient darkness to murmurs and claps.

Flashbulbs were explosive, popping off like gunshots as Egyptian workers in white robes and turbans carried out artifacts of ebony and gold under the direction of lead archaeologist Frank Carson. Coptic jars, statues, and mummified meats wrapped in white cloth. They loaded the items on carts as more pictures flashed.

By evening, the event was over, but the reporters remained to further document the dig, seated around a massive bonfire teeming with workers, temperatures plummeting into the low fifties. The dark was deep and heavy, no light pollution to soften it, especially in 1923.

Meat sizzled on spits, aromatic drift of wood smoke and turmeric mixing with the sharp tang of fresh coriander leaves and earthy scent of cumin. The dig team drank port from tin cups and ate roasted mutton with their fingers as they told stories, embers wafting like fireflies through camp.

Harry sat in front, cup of port in hand, his mellow, bright voice telling tales about Vikings above the crackle of the fire. Even in the glow of firelight, his face looked pale. But he kept shaking his fingers and laying his hand against his chest.

Was he in distress?

She moved toward him, but he bolted up from his seat, cup in hand, and an arm across his gut. He rushed toward the first tent where he'd taken her earlier but ducked behind it.

Ever hurried after him, but a piercing shout rose from behind the tent.

When she raced around it, Harry lay motionless on the ground, port spilling into the sand.

Bertie, the older Brit, knelt beside him, shaking Harry's shoulder.

"Harry! Get up! What's the matter with you, old chap?"

No! Harry Lawrence was dead.

The world began to shift around her, shuddering and twisting. And she couldn't stop it.

Ever grabbed hold of the tent flap, but the force of the tilt dragged her out of 1923.

She found herself back in her Vegas apartment, Harry's tool wrap still unrolled on the tile floor beside the cardboard box where she'd left it.

Grabbing her laptop bag that set beside the sofa, Ever fired it up, accessing every article she could locate about the death of archaeologist Harry Lawrence.

Whatever her little jaunt to the dig site had done, it had produced a lot more articles about Harry Lawrence. And his death.

She found an article in *The London Times* that mentioned a dispute between Harry and some of the other archaeologists regarding a medallion that had turned up missing from the tomb's cataloged items. From the quotes attributed to Harry, he seemed suspicious of his fellow archaeologists—including Frank Carson.

Then she looked up the symptoms Harry had exhibited. He'd been shaking his hands. Holding his chest. And then his gut.

Had it been a heart attack?

After not finding anything but the medallion lead, Ever moved back toward the tool wrap. Determined to go back to 1923.

And follow Harry out of the tent this time.

With a deep breath, Ever bent down and picked up Harry's trowel that rested on top of the other tools.

Time whispered around her in a rush of images that churned into a maelstrom of light and shadow and silence. Until the trowel fell from her hands, propelling her back again.

Back to 1923.

What the hell? Into the exact moment she'd entered the first time?

Egyptian workers crowded around her, blocking the sun, and chattering in Arabic as Harry Lawrence leaned over her, skin sun-bronzed and hair golden blond. Animated green eyes lit by a devilish smile and smoking hot looks that made her breath catch. Same white cotton shirt and shorts. Same dusty brown boots.

"Miss? Are you all right? Miss!"

Harry's bright baritone voice and smooth British accent slid across her ears like silk.

Same question.

"Making the ladies swoon already, Harry?" asked Bertie, Harry's older Brit colleague, in a rough but jovial voice.

It was all the same, the crude rock wall surrounding the hole where the dark passage led into Tutankhamun's tomb. The workers scurrying past, a donkey's sharp bray.

Like everything had restarted. But why? It made no more sense than her traveling back to 1923 at all.

She sat up.

"Harry Lawrence?"

She almost said the cheeky words along with him about liking her tank top and shorts. Probably hadn't seen a woman dressed like her before today.

Again, she told him she was a reporter for *The Los Angeles Daily News* and that she'd come a long way to interview him.

On cue, his colleague shouted the word, *rubbish* and shot a light-hearted dig at Harry who assured Bertie that he was famous in

America. His colleague grumbled about Harry's good luck as Harry helped her into the tent.

Just like before.

She waited for the canteen and drank as Harry sat beside her. She felt his heat and radiance again, wanting to touch him, hold him in her arms. She sighed.

And kiss him.

As she interviewed Harry, feeling starry-eyed as she stared into his green gaze, she knew that she would be taunted again with almost a kiss before the Egyptian boy interrupted them.

But she didn't mind. She ached to get close to him again, to hear him voice his passion for history and the past.

His words burned through her, his proximity intoxicating, and she fought down the urge to wrap him in her arms. Taking in his charm and wit and good looks was a privilege and she immersed herself in him. She comforted him this time when the sight of Lady Lillian Howe on Frank Carson's arm saddened him. Sliding closer.

His lips were a breath away.

She leaned toward him, brushing her lips across his, knowing she had only moments.

"I hope you find the woman of your dreams, Harry," she whispered to him.

"I just did," he said, his lips against her ear, sending chills through her body.

He enfolded her in his arms, holding her like he was afraid to let her go.

"If I let go," he whispered, an ache in his voice this time, "Will you just disappear again?"

"I want to stay," she said and slid her arms around him, the beat of his heart thrumming against her chest, marking time with hers. "With you."

"Then stay with me this time, Ever."

His voice burned against her ear.

She pressed her face against his shoulder, his clothes smelling like wood smoke, dust, and the soft hint of clean cotton.

"Come, sir!" The boy shouted, tugging hard on Harry's shirt. "Come!"

Sighing, Harry hesitated and then finally let her go. He rubbed her arms a moment, glancing at his boots.

"I'll be back soon," he said. "Wait for me?"

"As long as it takes," she said, sliding her hand into his for a moment.

He squeezed it and let go, rushing out of the tent, the lanky boy fluttering around him like a moth as he disappeared around the rock wall.

She'd changed a few things. Would it be enough to change his destiny?

Sliding off the crate, Ever hurried out of the tent toward the rock wall. She peered around it as the sound of angry voices echoed.

"What do you mean, it's missing, Frank?" Harry demanded, arms folded against his chest as Lady Lillian and Lord Howe hung at a distance.

Bertie, the older Brit, looked disgusted. Two other archaeologists that Ever didn't recognize shrugged and kept quiet, looking as confused as Lord Howe and his daughter.

"The medallion from the outer chamber!" Frank shouted, arms flailing. "It's bloody missing!"

"How?" Bertie demanded. "I cataloged that piece myself to hand over to the Egyptian government."

Harry's gaze narrowed and he glared at Frank Carson.

"Bloody explain that one, Frank," Harry snapped. "Since you demanded to oversee the delivery of those artifacts."

"All I know is that it's missing," Frank said, his voice quieter.

"It? There were two of those sodding medallions, Frank!" Harry was in Frank Carson's face now. "Two! Remember? They were a set. How is one missing?"

Bertie shook his head, looking disgusted.

"I don't know!" Frank Carson shouted. "All I know is that two were cataloged and one is missing."

Harry glanced from Frank to Bertie and then slapped his arms against his sides.

"Let me know when it bloody turns up," he said with a growl. "Now, I have work to do."

———

The opening of Tutankhamun's tomb went exactly as it had the first time that she observed it. Harry nearly outshone the gold and ebony artifacts recovered from the tomb as flashbulbs popped in bright blue strobes, the sun low on the horizon by the time it was over.

When night enveloped the Valley of Kings, stars filled the heavens like someone had spilled sugar across the vast expanse as Ever hurried to the bonfire gathering.

Looking for Harry Lawrence.

Meat sizzled on spits, aromatic drift of wood smoke and turmeric mixing with the sharp tang of fresh coriander leaves and earthy scent of cumin. The dig team drank port from tin cups and ate roasted mutton with their fingers as they told stories, embers wafting like fireflies through camp.

Harry sat in front, cup of port in hand, his mellow, bright voice telling tales about Vikings above the fire's crackle. Even in the glow of firelight, his face looked pale.

He shook his fingers and pressed his hand against his chest.

She rushed over to him.

"Harry, what's the matter?" she asked, laying her hand on his shoulder.

He looked up at her, tin cup in hand, looking distressed. Ghost pale.

"Suddenly, I'm not well," he said in a quiet voice, his hand still against his chest.

"Are you having chest pain?" she asked.

He shook his head, face flushing. "No…my heart's—fluttering." He glanced at his left hand and shook his fingers again. "And my hands have gone to sleep."

She helped him stand. "You need to lie down," she said and steered him toward the tent.

In a moment, he doubled over, grabbing hold of his gut.

"Harry, what's the matter?" she cried.

He pulled away, lurching around the tent.

"Harry!"

She ran after him, but Bertie's shout halted her steps in mid-stride, her heart smashing against her rib cage.

Harry lay motionless on the ground behind the tent, port wine spilling into the sand.

Bertie dropped to one knee, shaking Harry's shoulder.

"Harry! Get up! What's the matter with you, old chap?"

Her hands flew to her mouth, her chest twisting into knots.

Harry Lawrence was dead. Again.

She hadn't changed anything.

The world began to shift around her, shuddering and twisting. She grabbed hold of the tent pole, trying to hold onto 1923 again, but the force was too great. Pulling her backward.

Dragging her out of 1923. Again.

For the second time today, she found herself back in her Vegas apartment. The sun was low on the horizon, casting fluid shadows through the apartment as she dropped to her knees beside Harry Lawrence's tool wrap on the sun-warmed terracotta tiles.

Her foot hit the tool wrap and it skittered across the tile, hitting the kitchen cabinets, and flipping over.

She dropped to the floor, tears rushing down her face.

For more than a decade, she'd been fascinated by Harry Lawrence. She'd read every article and watched every documentary about him.

But watching him die twice after feeling the heat of his hand against her face and basking in the glow of his passion for history and artifacts. She swallowed a breath. Sharing a moment of electric connection that had wrapped tight around her heart.

She knew now. She was in love with Harry Lawrence. And she wanted the chance to love him.

Reining in her pain, Ever wiped away her tears and righted the leather tool wrap. All the tools were scattered across the tile floor now. She squinted.

Including something small wrapped in old yellowed newspaper and crisscrossed rubber bands.

She scooped up the palm-sized bundle. The brittle rubber bands fell apart in her hand, the newsprint unfolding.

Ever squinted. *The London Times.* And read the headline. *Renowned Archaeologist Harry Lawrence Dies.* She read the tagline beneath it. *Country mourns loss but fears ripples of Pharaoh's curse.*

Carefully, Ever unwrapped the hundred-year-old newsprint.

A gold scarab medallion lay in the crisp folds, inlaid with lapis lazuli and some sort of polished yellow glass. A handwritten note was tucked behind it.

To my son, Albert,

Forgive me. I let my greed change me when I did the unthinkable. After my colleague, Harry Lawrence refused to participate in collecting personal spoils from Tutankhamun's tomb and threatened to inform the press, I did something terrible. I went along with the plan to silence him.

Forgive me, Harry. I hope there is peace for you on the other side, something I will only know in death. I wish I could turn back time and stop all of this.

To you, lad, I entrust this priceless but bloodstained relic in the hopes that you or your descendants may somehow atone for my horrific crime and remove the pharaoh's curse from my lineage.

Albert "Bertie" Rothesay II

Stunned, Ever stared at the letter. Harry's colleagues had all conspired to murder him because he refused to steal artifacts from Tut's tomb.

But how did Harry die?

She thought back to both trips to 1923, remembering Harry seated by the bonfire each time, eating and drinking alongside the workers and his colleagues.

Looking unwell.

Eating and drinking.

Both times, he'd died with a cup of port in his hand. All his colleagues had been drinking that port. Had they poisoned Harry's cup?

That was the answer! It would explain his symptoms and sudden collapse.

Maybe if she went back a third time and returned the medallion, she could save Harry?

She had to try. She loved him.

She turned to her laptop on the sofa and typed in a search of Harry's symptoms which led her down a rabbit hole of information—and something obscure she could use.

Sliding the medallion into her shorts' pocket, she rushed over to the overturned dig tools.

Taking a deep breath, she reached down and scooped Harry's trowel off the tile floor.

She tried to hold onto it, but the trowel fell out of her hand as she sank into a rush of images that churned into a maelstrom of light and shadow and silence.

And for a third time, she opened her eyes to the same moment in time. To shadows hanging over her. A flood of voices chattered in Arabic above her as the Valley of Kings burned bright in the sun.

"Miss? Are you all right? Miss!" Harry's warm baritone voice and smooth British accent slid across her ears like silk.

"Making the ladies swoon already, Harry?"

Harry's beautiful smiling face hung over her. Enchanted. Radiant.

Her heart fluttered as her eyes welled with tears. Harry!

Around her, hard-packed pyramid-like mounds of dirt and rock cast dark, heavy shadows across the sandy ground, Egyptian pyramids towering around the dig site. Distant bray of a donkey squawked above the hiss and scrape of shovels moving dirt and the tangle of more voices speaking Arabic.

"Harry!" she cried and threw her arms around him.

He held her close. "I…think I…know you. Don't I?"

His arms around her felt like sunbaked clay, like a hot car seat in August. She swallowed a breath. Like Fourth of July fireworks in Vegas.

She brushed her lips against his ear.

"I'm Ever Maine," she whispered.

He closed his eyes a moment, a sigh rising through his chest—like he'd just recalled a fond memory.

"The feel of you is so familiar," he said. "And comforting."

She'd changed something. Felt their mutual attraction. That Harry had just displayed in front of the entire dig.

"Let's get you out of the sun now, shall we?"

He lifted her in his arms and carried her through the crowd into the first tent closest to the rock wall. And set her on the crate.

Again, Ever threw her arms around him, trying to erase the memory of his lifeless body behind this very tent, port spilling like blood across the sand.

"I…can't explain it, but I haven't felt myself until you—returned?" He shook his head, a haunted look in his electric green eyes. "It was as if time was stuck in place. And I wasn't myself until I—" He pulled in a breath. "Until I felt its ripples…when you arrived. And I felt your presence around me again."

She was just going to lay it all out for him. If he knew what was coming, maybe he could stop it somehow.

"Harry, listen to me," she said in a quiet voice as she gripped his shoulders. "Your colleagues are stealing artifacts from the tomb. They know you won't go along with these thefts, so they're going to silence you."

He frowned. "Silence me?" he said with a hiss. "I don't think Frank would—"

"Harry!" she shouted, shaking him hard. "They're all in on it. But it isn't just Frank."

He pulled away from her, slowly shaking his head.

"No," he said. "No…it's not true. It can't be true." He winced, an anguished look burning through that beautiful, handsome mask. "Not —not Bertie."

Ever gave him a decisive nod.

"Blimey! Not Bertie. He's been like a father to me."

"Until a fortune was at stake," said Ever. "You can't trust him now." She pressed her lips to his ear and spoke as quietly as she could whisper. "Harry, they're going to kill you tonight."

He pulled away, a horrified look in his eyes, face turning pale.

"I've seen it," she insisted.

Her words stunned him into silence.

A young Egyptian boy with tousled dark hair rushed into the tent, chest heaving.

"Sir, sir!" He called and waved his arm toward the tent flap. "Come!"

Ever grabbed hold of Harry's arm.

"Harry, don't go. Please."

Harry glanced out the tent flap and then back at her.

"Frank's opening the sealed tomb."

"To rob it!" Ever fired back at him.

She shifted her weight, feeling the scarab medallion press against her thigh. It felt so heavy. But she couldn't give it to him yet. It didn't exist in his world until they opened the tomb.

Harry wrapped her in his warm embrace and she held onto him, not wanting to let him go.

She had to change it this time. She couldn't watch the man she loved die a third time.

Could the medallion stop all of this?

"Come, sir!" The boy shouted, tugging hard on Harry's shirt. "Come!"

Sighing, Harry let her go. He reached out and caressed her cheek, his fingers summer-hot against her skin.

"I'll be back soon," he said. "Wait for me?"

"Forever," she said.

Harry rushed out of the tent, the lanky boy fluttering around him like a moth as he disappeared around the rock wall.

To argue about a missing medallion. Ever prayed it was for the final time—because she had changed it. Because she had saved him.

For the third time, meat sizzled on spits, aromatic drift of wood smoke and turmeric mixing with the sharp tang of fresh coriander leaves and earthy scent of cumin. The dig team drank port from tin cups and ate roasted mutton with their fingers as they told stories, embers wafting like fireflies through camp.

Harry sat in front, cup of port in hand, his mellow, bright voice telling stories about Vikings above the fire's crackle.

Ever rushed toward him.

Laughing, Harry brought the cup toward his lips.

Ever snatched the cup out of his hand.

Frank Carson and Bertie jumped to their feet, a mix of anger and fear hovering in their eyes.

"What are you doing?" Bertie shouted.

Harry was on his feet now, staring at his colleagues and then Ever who carried the cup to the bonfire and sat it in the embers.

The tin cup began to heat.

"I learned something funny today, Harry," she said, glaring at Frank and Bertie.

Harry frowned. "Something funny?"

She nodded, watching the port begin to bubble.

"See, when arsenic is heated in the sun or over a flame, it gives off the distinct smell of garlic."

Frank and Bertie fidgeted.

Already, she smelled the savory scent of garlic.

She let the port heat a moment or two longer and then lifted the cup out of the embers with two sticks.

She carried the steaming cup over to Harry, wafting the warm, heady scent of garlic in her wake.

And held the cup out to him.

He sniffed, his face turning pale, eyes igniting with fury.

"I smell garlic," he said through gritted teeth. "Lots of garlic."

Frank glared at Harry as Bertie held up his hands.

"Harry, I…"

"You were against us, old boy," said Frank.

Like that made it okay.

"You stole artifacts! From the tomb!" Harry shouted.

He threw down the cup and walked away. Into the tent.

Ever followed.

"Harry, wait!"

He paced inside.

"I trusted them! Now, we'll never recover that sodding medallion."

When she gave him the medallion, she knew the strange corridor between her time and his would close. She smiled. An adventure awaited. She belonged here—with him.

She slid the medallion out of her pocket. "This one?"

He whirled around.

"Ever! How did you get that?" he cried, grinning.

"I'll tell you all about it," she said. "If you have fifty or so years free."

He flashed that devilish grin and pulled her into his arms.

"I do," he said. "Because I'm in love with you, Ever Maine."

She grinned and pressed the medallion into his hand.

"And I've already loved you for a hundred years, Harry Lawrence. Time to catch up."

The medallion glowed as he smashed his mouth against hers in the hottest kiss she'd felt in more than a century.

Beauty, Captured and Framed

Twenty-first-century ghost hunter, Jackson Mayfield pounded up the dark redwood stairs of Port Townsend's Peninsula Hotel, frantic to save the woman he loved.

Gaslights pooled pallid yellow along Water Street, the dark winter night eerily quiet. Scent of burning coal and wood smoke hung above the scent of orange oil as he pulled in a hurried breath.

Wood floors creaked with every slick step, top floor painfully quiet except for the steady clack and tick of the dark oak grandfather clock against the hallway's ivory wall. It lamented seven o'clock's arrival with seven mournful notes, a requiem that rose in layers through the empty hallway as he reached the top step.

His stomach dropped, heart beating faster. The door to her hotel suite was wide open and dark, lit only by gas lamps below on Water Street.

"Ophelia!" he shouted, fear turning his hands to ice.

His heart pounded in his ears, stomach burning as he brushed past the polished redwood balustrade, the tails of his black tuxedo jacket whipping against the baluster.

"Ophelia, where are you?"

He couldn't be too late! He couldn't! She meant everything to him.

"Please!" he called, "Tell me you're still here. Ophelia!"

He rushed into Ophelia's suite.

As the last moan of the clock faded to steady ticking, heavy sounds of fluttering overpowered the painful quiet.

Horrified, Jackson turned toward the sound, toward the picture windows that lined the south wall overlooking Port Townsend Bay and Water Street below.

A surge of cold air stung his face, his gasping breaths fogging the air as his brain began processing details. His heart beat a wild staccato against his rib cage.

The window! February's chilly wind fluttered against white muslin curtains. Like topsails on a sloop. At last, he realized it.

One of the windows was open!

His heart dropped and for a moment, he couldn't breathe. He gasped. "Ophelia, no…"

He rushed over to the open window, rain misting Port Townsend's dark, cast-iron skies, the bay a black mirror. And looked down through the gaslights' yellow haze to the street below as shouts and commotion rang out. Rising above the clock's steady ticking and the rustle-clomp of horse-drawn carriages.

A shrill police whistle cut through his pain, dispersing the crowd.

At last, he saw the hazy dark figure in the street. His eyes filled with tears as he sucked in a breath and turned away.

"Oh, God, no—Ophelia," he said through gritted teeth. "No!"

His knees buckled, body aching all over. Desperate to feel her soft, calming presence, to hear her gentle, lyric voice telling him she was all right.

The heaviness of her growing absence broke him with every step away from the window.

He smashed his stinging eyes closed, shaking his head. No! He couldn't look at her lying lifeless in the misty yellow darkness, not one moment longer. He wouldn't have his last image of Ophelia Swann dead and broken in the street below.

Defeated, he dropped to his knees, shuddering as he wrapped his arms around himself. He had never loved anyone like he loved Ophelia Swann. Ever.

He felt sick inside. He'd traveled back 124 years into the past to save her. And failed.

Something glowed purple to his right. The blue flower pot sat on a small drum table, daffodils in full bloom, glowing purple. He plucked one glowing blossom off the plant, resisting the urge to crush it. He never even got to use it.

The newsprint page covering the planted bulb lay on the damp floor. Face up, mocking him with its February 29, 1896 date. And its headline read, *International Opera Star Leaps to Her Death.*

The strange warning had given him four days to save her, but he'd failed. Miserably. Tears slid down the sides of his face and he balled his hands into fists, gritting his teeth.

He winced, aching to hear Ophelia's clear, melodic soprano voice, part songbird and part angel. Her touch had softened the painful loneliness he'd hidden from the rest of the world. And the strange crossover with his fourth-great-grandfather, who thought Jackson was his youngest son, grown up. Also named Jackson, the boy drowned at age six around 1880. He played along when he'd arrived through the portrait—until the man tried to hurt and control him.

Jackson sank to the slick hardwood floor, wet with cold rain misting through the window. Shadows danced along the suite's ivory walls as he played everything back in his head, his heart crumbling.

Where had it all gone wrong? Why couldn't he save her?

Everything started to go wrong with the phantom news story. Or was it the daffodils? No, everything started with the painting.

Port Townsend, Washington
      Wednesday, February 26, 2020

The Port Townsend Spirit Seekers, led by Jackson Mayfield, met at the Gothic Ghost, a pub just blocks from the once famed, Victorian Northwest Opera House, closed more than fifty years now. And prime ghost-seeking real estate. Especially now that he'd learned about the six, strange Victorian oil portraits locked up in a small office. One of them was the famous portrait of Ophelia Swann.

Forgotten until his cousin discovered them as the property's new security guard. Around midnight, Darren had agreed to let Jackson and his four other ghost seekers into the place. To see hers and the other paintings.

And finally test the local Leap Day legend, something no other ghost hunter had ever done. On Leap Day in 1896, international opera star and Port Townsend native, Ophelia Swann leaped to her death from a hotel near the opera house.

Over a lost love, some said. To escape her corrupt, embezzling manager said others. He wanted to find out the truth. Set the mystery to rest.

No, he wanted to save her.

After 124 years, it was time.

He'd studied Ophelia's portrait and researched her mystery for over a decade. Since middle school and a local history project and later, with Marti and the Spirit Seekers crew. Until a year ago, when the portrait disappeared without notice from the local historical society.

Just last month, it resurfaced. Back in the old opera house where it'd originally been found. Ignored and forgotten in a back room of the derelict building, along with the other unusual, full-length portraits. It made no sense.

Jackson wanted answers.

The antique brass and mahogany pub smelled warm with oranges and cold with brine from the sharp winds coming off Port Townsend Bay as he slouched his tall, lanky frame into a wooden captain's chair around an eight-top table in the bay window overlooking—well, the bay. Made sense. He loved this gothic little seaport in the Northwest's misty grey heart, with its porticos, cupolas, and widow's walks. Perfect setting to hunt ghosts.

The light was low in the brick and glass building with dark hardwoods and wooden booths lining three walls. Candles flickered on all the tables and booths. The U-shaped bar lit up the back wall. It was draped with brass piping and milled Victorian flourishes of leaves, vines, and swirls. Three large mirrors shaped like gothic cathedral windows reflected the entire room. Strings of gold lights lit the bar and its mirrors. Rows and rows of colorful, glowing bottles made it look like an alchemist rather than a bartender tended the elaborate bar. Tall, padded captain's chairs with brass footrests lined the shiny cherry wood bar.

Along the mirrors, over two dozen tap handles represented some of Jackson's favorite microbrews, Pacific Northwest and Alaskan beers, and seasonals. Nothing like having to choose from Fremont and pFriem Winter Ales and Rogue Yellow Snow.

Before a ghost investigation though, he always preferred his go-to, tried and true Pyramid Hefeweizen.

He brushed his fingers through windblown, blond hair, his pale blue eyes (a Mayfield trademark trait) reflecting back at him from the brass fixtures. He leaned back in the creaky chair as the stained-glass light above his head cast rivulets of blue, purple, and yellow lights across the table. Waiting for the rest of his ghost-hunting team to arrive. He wore a blue and grey plaid shirt over jeans, black boots, and charcoal grey Gore-Tex coat.

He ordered a draft Pyramid and nursed the ice-cold beer until Stan Westbrook and his wife, Marti arrived. Thirtysomethings to Jackson's twenties, Stan and Marti both wore black Spirit Seeker T-shirts underneath matching puffy red jackets. Stan wore jeans and Marti wore black leggings. Stan was five-six to Marti's five-eleven, leggy frame. Dark-haired and stick-thin to Marti's thicker athletic frame and short white, highlighted bubblegum pink hair.

"Hey, Jackson," Stan called, following Marti over to the table.

"Stan," he said with a nod. "Hey, Marti, love the pink hair."

"Thanks, Jackson," she said grinning, warm brown eyes bright as she sat down beside Stan. "Stan here says it's too much."

Jackson rolled his eyes. "What does he know? Looks great."

Marti poked Stan's shoulder. "See!"

Stan sighed and ordered two chardonnays as fiftysomethings Scott and Nancy Branson hurried out of the cold rain and mist, brushing off their coat sleeves.

"Jackson, what's up?" Scott shouted, his loud voice carrying through the half-full bar.

For 10:00 P.M. on a Wednesday, the Gothic Ghost was pretty full.

Black parka, black Spirit Seeker T-shirt, and jeans, Scott plopped into the nearest chair. His mop of curly dark hair was unruly, Van Dyke beard trimmed short, hazel eyes warm as he smiled at Jackson. Nancy slid into the chair beside Scott, wearing a wool blue coat. She was petite and thin, five-foot-five to Scott's five-foot-nine. She had a short, black bob and small, kind green eyes. She wore a grey Spirit Seekers T-shirt over navy blue leggings.

"Hey, where's your T-shirt?" Nancy asked, leaning against the table.

Jackson ignored her question, glancing at the empty chairs to his left and right. Where Ava would have been tonight if she hadn't walked out on him. Now, he was the group's fifth wheel. Damn, it hurt to be surrounded by happy couples. He and Ava had been together for three years. He was hoping to propose to her in May. When he paid off the ring.

She moved out while he was at work. He came home to a half-empty apartment and Ava with her pink coat on and suitcase in hand. Looking like she was going on the trip of a lifetime. Without him. She'd given him the classic, *it's not you, it's me* speech. And every word hurt. So damned short it could've been a text message.

Now, he hated nights alone in the apartment, frozen dinners for one, his voice the only thing staving off the silence. And all the questions—like why she didn't want him anymore?

"Jackson?" Nancy repeated. "Where's your T-shirt?"

Frank Estes, the stocky, bearded bartender waved at Scott and Nancy. Old friends. That's why the team haunted the Gothic Ghost before and after investigations. That and its killer view of the bay. Okay, it was also the amazing beer selections and pub food.

"Wanted to look inconspicuous," Jackson replied and took a long pull from his frosty beer glass.

Scott frowned, casting a worried look at Nancy who watched Jackson with a wary gaze.

"What are you up to, Jackson?" Nancy asked, her alto voice sounding concerned as she exchanged a look with Marti. One that Jackson couldn't read.

He shrugged, glancing at his glass.

"You okay, dude?" Scott asked, a hand on his shoulder. "This about Ava? Guess she was tired of sharing the apartment with you *and* Ophelia Swann all these years."

Scott laughed, the warm timbre filling the expanse until Nancy smacked him on the arm.

"Not funny," she said with a growl.

"Just kidding, Jackson," said Scott, looking contrite.

"Forget it," said Jackson.

Why would he say that? Had Ava said something to Scott about how much time he spent investigating Ophelia Swann's death? Had she confided in Nancy? Why hadn't Ava said something to him about it if it bothered her? She hadn't said a word about anything. Not even his cooking.

"If you need to talk, you know our door's always open, bro," said Stan. "Always."

Marti reached across the two empty chairs and gripped Jackson's forearm. "Any time day or night, Jackson. I mean that."

"Ours, too, dude," said Scott, leaning back in the creaky captain's chair. "Nancy and I won't let you go through this breakup alone. Hell, it's only been two months."

Monday, December 7th at 6:08 P.M. Jackson sighed, not looking up. Didn't they understand?

"Gotta get used to being the group's fifth wheel again."

The group had been together for six years. Twice as long as he and Ava.

"What? Fifth wheel? That's ridiculous!" Scott shouted as the bartender carried over two chardonnays, a Fremont Winter Ale, and a Merlot for Nancy.

Jackson looked up from his ale and forced a smile, his voice quiet, making everyone lean closer.

"Figured it was a good time to test the Port Townsend legend of Ophelia Swann's portrait. Tonight. During our investigation."

The table went deathly quiet, Scott and Stan exchanging unsettling glances while Marti and Nancy froze, staring wide-eyed at each other.

"Jackson, you can't!" Scott set down his glass of Winter Ale. "Dude, seriously. Nobody knows how it works. *If* it even works. And if it does…nobody knows if you can come back through again. Or how."

"Dammit, Jackson!" Marti shouted, slapping the table with her hand. "This is the most dangerous thing you've ever suggested! What if you get trapped there?" She pulled in a breath. "Or die."

"Marti's right," said Stan in a quiet voice. "We only know the basics since you brought up doing this investigation. We've barely learned how the mechanism works. And none of us has done any testing yet. Much less actually scanning for portals in that old opera house. Took that long just to get permission to enter the place."

"My cousin, Dylan's running security for the building now. He's gonna get us into the room with the paintings. That's where the Ophelia Swann painting ended up."

"When were you going to tell us they'd found the painting?" Marti demanded. She crossed her arms. "After you went through it?"

Scott adamantly shook his head. "None of us has even seen the Swann portrait—except Marti—much less investigated those other damned paintings! You've never even seen the other paintings, just heard about them."

It was true. He'd overheard an employee at the historical society talking about the other creepy portraits, all full body height, but there was little information on the artist and none on the subjects. The older woman confessed that she felt uncomfortable around these portraits— even the one of Ophelia Swann. They creeped her out, she'd said in a sharp whisper.

He'd never understood that woman's reaction. He'd always found Ophelia's portrait breathtaking. He wondered if that woman was the reason the portraits disappeared from the historical society without warning.

"And no one's even taken EMF readings!" Scott continued. "Not a single EVP or even a spirit box session!"

Jackson sighed. Still yelling at him.

Scott motioned out the window toward Water Street. "We've never even been in the building. Hell, tonight's our first visit there and you wanna go try some untested portal without any information about it! And there's only two days until Leap Day. You'd only have forty-eight hours." His face lit with anger. "That's irresponsible as hell, Jackson. Even for you."

"You done?" Jackson asked, making Scott even madder.

"Bro," said Stan, setting down his glass of chardonnay. "Listen to Scott. It's not safe. You're legendary for charging alone into dark places with only a flashlight and digital recorder. But we won't let you get yourself killed or maimed tonight over that painting. Forget it!"

Scott took a big drink of his ale and wiped his mouth with a paper napkin. "What Stan said. Besides, this is Spirit Seeker's biggest investigation to date. Now, how would it look if we captured our founder getting killed tonight on video? Not good for our regular streamers or our YouTube ratings."

"I don't know…ratings might spike," Jackson said with a chuckle.

"Not funny," Nancy replied.

"Our competition would love just that," Marti snapped. "And the thrill seekers out there. But we're not filming for them. And we aren't letting you go in there all kamikaze, Jackson."

Scott crossed his arms. "And that's final."

Were they planning to stop him from testing out the stories about Ophelia's portrait? He had to be on guard for that possibility. Together, Scott and Marti could probably keep him away from the paintings. He'd have to be quick.

Nancy's eyes were wide. "They're right. You can't just charge in there blindly, Jackson! *If* there's an open portal in that place. You could be lost forever."

He sighed. He was already lost. Besides, Ophelia Swann was all he thought about anymore. If there was a chance to go back and meet her —save her—then he was taking it. Risk or not.

"If there's an open portal," said Marti. "If there is, it closes at midnight on March First. If you don't come back through by then, you'll be trapped in the past. Think about that."

The table fell painfully silent.

Marti cast a sobering glance at Stan and then Nancy as rivulets of stained-glass colors illuminated their faces. "Our first chance to even attempt a rescue wouldn't be for four years. Four years, Jackson! It's a leap year!"

That was the whole point. A leap year—Leap Day—was the only time the portal opened. Or so went the stories.

"I'll be careful," he said, glancing around the table at his concerned friends. Hoping they wouldn't see through his lie. "And I won't do something stupid."

He would if that's what it took to get to 1896. He'd do anything to get there.

Scott didn't look convinced, but the others relaxed and focused on their drinks as Stan set a tablet computer on the table, displaying a map of the opera house. Only the safe spaces. Excluding the locked office where they kept the paintings.

Stan was the tech guy for the team. Nancy handled logistics and scheduling. Scott was the main camera guy and also the video editor. Marti researched their locations. Jackson was the founder and managed the website, also backing up Stan on the tech. They all worked well together. Known each other for almost a decade.

"So, your cousin, the security guard will let us in tonight," said Nancy. She set down her glass of Merlot, studying the opera house map. "And lock us in until morning."

Jackson nodded, glancing from Marti to Nancy. "So, according to Stan's map, we've got entryway and office access, right? Including the stage?"

Marti nodded. "Except the office with the portraits." She let out a heavy sigh. "But I'm guessing you've already weaseled access to that room—without telling us. Through your cousin."

"I was just going to tell you about accessing that room," said

Jackson, picking up his glass of ale. "As long as we're careful, the portraits won't be harmed and no one will be wiser." He took a drink.

"What about harm to you, Jackson?" Marti asked.

"Look, everyone, stop!" He set down his glass hard enough to startle Nancy. "I'll be fine, so stop all the worrying. It's going to be fine."

"What about filming in that room?" Scott asked, eyes narrowing. "We are going to film, aren't we?"

Jackson nodded. "We'll film that room tonight and worry about the rest later. But don't add any of that footage into the normal investigation when you edit the footage, Scott."

"And risk getting sued?" He cried, his loud voice booming through the pub. "Forget about it!"

"Okay, then, we doing standard teams like always..." Stan's voice trailed off when Jackson winced.

He waved Stan off, trying to mask the pain. "It's fine, Stan," he said, motioning to Scott and then Marti. "You and Marti are a team and so is Scott and Nancy. I'll just GoPro it alone. It'll be fine."

Scott shook his head. "No way, dude. Not happenin'. We'll do two teams tonight and divide up the building. Upstairs is blocked off. Stage catwalks aren't safe either, so we're pretty limited to the entryway, the stage, and some offices. Everything else is off limits according to Marti and Nancy."

"That's correct," said Nancy, pointing at the map. "Stan's already laid out the safe areas we can access. So, follow Stan's map and come out alive."

Everyone nodded.

She pointed at Jackson across the table. "That goes double for you, Jackson. No Indiana Jones shit."

It was well after 11:30 P.M. when Jackson finished his second Hefeweizen and waited for the others to finish their drinks before he pulled on his grey coat. He paid the tab for the group and followed them out to Stan and Marti's blue van. They had motion capture and infrared cameras to setup and EMF meters, spirit boxes, wireless mics, and digital tape recorders to equip as they drove down a few blocks to the old, dilapidated opera house. Its three-story red brick and glass architecture had been boarded up, looking more gothic and apocalyptic as they pulled up to the curb.

Everyone piled out and headed to the back of the van, carrying in tubs of equipment and folding chairs and tables to the door. A hint of charcoal and ozone hung in the night air.

"Yo, cousin, how are ya?" the deep voice called to Jackson from the building's dark doorway.

Jackson turned around. Dylan Mayfield. Dressed in a dark blue, cop-like uniform, a stainless-steel security badge pinned above his heart. He had a 9 mm Glock strapped into a black side holster at his side, partly hidden by a long, black Gore-Tex duster. The air coming off the bay was cold, smelling of seawater as his brown-haired, nineteen-year-old cousin led him to the heavy oak door and unlocked it.

"There's electricity inside," said Dylan, running his hand over his short, clippered hair. He was lanky like Jackson, but shorter. About five ten. "No lights or heat though, so be careful in here, guys.

Dylan held open the heavy door as Stan and Scott carried in grey plastic tubs and hard-sided cases, Marti and Nancy wrangling the folding furniture. A musty smell like old rubber mixed with the smoky ozone and cold sea air as the building's thick darkness loomed.

"What about the portraits?" Jackson asked in a whisper, studying his young cousin who grabbed a flashlight and shined it into the dark entryway.

Dylan shushed him, nodding toward the open door as the Spirit Seekers carried in equipment and began setting up in the pitch black, high-ceiling entryway. Computer lights glowed a soft blue, bright white photography lights winking on in the darkness.

"Here," Dylan whispered, handing him a key. "Door at the end of the long hallway."

Jackson slipped the key into the front zippered pocket of his grey jacket and grabbed the last in-bound tub, carrying it into the dark entryway. Stan was setting up a couple of laptops and large-screen monitors while Scott attached cabling for the motion capture and infrared cameras. Nancy and Marti worked together, carrying cameras through the dark expanse and setting them up for Stan to connect and test.

The famed Victorian opera house was empty and freezing, its silence heavy as Jackson closed the front door, the last vestige of streetlights disappearing into thick darkness. Dylan locked the doors and left them to their investigation.

Jackson glanced at his old school wristwatch, dial illuminated. Six minutes past midnight. They were making good time. Enough for him to slip away. And test out his portal theory.

The one in Ophelia Swann's portrait.

With flashlight in hand, misty beam cutting through the silence and dark, Jackson put on his wireless mic pack, chest mount, and body camera. He turned on his mic.

"Jackson to Oracle. Over."

"Oracle responding. Coming through strong, Jackson," said Stan, through the earpiece in his right ear. "Video's clear, too. Already in the office hallway, I see." He rubbed his forehead. "Big surprise there."

"Right behind him," said Scott, his voice sharp in the dim lighting. "No worries, Oracle. Not letting him out of my sight."

Jackson sighed and moved out of the darkness as Scott flicked on the video lights. With Scott trailing him, he headed down the long hallway, old wood floors creaking.

Toward the offices. And the room with the portraits.

Ivory painted walls peeled, revealing old Victorian wallpaper beneath where they'd just painted over it. It was an intricate white and silver damask print that sparkled against his yellow flashlight beam. The air smelled like raw earth and old rubber, white five-panel doors faded and greyed with age as he moved toward the door with the large padlock.

He flicked the key in the lock and removed the padlock, hanging it on the wide metal latch that rattled like chains.

"Figured you'd already have the key," Scott said with a sneer.

The hair on the back of his neck stood up as the door creaked open without him touching it.

An EMF meter alarm went off behind him.

He whirled around.

Scott stood there, red flashing EMF detector held out in front of him, the handheld device whining as the needle bounced into the red and stayed there. High EMF readings.

"Dammit, Scott! You scared the hell outta me," said Jackson, grabbing his chest.

Scott grinned. "Think I'd let you go in there alone without taking some readings first," he said, staring at Jackson over the meter.

Gold light filtered out of the long, narrow room, floorboards scuffed and broken, ivory walls peeling, revealing more blackened wallpaper and bits of the silver and white Damask.

Something rustled in the dark.

"You hear that?" Jackson asked, pointing toward the empty, dilapidated room.

"Please let it be a full body apparition," Scott replied.

Then Jackson saw the portraits. Against the far wall. Thick, heavy gold frames, intricate with vines and swirls, each one covered with grey canvas. At least six feet tall, they leaned against the wall. Six of them. The middle one glowed with an ethereal gold light beneath the tarp.

"You getting' all this, Scott?" Jackson asked.

"Damned right I am," said Scott, high-end digital camera capturing the strange lights and the glowing portrait. "Oracle, this is Scott. Look what we're seeing down here."

"We're still setting up," Stan snapped. "We haven't even gone to blackout yet. Told you guys not to wander off."

"Stan!" Jackson shouted at his wireless microphone. "Look at the live footage and tell me you guys are capturing this through our body cams, too. Over."

"What the hell is that?" Stan shouted.

Jackson approached the painting that pulsed with otherworldly light, a dull thrum echoing through the barren room. He reached out a shaky hand and slowly pulled away the stiff, grey tarp. Revealing an incandescent painting. A portrait that looked so real that he expected her to move within the frame. One he'd seen so many times that it was branded in his memory.

"Wow," said Scott in a quiet voice. "Incredible."

Draped in a diaphanous, empire waist white dress, its translucent folds settling in gossamer layers against her lithe body, Ophelia Swann leaned her hands against a tree trunk, luminous, pale mint, doe eyes full of wonder. Her pensive smile enchanted him as she looked toward him, soft light filtering through the tree branches. What thoughts and dreams lay behind those pale green eyes?

"She's still breathtaking," said Jackson, moving closer to the portrait.

Scott followed. "Careful."

Her thick, coal-black hair glimmered, swept up from her heart-shaped face in that old-fashioned plume. Marti called it a Gibson Girl? She was magic incarnate, part nymph and part siren. The entire canvas had an almost ethereal gleam, the realistic details overwhelming in their luster and accuracy. Almost like a photograph. After more than a century.

He'd seen this portrait hundreds of times, but never with this otherworldly glow.

Bright and bewitching, yet sweet and innocent, she glowed with life. The layers of glistening white silk draped her slender body like an angel taking flight. She looked so real. And so sad.

Jackson stared at the portrait like an old friend for several moments.

Noticing that her expression had changed. A chill surged down his spine.

She was staring straight at him, her image turning ghostly, translucent as she reached toward him.

"It's you again," she said, a surprised look on her face, her fingers reaching toward his face.

The scent of lavender was strong, permeating the air with a clean, pungent scent.

"You smell that?" Scott cried. "Holy shit! Apparition!"

Jackson was mesmerized. He couldn't turn away as Ophelia Swann stepped out of the painting. Like a specter.

"Oh, God, Stan!" Scott shouted, moving closer to the portrait. "Please tell me you're seeing this, too."

"Damn…" said Stan. "Uh, checking cloud data backups. One sec."

"It's too dangerous," Ophelia whispered, stepping back into the painting. "Turn back. Turn back!"

In an instant, her ethereal form disappeared back into the painting. Jackson's heart fell.

"No, come back! Ophelia! Wait!"

He reached out toward the portrait, wanting to feel paint against canvas, wanting to know it was just a painting.

But the surface melted against his fingertips, rippling like water. It was true. Two days before Leap Day, a portal into Ophelia's world opened.

He pulled in a deep breath. Time to go.

"Jackson, don't!" Scott shouted and rushed toward him.

But he was already moving. Pitching forward through the painting.

Jackson stepped through the portrait into the opera house lobby, bustling with people. Dressed in Victorian clothes. The warm air had a tinge of sulfur to it. And ozone that was beginning to dissipate. He stood in front of the covered, full-length oil painting of Ophelia Swann, hometown native and international opera star. Port Townsend's Northwest Opera House lobby was bustling with people. Sunlight trickled into the airy space that bustled with activity, men dressed in 19th century suits and women in long skirts and corseted blouses.

He'd done it! He was here—her time. He'd traveled 124 years into the past through Ophelia Swann's portrait. Back to February 27, 1896. Two days before she leaped to her death on Leap Day. Strange magic swirled around the portrait, only months old here, in 1896.

From his research, he knew that Ophelia Swann had funded an almost magical renovation of the sprawling Romanesque Revival building. Replacing some of the structure's overwhelming heavy, dark brick elements, softening some of the forbidding Gothic features with glazed glass panels and white marble and glass arches. The airy elements created a delicate sense of peace and wonder as they gathered the sunset. And illuminated Port Townsend with its light.

It bore no resemblance to the rundown ruins of 2020 he'd just entered. Here. Now. Was breathtaking. He smiled at the covered portrait. Underneath that grey silk covering lay Ophelia Swann's mesmerizing beauty, captured and framed. And this strange magic.

The opera house's crystalline structure gathered the sunsets' intense blues, pinks, and reds and reflected them along archways that gleamed pearly white and gilded gold and draped silver. Vaulted ceilings of frosted glass, and spires glistening with gossamer fish-scale shingles awash in the Puget Sound's calm, radiant surface filled the expanse. These renovations rivaled the opera houses of the time, even Seattle's opera house, and filled half a city block when it reopened on Port Townsend's famous Water Street. The jewel of the City of Dreams —what they called it in 1896.

Tonight, Ophelia Swann performed for the opera house's reopening. At last, he'd meet her in person. And do everything in his power to save her.

The newly reborn opera house's beauty paled against Ophelia's delicate splendor. Even in his memory, she took Jackson's breath away.

Gas lamps pooled warm gold light across the opera house's dimly lit lobby and polished maple floors, casting fluid, early evening shadows along soft blue velvet curtains and the new full-length oil painting of Ophelia Swann, six-foot-tall canvas hidden beneath swaths of grey silk. The tall, ornate gold frame stood on a stand to the left of the half-moon ticket counter, its burled maple polished to an almost mirror finish. The shiny frame cast reflections throughout the lobby with its vaulted crystalline arches of frosted glass and white and silver Damask-papered walls.

Almost dancing in the gas flames.

A crowd gathered beside Jackson at the half-moon desk, waiting to purchase tickets, he realized. No one had even noticed that he'd stepped through Ophelia's covered portrait like it'd been an open doorway.

A short, balding man stood behind the counter, clean-shaven, round wire-rimmed glasses perched high on his Roman nose as he watched the clock. His red attendant's jacket and white shirt looked pressed and spotless, collar and cuffs starched stiff, and black pants creased to a razor's edge.

Traces of warm coal oil, damp wool, and brine combined with a mix of bay rum, sulfur, and mossy leather scents. Jackson rubbed his face, eyes watering and nose itching.

As the lobby filled, the man at the counter gazed warily at the wall clock, its loud tick announcing every movement of the small hand toward half past six o'clock. Just after sunset. The sign on the counter indicated that the brand-new portrait would be unveiled when tickets to Ophelia Swann's performance went on sale.

Jackson extended his elbows to keep his place in front of the covered painting, but the crowd began to push forward against his lean, six-foot build. Men carrying umbrellas pushed and shoved. Women in sharp-heeled shoes, bustled skirts, and quilted jackets over tight corsets were more like soldiers, weathering shoves and clumsy-footed patrons. Lavender, rose water, and violets hung heavy above the other scents in the lobby. Almost overpowering him, but he held his place, pushing back against the tangle of woolen frock coats and floppy, feathered hats.

The clock chimed half past six. As the alto notes reverberated through the large lobby, a din of voices erupted, the crowd flowing toward the ticket counter like migrating starlings.

Jackson planted both feet as the sea of people pushed toward the ticket counter. And him.

"Settle down and queue in orderly fashion or they'll be no tickets sold tonight," the attendant shouted in a stern voice.

Waiting for the painting to be uncovered, Jackson leaned forward and stared at his reflection in the painting's thick gold frame. Shocked!

His modern-day clothes had morphed into period clothing. Without his flashlight, body camera, and wireless microphone, too. He felt in his pants pockets for his cell phone, but it was gone too. His blond hair was still tousled and windblown, pale blue eyes bright. Winter in the Puget Sound was all wind and rain, so hair pomade kept it neat. Most of the Victorian men around him had slicked down hair and mustaches. From the bay leaves-like scent, they probably used bay rum oil. He preferred his hair—and face—without all that junk. And smell.

He took a quick inventory. Grey rumpled frock coat. Dark blue waistcoat, an unusual color from the blacks, tans, and greys around him. Charcoal grey pants and white shirt, creased in all the wrong places. Shirt collar starched, stiff, and scratchy.

How badly did he stand out against all these smartly dressed people?

A slight young man in a black woolen suit walked behind the ticket counter. Dark hair oiled and parted down the center, brown eyes wide, he approached the painting with shaky hands. He stood beside it and looked over at the attendant.

In a few moments, the attendant gave him a nod. The young man reached up for the grey silk covering.

"And we are pleased to present a new portrait of our hometown, international opera star, Miss Ophelia Swann," said the attendant behind the counter as the young man removed the cloth from the painting. "It will reside here in the opera house."

Jackson was transfixed. Like his very first time seeing the portrait.

Her lithe body was all light and grace. Pale mint eyes animated, full of wonder, looking through him. Into his heart. Her smile enchanted him, filled him with warmth and belonging. Had she dreamed of someone that ended up breaking her heart? Shattering it until she couldn't put the pieces back together. So badly that she leaped to her death two days later?

And why had she told him to turn back in his own time? What did she know that he didn't?

Her thick, coal-black hair glimmered with ethereal light, swept into a shiny, loose Gibson Girl hairstyle, as Marti called it.

Even through the newly painted canvas' luster and shimmery gold frame, he felt the portrait's magic—like he had in his time. Felt Ophelia's siren-like pull washing over him. As if she'd walk out of the painting like he had and stand before him in all her magical glow.

Like she had back in his time, if only for a few moments.

Bright and bewitching, yet sweet and innocent, layers of glistening white silk like an angel taking flight. She looked real. He sighed. And so sad. Every masterful stroke of the brush had captured the most realistic, full length portrait he'd ever seen. Photorealistic resolution. Skin so dewy he expected to see her chest rise and fall with breath.

It was spooky. He'd already seen her come to life once in this portrait. In her time, she was still alive. Maybe the magic hadn't happened yet?

He touched the canvas, expecting to feel the soft, glossy white folds of her silk dress slide across his fingers. But he only felt layers of dried paint and stiff canvas. Was the way back to his time through this painting? Or had this all been a one-way trip? Maybe Scott and Marti were right? He hadn't done any investigation beyond confirming the portal's existence.

Regardless, he wanted to save Ophelia Swann. And maybe if he saved her…she'd save him, too?

His heart raced, his gaze darting to the lobby curtains. Was she standing just beyond those curtains right now? Practicing for tomorrow night's opening? Running scales through all those octaves? About to step out and sing for her crowd of fans.

The sudden scent of roses and fresh-cut lilies pulled his gaze back to the portrait again. Back to Ophelia. The portrait was reminiscent of Raphael or Titian—a work of delicate light and shadow born in the Renaissance. As if she'd been painted to life by its grand masters.

He couldn't look away from her beatific face.

A face revered all over the United States at the time, gracing stages here and all over the world. A voice adored in Europe, Prussia, the Russian Empire, even the Orient. According to old newspaper and magazine articles Marti had given him. Including the modern-day ones still talking about her legend and how her young life ended on Water Street's brick façade.

When she leaped to her death. On Leap Day, 1896.

On this night, she'd returned home to Port Townsend from two years in Europe. The performance was to be her Winter Homecoming Revival. One she wouldn't live to do.

He stared at the painting, enchanted by her incredible beauty, almost feeling the weight of her gaze staring back at him. As if following his every move. If only he could step inside it and carry her out in his arms. Protect her from whatever broke her over these next two days. He understood that frailness. He'd begun a slow fracture when Ava left him in January, the cracks lengthening and deepening until he felt the seams ripping.

He understood Ophelia's leap more than most people. And he'd do everything in his power to save her.

February's winter sky was gunmetal grey, darkening quickly now that the sun had set, thin wisps of pinks and purples fading into the bay's silvery mirror calm. Gas-lit streetlamps shuddered to life, casting pools of gold light along the dusty street. Carriages creaked, horses clomping and nickering past the opera house. The scents of bay rum and bergamot were cloying against the dry scent of wool, sulfur, and the bay's salty tang. But comforting against the stench of horse dung.

He met Ophelia's fixed gaze again. Enchanted by her portrait's soft innocence. The whisper of hope still on her lips. In her luminous green eyes staring back at him.

Until she winked at him.

Jackson gasped and stumbled backward, heart racing, mouth agape. Was there more magic beyond the portrait's portal? In her own time period?

He shook his head, certain he was seeing things when a hand clapped against his shoulder. Startled, he turned.

From Marti's research—and grandma's photo albums—he recognized the long, thin, angry face glaring at him. Younger than the photos. His fourth-great-grandfather, Orson Mayfield. About forty-two, according to genealogy records.

"Jackson!" he shouted, an anxious look on his face. "I knew I'd find you here."

How did this man know him? Then he remembered the man's two youngest sons were Arthur (Jackson's third-great-grandfather), and Jackson, but Jackson drowned in the bay at six. Did this man somehow think he was his dead son?

"You should be at the manor. Helping entertain our party guests, as you assured me you would be."

Jackson stared at the man, feeling tongue-tied. He had no idea what to say. At six feet tall, Jackson was two inches taller than Orson

Mayfield. The man's short ashen hair was traditional, properly oiled, and parted in the center, every single hair in its proper place. Thick eyebrows and close-cropped beard gave him an ordered and commanding appearance, softened only by his pale blue Mayfield eyes (that Jackson had inherited generations later). He wore a freshly brushed black frock coat, pristine white shirt, waistcoat, and pressed white ascot. His annoyed expression was as ubiquitous as his black bowler.

"I…wanted to get—tickets to the opera," said Jackson, hoping to placate his quadruple great-grandfather's anger.

He'd just play along with the whole son thing. Must be a weird effect of the portal. It's not like he could have googled portrait portals do's and don'ts beforehand.

Mayfield sighed, eyes closing, head shaking. "Why did I know you'd be here pining for this little theatre trollop."

Jackson glared at him, shoulders stiffening. He started to respond back when a scabby looking man with slicked back, thinning black hair ducked behind a lobby curtain, holding something wrapped in a white cotton sack. He had a hooked nose and five o'clock shadow, wearing a tan jacket over an ivory shirt, worn green waistcoat, and wrinkled brown tie.

Jackson squinted, catching the royal blue markings on the cotton sack. From grandma's papers: the Mayfield crest. What was that about? The outline of the sack's contents looking suspiciously like a stack of money.

Something felt very wrong here. Mayfield calling him son and Ophelia's portrait winking at him? It made no sense. Had someone bumped the painting? A visual trick caused by gas lamps flickering? And why did Orson Mayfield think Jackson was his dead son? And why was that strange man walking around with a sack of his ancestor's money?

What had he walked into?

"You fancy this little tart, don't you, Jackson?" Mayfield's tone was sharp as he nodded at the portrait and Jackson bristled. "Like most young men in Port Townsend. Including her slimy manager, Horace Tetrault, skulking about the lobby like a common criminal."

That man was Ophelia's manager! But what did it mean?

"Make sure you take a number, boy," said Mayfield with a smirk. "Don't want to lose your place in her line."

Jackson gritted his teeth, shoving the man backward. "Don't you dare talk about her that way! She has the voice of an angel and a reputation to match."

The crowd went quiet, everyone staring at them.

"You are expected at home," Mayfield said with deadly calm, a hollow smile on his face. "To greet our guests and handle other duties. Like your brothers."

Jackson let out a hiss of breath, fingers clenching into fists. Dammit! This dick baited him into pushing him in front of this crowd. Now, he looked like the aggressor.

And what the hell was this party Mayfield expected him to attend? Conveniently timed during Ophelia's return home. Victorians loved arranged marriages. Was Mayfield trying to marry off his sons to money and keep him away from the hometown opera star? What the hell had he walked into the middle of here? Through Ophelia's portrait. Apparently, Ophelia's theatre money wasn't good enough for Orson Mayfield and his sons. What was this dude up to?

"What other duties?" Jackson snapped.

"Jackson," Mayfield began, that all-too-calm demeanor infuriating. "You've known about this party for weeks." Mayfield put his hands on his hips, glaring. "I know you loathe them, but as my youngest son, your attendance is mandatory." Mayfield wagged a finger at him. "I also expect you to escort Clara Wexbright tonight at the party."

Jackson groaned. "Who is Clara Wexbright?"

Mayfield sighed. Shaking his head. "Why are you being so dense? The attractive, nineteen-year-old brunette you met last month at the Wexbright's Winter Gala." He spoke like Jackson was a slow five-year-old with head trauma. Jackson scowled at him.

This chick sounded like a rich socialite. And he hadn't agreed to anything.

"For how long?" Jackson demanded.

"Until the party concludes, of course," Mayfield replied, smirking again.

Until Ophelia left Port Townsend, of course. This guy was as transparent as glass. And ancestor or not, Mayfield was pissing him off!

"Why not introduce her to Arthur instead?" Jackson asked with a groan. "Or my other brothers?"

Arthur was his third-great-grandfather. He hoped he didn't do anything to screw up his own eventual existence. He'd always heard you couldn't go back in time and kill your own grandfather. But what if he stopped the dude from marrying his third-great-grandmother? He hoped not.

"As my youngest son and heir," Mayfield began, his voice low and sharp.

Jackson cringed. He knew the wind up for the classic obligations speech. Every generation ever had heard this one. Why he was obligated to do something he didn't want to do.

"As a pioneer graduate of Leland Stanford University, that I paid for, you have obligations to fulfill," Mayfield continued.

Sweet! He'd graduated from the pioneer class at Stanford. Not bad for a dead kid. Had Jackson's traveling through the portal somehow displaced his great-times-three uncle and caused him to…well, not be dead? Still, he'd have to locate the Stanford diploma and carry it back through the portal. Might look better on his wall than his community college degree in IT.

"And you will do my bidding as long as you live under my roof, work in my businesses, and live off my funds. It's your duty. Cross me, boy and I will remove you from the will. And that's just a start. Do you understand me, Jackson?"

Funny how every obligations speech always ended in threats. Disinherited. Cut off from the family bank accounts. And…bodily harm? Wouldn't put it past this guy. Jackson remembered from Marti's research that this guy had been married like five times. She'd shown him images of some Victorian study or den with a bunch of full-length oil portraits hanging on the walls.

Wait a minute! Had those other paintings in the opera house been of Mayfield's wives? Were they the ones hanging on Mayfield's den wall? How had they gotten there? How were they connected to Ophelia Swann? He had to find out.

Mayfield grabbed his right shoulder again. "Jackson? Are you listening to me?"

Jackson ducked out of his hold. He wouldn't let this guy put hands on him. He'd deck the man first.

"Not really," he replied.

Mayfield's face darkened, anger sharp in his eyes. "You will chaperone Clara Wexbright at the party and that's final," Mayfield said, his voice a quiet demand now. "And you will keep her happy while her parents and I negotiate a contract with the city."

"Contract?" Jackson asked with a frown. It *was* about money.

"Yes, a building contract, if you must know," Mayfield replied in a calmer voice.

Jackson's stomach roiled. This dude had some underhanded stuff planned. Something that now involved him.

"And what else?" Jackson snapped, glaring.

Mayfield pulled in a deep breath and fixed him with his piercing gaze. This dude had already convinced himself that whatever he'd been plotting was best for everyone involved. Even when they wanted no part of it.

"Once the contract is signed, I think Ephraim Wexbright and I can come to an arrangement."

Jackson set himself. Waiting for the other shoe to drop. On him.

"What arrangement?" Jackson demanded.

"Why, marriage, of course," Mayfield stated, as if only a fool could possibly disagree with such a perfect plan that benefitted ~~him~~ everyone.

Except Jackson. He held in a sigh.

He traveled 124 years into the past to meet and save Ophelia Swann. And he only had two days. He refused to spend those two days at some stupid party, escorting some vacuous, self-absorbed socialite. Even for his ancestors.

This trip was Ophelia's last chance. And maybe his too?

Marti said that Ophelia had performed all over the world, singing for presidents and royalty, even the Emperor of Japan. Her wealth was more than the Mayfield and Wexbright holdings combined. She didn't need a suitor. Was that why Mayfield refused to let his sons court her? Maybe he'd tried to arrange something and failed?

Jackson looked up as the young man with oiled hair and black wool suit picked up the portrait and took it away.

"Wait! Please!" Jackson called, but the young man and the painting disappeared behind those blue velvet curtains.

Mayfield grabbed him by the arm and jerked him back. "Jackson, you disobey me at your peril," the man said through gritted teeth. "My reach is much farther than you realize, boy." His face twisted in disgust as he motioned at Jackson's bare head. "Where's your hat? And you haven't combed your hair. Did you forget all propriety while at Stanford? You look like a street urchin."

Jackson just smiled, enjoying this dude's frustration over his lack of control.

"It's the Casual Cali look," he said with a chuckle. "It's all the rage at Stanford."

Mayfield looked less than amused.

"I expect you home shortly," Mayfield snapped, turning around. "Or else." Fuming, Mayfield slammed the opera house's front door and left Jackson standing in the lobby.

"Excuse me, sir," said a timid voice.

"Yes," Jackson replied, turning around.

The young man that had removed the painting stood in front of him, extending a crisp white business card.

"I was asked to give you this calling card." He pointed toward a small opening in the blue velvet curtains.

Ophelia Swann's calling card! His hands shook as he stared at her name engraved in silver, flowing script. She'd written in black ink, *Peninsula Hotel, Room 301.*

He could hardly breathe as he walked toward the curtains, hands still shaking. Slowly, he pulled back the curtains, scent of fresh-cut lilies and rosewater wafting toward him. He was weak in the knees when he stepped into the small cubbyhole where ushers sometimes waited, surrounded on all sides by those heavy velvet curtains.

And saw Ophelia Swann in person. For the first time.

She wore the white dress from the portrait, silky layers draping her body. Her Gibson Girl hair was a crown of soft black hair swept into a loose tie on the top of her head. Her large, pale green eyes were luminous, haunting as he stared into her beautiful alabaster face, that smile the brightest light he'd ever seen.

Jackson's eyes stung with moisture. "Ophelia," he whispered, his voice catching in his throat. "It's you." After all these years, it was really her. Right in front of him, at last.

Her eyes widened, but she smiled. "You're the man that stepped through my portrait. Despite my warning."

"Guess you saw that," He said, moving toward her.

She nodded. "Why have you come here, ignoring the danger? To my time?" she asked, her soprano voice lyrical. Every word like an aria, aching through him.

"To save you," he said, his voice almost a whisper.

"Save me?" Her eyes welled with tears. She laid a hand to her mouth. "We've never formally met, but...I feel like I know you, Jackson Mayfield."

His mouth fell open. "You know my name?"

She nodded, a shy smile returning to her face. "You've spent a lot of time studying my portrait. You're like an old friend I've just met."

He'd been fascinated by her for so long, wanting to meet her. Talk to her. Save her.

"You've seen me through your portrait?" he asked, surprised.

She nodded again, voice soft and inviting. "Many, many times. I'm so happy to finally stand beside you, breathing the same air. Feeling the same emotions."

His smile widened into a grin and all he wanted was to hold her in his arms. "I'm not exactly sure how I was able to walk through your portrait to here and now, but I've dreamed of this moment for more than a decade," he said, his voice thick and gravelly.

"For one hundred and twenty-four years," she whispered, her eyes turning glassy. "A lifetime. In all that time, you're the only one that came back to my portrait. Again and again. Why? Why have you come?"

She reached out and took his hand.

Dear God. Sparks! Like Carburetor Day at the Indy 500! Heat lightning on a New Orleans summer night. Fireworks on the Las Vegas strip.

He gasped, the rush of heat and attraction burning through his veins. Something he'd never felt before. Was this obsession why Ava left him? Had he mistaken comfort and caring for love?

Had she been smarter than him, getting out before he did something stupid? Like propose?

For almost half his life, he'd obsessed over Port Townsend's legend of Ophelia Swann. It all ramped into high gear last year when he brought the mystery to the Spirit Seekers, suggesting an investigation. He'd read everything he and Marti found, studied every Port Townsend landmark. Listened to recordings of her singing opera, her delicate, crystalline soprano voice sending chills across his skin. He sighed. Even visited her grave. The more he focused on Ophelia and the investigation, the more distant Ava became. He hadn't realized that until right now. Scott had, apparently, but he'd never said anything.

Her first clue to him that something was wrong had been her "it's not you, it's me" speech as she departed. With half the apartment.

Had Ava been jealous of a ghost? Or did she know something he hadn't all that time. He understood why Ava left him now.

"Jackson?"

Ophelia's musical voice pulled him back to the present.

He squeezed her hand, struggling how to answer her pointed question. "Something…bad happens here. I've come to stop it."

"Something bad?" she asked.

He flinched at the intensity of her stare. "I don't know exactly what, but I have two days to stop it. Before it—hurts you, Ophelia. That's why I came through the painting."

He didn't know what horrible thing happened to her between now and February 29th. All he knew was the ending. That he had to change it. He was terrified for her. And at this moment, he didn't want to lose her. After finally meeting her in person.

She let go of his hand, reaching toward him with both arms. And he stepped into her embrace. She was all warmth and joy as he enfolded her in his arms and held her tight against his chest.

"You're shaking," she said.

"Ophelia," he said again, his voice breaking, overcome with emotion. "I—care about you. And don't want to lose you."

"That's so sweet, Jackson," she whispered in his ear. Her words burned through him. He felt her trembling now, tears in her voice. "I've thought about you every day since your first visit to my portrait."

"You have?" he asked, shocked. He held her tighter, feeling suddenly cold. Protective.

"Teasing him, are we?" someone called from behind the curtains. "You know what happens when you don't listen."

Ophelia looked terrified, pulling away. She slipped behind Jackson and wrapped her arms around his waist. Hiding. What had these cretins done to her? Jackson's blood began to burn.

"Who's there?" Jackson demanded. "Show yourself."

Tears ran down her cheeks, her body trembling. "That's my manager, Horace Tetrault. I signed a contract. He's a—"

The curtains peeled back, chains rattling as a short pudgy man in a tan suit, big belly stretching his brown waistcoat, and his dark hair wild stepped into the small space. A cold wind blew over him and he shivered as Tetrault reached toward Ophelia.

Jackson shoved the man back, his fingers suddenly chilled and stiff.

"Who are you?" the man demanded.

"Jackson Mayfield." He glanced back at Ophelia and smiled. "Ophelia and I were just leaving to attend the Mayfield winter party. She's our guest of honor and I will be escorting her to and from the event. Sorry, but you're not invited."

Tetrault crossed his arms over his belly as he let out a guttural laugh. "Well, now, isn't that grand," he said in amusement. "I'll have to have a talk with your father, brat."

Again, with this father stuff. "Do that," said Jackson.

"Besides, she'll be singing quite a different tune come sunrise. I'll just let Cinderella's evil twin tell you all about it."

Jackson glared at Tetrault and kept Ophelia behind him.

"There is something I need to tell you, Jackson," Ophelia said in a pained voice.

"Either way, she's coming with me," Jackson replied.

Tetrault let out a belly laugh. "For a while. The little beauty always come back to me though."

Jackson slid his arm around Ophelia's waist and together, they backed out from behind the curtains. He slid off his frock coat and helped Ophelia's arms into it. Together, they hurried out through the double wooden doors and into the night.

Jackson and Ophelia rushed down Water Street, February's winds chilly as they dodged carriages to cross Water Street's corner onto Taylor Street. Nothing looked the same, but he followed Ophelia's lead. To the carriage stop. The thickening mist rolled off the bay and billowed ashore, giving the burgeoning seaport a foreboding air. Ophelia held onto his right arm with both hands as the rocky shoreline vanished and reappeared in the thickening mist. The bay was choppy with waves.

He nearly collided with a middle-aged woman selling flowers from a stand beside the Taylor Street carriage stop. Baskets of fresh flowers sat on the sidewalk and she carried one in her arms. She was petite and walked with a limp, her blond hair in a curly chignon beneath a wide-brimmed hat that obscured her face. She wore a dark skirt and white blouse, a pink shawl tied around her shoulders. The air smelled of ozone and daffodils as he gazed at her coppery hazel eyes that had almost a gleam to them.

There was magic here. And it frightened him.

"Forgive me, ma'am," he said, bowing.

She stared at him a moment, her face long and tired, pale as the mist coming off the bay.

"That was some argument in the opera house lobby tonight," she said, pointing a curved index finger at him. She set the flower basket down at her feet. "These are difficult times for you. And your lady."

Jackson frowned. Good news traveled fast here. Ophelia slid her arm in his and huddled against him. He was already cold without the coat.

"Yes, they are," Jackson said.

He stared at the basket of flowers she carried, glistening in the wash of gas lamps. Pink carnations, red roses, lavender, purple tulips, daffodils, sunflowers, and orchids in several colors. Almost pulsing with light—and something else.

The smell of ozone was strong, sharp, as she reached down and rummaged through the flowers as the night sky darkened, fog roiling across the bay and whispering ashore. She plucked something from the basket and held it out to him.

A dirty, brown thing, like a freshly harvested potato. It began to glow a soft purple in the shrouding haze.

The mournful call of a fog horn lamented through the chilly mist above the bay water lapping against the shore. A bell chimed near the wharf. Seagulls chittered.

"Take it already," she cried, pushing the dirty, glowing thing at him.

"What is that?" He held up his hands, not wanting to touch it.

She nodded at Ophelia. "You love her, don't you?"

Could she somehow read his inner thoughts? He blushed and glanced at Ophelia who looked pleased by the woman's question.

"I think I do," he said, reaching out to touch Ophelia's face. "Since the day I first saw your portrait staring back at me."

Ophelia took his hand in hers, bringing his cold fingers to her lips. Kissing them with her warm lips. He wanted to melt right here in the cobblestone street.

The flower woman shook the shriveled thing at him. It was crusted with dirt and looked like a small malformed potato. Except for its otherworldly—unnerving—purple gleam.

"Fine," she snapped, sliding a newspaper page out of a basket. She wrapped the shriveled brown thing up and handed it to him.

He accepted the wrapped item.

"I think I love you, too—Jackson Mayfield. From the future. From the moment I first saw you. Dreaming of me."

The flower woman smiled at Ophelia, reaching out to take her hand. She patted Jackson's arm with her other hand. Suddenly, he felt warm.

"Your torch burns long and bright, Jackson Mayfield. Like Miss Swann's. But she is doomed."

The heat of embarrassment flushing his cheeks quickly burned to anger. How could she know Ophelia was doomed? And why say it in front of her?

"I know the truth of it all. But I have the magic to fix it. If you're brave enough to try."

What truth? What magic? He frowned. Like fairies and witches? Merlin to King Arthur? He didn't know the problem, much less how to fix it.

The flower woman held out a small, blue flower pot with rich, dark soil. Wet from all the rain.

"Plant that bulb in this pot, Jackson Mayfield," she said in a quiet voice. "It will bloom quickly. Find out why Ophelia returned to Port Townsend. To her hometown."

"I am right here," Ophelia said, frowning. She propped her hands on her hips. "And none of that is a secret. My manager has been stealing from me and—controlling me against my will." She glanced up at Jackson, her eyes filled with hope. "People like Jackson—" She hesitated. "Are…old friends. Someone that can help me escape him."

The woman shook the pot at him. "Jackson. Take the pot. Plant the bulb." She leaned in close until he smelled hot tea and honey on her breath. "When it blooms, you'll know what to do. Reflect on it. You'll know when the time comes."

"You're not making any sense," said Ophelia in a quiet, concerned tone.

"Please, we need more information," he said, his brow furrowing, mouth flattening into a grimace. "How do we fix whatever it is we're trying to uh, fix."

"Do you feel it?" the flower woman asked in a hoarse whisper, glancing up at the sky. "Lost souls stir along the bay."

He felt a chill rake his spine as the fog horn called out across the dark, luminescent waters again.

Something stirred in the mist. Jackson shuddered, cold dancing across his skin.

Something dark and malevolent. Something he'd never felt before.

"It has arrived," the flower woman said in a harsh whisper, pulling away from Jackson. She brushed a hand across her face, her breath quickening.

"What's arrived?" Jackson snapped. "Answer me!"

"Dark magic. Stand in the light and count the shadows. There will be more than one." She patted his hand that held the flower bulb. "When it blossoms, the magic will bloom. I must go now."

"Wait—who or what are these shadows?" he demanded.

"You will know them by the cold," she answered.

"The cold?"

The woman disappeared into the fog that grew thick and soupy.

Something moaned in the dense, briny mist, an almost keening sound, grating like an ice pick against slate. Jackson gripped Ophelia's hand as a black carriage creaked to a stop.

"Climb aboard, young master Mayfield, Miss Swann," said the driver with grey hair and heavy mustache. "Are you headed to the manor house?"

Young Master Mayfield? What was this carriage jockey guy smoking up there on top?

"Yes, we are," he said. "How much?"

"One dollar, sixty cents, Master Mayfield."

He reached into his right front pocket, knowing he had some dollar bills there before he stepped through the painting. It jingled. Surprised, he pulled out two Morgan silver dollars.

He handed them up to the driver. "Keep the change, dude."

"Dude, sir?" the man replied. "This isn't Seattle, but thank you, sir."

He shrugged. Guess dude meant something way different back in 1896.

As the moans from the bay grew louder, he and Ophelia climbed into the carriage and slammed the door. The carriage lurched forward through the fog.

What had that flower woman called up from the sea? It chilled him to the bone.

"Now, tell me," Jackson said with a sigh, turning to Ophelia, "What the hell's going on here?"

Tears streaked down her face. "It's so awful, Jackson...I—I don't even know where to start."

He took her hand in his. "Start with the Cinderella's evil twin comment and this contract you signed."

"I am in an awful situation and I don't know how to escape it." She sighed heavily. "The contract wasn't at all what I agreed to and the words seemed to change after I signed it."

"Dark magic perhaps?"

She shook her head. "Worse. After signing, we drank a toast and my champagne tasted...strange. Everything began to move slowly and I heard Tetrault reciting something...dark. A black mist rose around me and I blacked out. And—this is the most incredulous part. I found myself trapped inside that—that painting. It's horrible, Jackson."

"What?" Jackson cried. "So, you did wink at me from that painting."

She nodded. "Once the sun sets, I can move. And step out of the painting. Until sunrise, but only in my own time. No matter what I do or where I go, I will always return to the painting." She shuddered. "Forever."

Jackson put his arms around her as she began to cry.

"I don't understand most of this, but I'll do whatever it takes to free you."

She lifted her head and pressed a soft, enveloping kiss against his lips. That burned through him. "I love you, Jackson. For all these years."

Could she really love him? Had she felt the same way he had, every time he spent the day at the historical society. Studying her portrait. Daydreaming. Wishing she'd step out of that painting into his life?

He returned her kiss, sipping her lips, stroking her hair. He held her so close he felt her heart beat against his chest. She smelled soft with rosewater and lilies. The thump of the clay pot against her shoulder reminded him he was still carrying that wrapped bulb and flower pot.

"Sorry," he said, letting her go. "I should plant this before I lose it."

"Let me help," said Ophelia, taking the blue pot from his hands.

He unwrapped the glowing bulb from the newspaper wrapping as the carriage turned down a well-lit street. In the flush of gas lamps, he saw the newspaper headline and his blood turned to ice.

International Opera Star Leaps to Her Death from Peninsula Hotel Window. Dated Saturday, February 29, 1896.

That was only two days away!

That flower lady had given him this article. He'd never seen this article, despite all his research.

His breath quickened as he read through the story, horrified at the details. Ophelia spent Saturday night alone after an altercation at the theatre, one involving her manager and an unidentified person. In her suicide note, Ophelia left her fortune to Tetrault and cited an unrequited love was behind her suicide. The article hinted that her beloved had been forced into an arranged marriage.

"Jackson, what's the matter?"

"This," he said in a shaking voice and held up the page to her.

Ophelia stared at it a moment. "Ophelia Swann Returns Home for February Concert. Is that what you read?"

"What?" he cried, turning it back around. The headline was the same one she'd read. Had this strange bulb given him a glimpse into the future? He wadded up the newspaper page and shoved it into the pocket of his coat. That Ophelia still wore.

He took the bulb and laid it in the hollowed-out hole Ophelia made. He covered it in dirt.

"We don't have much time," he said, taking the pot from her hands.

She nodded. "You have to get me back before sunrise, Jackson."

"Where will the painting be?"

"In my suite at the Peninsula Hotel."

The carriage plodded up to the towered entrance of Mayfield Manor, mists swirling along the grounds overlooking Port Townsend Bay. Grey brick rose into forbidding cupolas like a Gothic castle that could have inspired Bram Stoker. It looked like a movie villain's lair. Gas lamps lit the portico and large, curved wooden door carved with vines and swirls. The house was lit with newly installed electric lights. It could probably be seen from Vancouver Island.

Jackson got out first and helped Ophelia off the carriage. He picked up the flower pot and slid it into the roomy right pocket of his frock coat that Ophelia still wore. He held out his arm to her and she took it. Together they walked down the portico, wisteria brown and hibernating, dark, twisted vines following them to the front door.

A tall, spindly, dark-haired man with a warm smile and grey eyes greeted him. He smelled like soap and mineral oil. Late fifties, balding and grey, he wore a black, tailed tuxedo jacket, starched white tuxedo shirt, and black pants. Butler?

"Good evening, Master Jackson," he beamed, a smile lighting the older man's long, lined face and deep grey eyes.

"Good evening, Harris," said Ophelia, glancing at Jackson, cueing him into the man's name.

Harris' eyes widened, a grin appearing on his face. "Miss Ophelia, it's grand to see you again! I dare say you're a household name these days."

"It's good to see you again," she answered with a nod.

"We're all looking forward to tomorrow night's opening performance," said Harris with a bow as he ushered them into the party. He lowered his voice. "And it's grand to see you on Master Jackson's arm. Arthur will be thrilled."

"Arthur?" said Jackson. His ancestor.

"Yes, Arthur loves opera," said Harris, a twinkle in his grey eyes. "And matchmaking."

She smiled at him and then Jackson. "Follow my lead," she whispered.

Jackson gripped her arm tighter as she steered him toward the ballroom ahead, the burled walnut floors polished to a diamond sheen and the crystal chandeliers dripped with light while a quartet played a Bach aria. And couples filled the dance floor. Dressed in tailed tuxedos and beaded gowns.

She led him past the ballroom and into the sitting room with two large, white sofas facing each other in front of a gigantic, roaring fireplace made from smooth river rocks. Several overstuffed chairs in blue and green set throughout the room, walls a soft yellow. Electric lights overhead illuminated a massive table of hors d'oeuvres. The scent of onions mixed with roasted potatoes and seared beef.

"Wow, nice spread," he whispered. "Must have cost Vlad the Impaler Mayfield a fortune. I mean, father."

She giggled.

The dining room was just beyond the sitting room, several long tables covered in red tablecloths, the walls paneled with walnut like the wood floors. The table sat about fifty people, laid out in fine white china rimmed black and gold with an array of crystal glasses and polished silverware that were almost blinding.

"Jackson! There you are."

He cringed at the sound of Mayfield's voice as he turned around with Ophelia.

But he did his best to hide his enjoyment when the man's face flushed red. Mayfield glared at her. Then him. He looked like a villain in his full, tailed black tuxedo, white tie and vest. A white tie event. And Jackson was under-dressed. That made him smile.

"May I present Miss Ophelia Swann," Jackson said with a nod.

"You may certainly not," Mayfield growled. "And you will go change into—suitable attire this instant."

He wasn't putting on a monkey suit for Vlad here. Mostly, because it pissed him off. Ophelia kept a polite smile on her face, but he saw her anger flicker to life.

"If you'll excuse us, we'll be in the ballroom."

"Jackson, did you hear me? Jackson!"

"Master Mayfield," Harris called, stepping between them. "One of the guests has asked to speak with you."

Mayfield's voice got lost in the hallway as a quartet drowned out the sound.

Harris leaned over to Jackson, pressing a key into his hand. "Take her down the hall to your Father's study," Harris whispered, pointing toward a hallway to the right. "He never goes in there in at night. She'll be out of sight there."

"Thanks, Harris," Jackson said with a nod and pulled Ophelia down the hallway. Toward Vlad's study.

"In here," he whispered as he reached the large walnut door at the end of the hallway.

Jackson turned the key in the lock and pushed open the door. Ophelia followed him inside as he closed the door.

The room was warm and covered in that same walnut paneling from floor to ceiling. The scent of orange oil hung in the air. A large mahogany desk sat in front of a red curtained window with only a small clock, a blotter and inkwell, and a wooden cigar box. On the wall behind the desk hung five paintings. A large black shade covered each one.

"What's behind the shades?" Ophelia asked.

A chill washed over him. Were these the other paintings in the old opera house? From Marti's picture. Frames looked the same. And their size looked right.

"Let's find out."

He moved toward a shade and grabbed the pull rope on the nearest painting. Then he saw a gold, engraved plate at the bottom of the frame. It read, Abigail Mayfield.

"His fifth wife," said Ophelia. "They divorced and she moved to France, according to the papers."

Jackson moved to the painting to the right. Read the bottom plate. "Ruth Mayfield." The painting right of Charlotte read, "Patience Mayfield." Painting right of Patience read, "Leta Mayfield." And the last painting read, "Cora Mayfield."

She shook her head as she moved toward the paintings. "Why would he want a constant reminder of all those failed marriages?"

Jackson shrugged. "It's kind of creepy if you ask me. Maybe that's why there's a shade on each one?"

Jackson reached up and pulled the cord, lifting the shades covering all five portraits, but Ophelia's gasp made him freeze.

"What's wrong?"

She tugged on his sleeve. "Look."

Jackson stepped back, looking up at the paintings, but he could only stare at them, his mouth open.

"Jackson…"

"They're empty," he finally said, his voice returning.

Horrified, he stared at empty backgrounds without subjects. None of Mayfield's wives ever left this house. He felt sick to his stomach.

Whoever imprisoned Ophelia in her portrait had done the same thing to Vlad's wives. Was Mayfield responsible? The dude looked more like a weasel than a wizard, but he was a rich weasel. Probably paid someone to imprison all five wives. Damn. That was harsh.

Shocked, his eyes stinging, he turned away, crossing his arms against his chest.

"That's some nasty retribution," he cried, a cold chill shuddering through him. "Gotta be the same magic used on you, Ophelia." He'd studied Ophelia's portrait since he was a teenager, not knowing it was a prison.

"But why?" Ophelia cried. "Why would he do this?"

"Because he's an evil prick," said Jackson. "Besides, who'd believe you if you told anyone?"

"No one, Jackson. That is the beauty of this spell." Mayfield.

Damn. The bastard was behind him.

Jackson and Ophelia turned.

Mayfield stood in the study's doorway, three men behind him. Damn. Had Harris set him up?

He grabbed Ophelia's arm and pulled her behind him as he backed away. Behind the desk until he felt the wall.

"Take the girl back to town," Father told the men. "Then interrogate my son. Away from Arthur, Robert, and William. Find out what Jackson knows, but don't kill him. This matter will soon be at an end."

Arthur, Robert, and William were Mayfield's sons. Jackson frowned. Guess he wouldn't be meeting his other ancestors this trip.

He stood his ground, keeping his body between Mayfield's thugs and Ophelia. "Touch her and I'll rip out your throats!" he shouted through gritted teeth.

"So, you're going to fight me even now. Stupid boy. Teach him some manners, first."

Jackson felt the window at his back. He slammed his elbow into the glass pane, shattering it as the men moved toward them. He shoved Ophelia out the window.

"Run, Ophelia!" he shouted and threw himself into the men.

He took down the first guy with a punch to the kidney, but the other two overwhelmed him. Their fists rained down, knocking him to the floor. His last sight was Ophelia running into the surrounding mist as he fell into unconsciousness.

Jackson awoke to sunlight filtering through a dirty, narrow window. A nasty old root cellar, he realized. He'd been in his grandma's enough times to hate these things. His hands and feet were numb from the constricting ropes gouging his wrists and ankles. The mossy sacks of grain beneath him were hard and smelled musty, the air cold and gritty with dirt. The ache in his head pounded out a furious rhythm against his skull, nauseating him. His face ached and burned.

He remembered the men hitting him, trying to get him to answer questions. Questions he had no answers for—not that he'd spoken anything to them anyway.

Footsteps tapped on the stairs, the old wooden door creaking open, sunlight and cold air flooding the cellar.

Jackson held a hand over his watering eyes.

"Good morning, Jackson," said Mayfield, a cheery note in his voice, hands folded behind his back. "I trust you've slept well."

Jackson glared at him, saying nothing.

He dropped down on his haunches in a grey frock coat and pants, black waistcoat, and white shirt. Black shoes so shiny that Jackson saw his bruised and cut reflection in them.

"I'm not sure what to do with you, boy. Things have changed now that you know about the paintings. Not that anyone would believe you, not even your brothers, but I can't risk anyone seeing them just the same. So that's why the paper will print a story today about your terrible accident and coma."

"Damned harsh treatment of your own kid, wouldn't you say? Vlad?" Jackson replied. "Not to mention what you did to all of your wives. Worst husband ever."

Mayfield glared at him. "Name-calling, Jackson? Really? They taught you that at Stanford?" The man shook his head. "I couldn't afford to pay for five ex-wives and send four sons to university, so I had them mounted instead. Alive, but mounted." He patted Jackson's head. "Your coma isn't all bad, son. It will gain me enough sympathy with the Wexbrights to sign that contract."

Jackson bared his teeth, wanting to tear this guy to shreds.

"Oh, and I'm sure you're wondering about dear, sweet Ophelia." He rose from his haunches, brushing off his pants. "She will fall to her death tomorrow, after deeding her fortune over to her dear manager. For me. Then I'll be the richest man in the world. If you're lucky, boy, I might spare you and sell you to a ship bound for the Orient. If not?"

"If not what? Vlad?"

Mayfield shrugged, splaying his hands. "Well, we'll deal with that when the time comes, won't we? For now, I'll let you discuss it further with my associates. Bad timing to be disrespectful, Jackson."

Mayfield stood up, smiling, bowler in hand. He tapped up the stairs and, in a moment, Jackson heard more footsteps on the stairs as the cellar door closed. Two men in dark pants and rolled shirt sleeves came at him with fists raised.

When Jackson opened his eyes again, he could barely see, both eyes swollen. His teeth chattered he was so cold, his ribs ached, and his face burned. He remembered making up something that satisfied Mayfield's men enough that they stopped hitting him and left him alone.

Light shone low through the narrow window. It was Saturday! Every nerve in his body went on overload. One day left. If he didn't get to Ophelia in time, she'd leap to her death. Did she really love him? Did she jump because she thought he was killed by Vlad and his men? Somehow, he had to get out of here.

Let her know he was still alive.

Footsteps on the stairs made him close his eyes and pretend he was still unconscious.

A hand grabbed him by the shoulders and struck him across the face. Jackson did his best not to react. Once more, someone hit him and he didn't respond.

"Told you he was still out, Mr. Mayfield," said a voice that was almost familiar. Tetrault maybe? "We made sure he'd be no threat today. I already made sure the girl knows about his accident. Without him, it'll be real easy to claim suicide."

"All right, let's go," said Mayfield. "There's work to be done."

Jackson didn't move until everything was still. He sat up, but when he heard footsteps on the stairs, he laid back down.

Timid footsteps moved toward him. "Master Jackson! What have they done to you?"

Jackson opened his eyes. Harris the butler hung over him, looking distraught. Guess the old guy wasn't the one that set him and Ophelia up after all.

"Harris," Jackson said in a broken whisper. "Are they gone?"

"Yes, the master and his men and that Tetrault fellow just left in a carriage for town. I'm so sorry, Master Jackson. I had no idea the master would find you and Miss Swann in the study. I thought she'd be unnoticed there."

Harris bent down and with a flip knife, he cut through the ropes until Jackson was free. He couldn't even stand when the circulation in his arms and legs started back again. Harris got a stable hand to help get Jackson inside and into the mud room, a cheery yellow room with shelving for shoes and hooks for coats. And a small hearth with a fire crackling. He set Jackson in front of the hearth and got him some fresh, warm clothes. Without blood on them.

"Harris," he said, his ribs aching with every breath. "Get me my tuxedo, please. Come hell or high water, I will be at Ophelia's opening performance tonight."

"Sir, you need a doctor," Harris said and set a plate of fried eggs and hash browns in front of him. And a white cup of coffee. "And an ice pack for your battered face."

"There isn't time. I've got to find Ophelia before they hurt her."

Jackson grabbed the fork and devoured the eggs and potatoes while Harris left, returning shortly with a black tuxedo with tails, white tie, and white tuxedo shirt. He struggled until Harris helped him into the tuxedo, including the black tail coat and a grey overcoat.

"Sir," said Harris, helping him comb his hair. "I overheard Master Mayfield talking to that scallywag, Tetrault, telling him to station men all around the opera house. In the event that you show up." Harris gripped his shoulders. "I'm so frightened for you, Master Jackson."

"Thanks for everything, Harris," he said, swallowing the cup of coffee in one gulp.

"Sir, Jennie the cook needs to go into town for supplies," said Harris with a smirk. "No one will notice that you're aboard her carriage."

Jackson grinned. "Harris, you're the best! Thank you."

"Please take care, young master. I just hope your father comes to his senses and stops all this intrigue. Hurting his youngest son like this is disgraceful. Arthur is beside himself. He and your brothers are out looking for you."

"When it's all about money, this douchebag can't help himself, Harris. It's his one great love. That's why I've got to stop him."

The cook gasped and Harris' face turned bright red. Whoops! Guess they weren't used to hearing that insult.

"Forgive my crude language," Jackson said in a sheepish voice. "After being beaten unconscious for a couple of days, I don't know what I'm saying anymore."

The smile returned to Harris' face as he patted Jackson's shoulder. "Given the circumstances, I might expect worse, Master Jackson."

A black carriage stopped at the mud room door and rang the bell. Slowly, Jackson got up and trudged toward it, the cook putting on a blue wool coat over her long black dress and white apron. He looked up at the white clock on the mud room shelf. Half past four. He didn't have much time. He had to get to Ophelia by sunset.

Harris gripped Jackson's shoulder. "I sent out two stable hands to find Ophelia that night," he said in a quiet voice. "They got her safely back to her suite, Master Jackson."

In an instant, he felt the lodestone lifted off his neck. He threw his arms around Harris and hugged him.

"I swear, Harris," said Jackson, grinning, "I'll find some way to repay you for this."

Harris smiled, shaking his head. "Remember, young sir, a kindness can never be repaid, only paid forward. Now, go—find and protect Ophelia."

Jackson hurried out the open door and struggled to climb into the back of the carriage. The cook, a tall, slender woman with kind brown eyes and a tight brown bun that made her thin face almost too thin, sat up front beside the driver. The driver was one of Mayfield's stable hands who looked about twenty-five with a head full of brown curls and dark eyes. The team of two chestnut brown horses whinnied as the driver tapped the reins and the carriage lurched forward, away from the manor.

The carriage brought Jackson to the edge of town, stopping suddenly.

"What's wrong?" he asked the cook.

"Harris bade us to ride fast and not stop," said Jennie, looking frightened, "but there are men up ahead, stopping carriages as they pass." She turned sideways, her face filled with fear as she motioned him toward the carriage door. "Master Jackson, they're searching the carriages! They mean you great harm. You must get out while we create a diversion."

"What sort of diversion," the driver asked warily.

Jackson opened the back door and slid out onto the paved road.

"This one," Jennie snapped as she jerked the reins out of the driver's hands and snapped them hard. The horses chuffed as she drove them hard down the road past the men.

While they chased after the carriage, Jackson hurried across the road toward the thick cedar forest. The trees ran to the edge of Port Townsend. He could make it unseen almost to Water Street. Slower route, but safer.

Rain misted the air, fog gathering, eddying around his shoes as he walked. His breath clouded the air as he hurried through winding brown brush and past the green firs and cedars. The scent of pine needles and sea air was sharp. Comforting. It was getting chilly, temperature falling, but Jackson kept his path headed north, watching the sun slip closer and closer to the western horizon.

The clomp of hooves startled him. Galloping hard from the east.

Jackson turned, slipping under the tall cedars' branches to stay hidden.

He froze, holding onto the cedar tree trunk and ducking his head to keep his ragged breath quiet. He held his breath at the sound of the voices.

Three horses rushed past him on all sides.

"Keep looking! He's gotta be here somewhere."

"Told ya, if we smacked that stable hand around a bit, he'd give up the little bastard's location."

Jackson kept as still as death, waiting until the crackle of twigs, rustle of leaves, and dull hoof beats faded into the distance. It felt like hours, the riders doubling back, covering the forest around the road again and again.

Finally, they gave up the hunt and rode off toward the south. To report back to Vlad, no doubt.

He veered east, weaving through the heavier woods as they fanned around the southern edge of Port Townsend. To the west, the sun was already dipping low on the horizon. He had to get to the Peninsula Hotel. By the time the sun had set.

Ophelia's life depended on it.

By the time Jackson reached the Peninsula Hotel, it was past sundown and getting dark. He turned down Water Street, expecting the Northwest Opera House to be lit up bright, but it was dark. A huge sign stood in front of the door. He crossed over to the other side of the street, dodging carriages and people, the air stinking with horse dung and sulfur.

In front of the opera house's double doors was a sign that read, "Due to death in family, Miss Swann will not perform tonight."

He ran two blocks down the dim-lit street, weaving in and out of the handfuls of people on the streets. He ran two more blocks, then three, his throat burning from the chilly air.

Someone grabbed him from behind and dragged him into a dark alley.

Jackson fought hard.

"Master Jackson, please! It's me, Harris—your butler."

Jackson turned to look at him, satisfied when he saw the thinning grey hair, long face, lanky build, and warm smile. Harris wore a grey frock coat, black waistcoat, and grey pin-striped pants. He smelled like hot tea and mineral oil.

"You scared the life out of me," Jackson said, leaning against a brick wall with an advertisement for Edie's Soda Shop painted in bright green and pink on the bricks.

The alley ran several blocks up the hill.

"My apologies. I got word from Jennie about what happened, so I came to town to help you. There are men stationed around the hotel. We'll need to be clever to get past them and get you inside."

Jackson shook his head. "Why are you helping me like this, Harris? I'm not the one who pays your salary."

Harris sighed and folded his arms against his chest. "Over the years, I've had to keep a blind eye to all of your father's nefarious doings. And I don't understand those hideous paintings in his study. I didn't understand him sending Arthur and his other sons overseas to apprentice either. After having some dark magic cast on Ophelia Swann. But tying up his youngest son in a root cellar and hiring thugs to beat him unmercifully? I can no longer serve this man in good conscience. Not anymore."

"Thank you for all you've done," said Jackson. "Now, I've got to get into that hotel before something terrible happens."

He bowed his head. "She thinks you're dead, Master Jackson."

"Dammit!" He gritted his teeth, hands balling into fists. "What if I'm too late?"

Harris shook his head. "Have faith, young master. There's an entrance in back of the hotel. Come, let me show you."

The butler trotted deeper down the dark alley and Jackson followed close behind him. With his collar up and head down, he hurried up a block and over three, turning left beneath the yellow wash of guttering gas lamps. Smell of ozone and sulfur heating the air. Charging it.

Up ahead was the pale blue, white columned back entrance to the famed Peninsula Hotel.

Jackson swallowed a breath. And two dark figures lurked outside. Waiting to pummel him, he realized.

His stomach dropped, heart racing as he and Harris approached the back door. He kept his head down and slid off his grey overcoat.

"One apiece, Harris," Jackson whispered.

"I look forward to it, sir," Harris replied, flashing a smile at him as he took a few steps ahead.

Harris walked right up to the first man in a black long coat and black wool pants, bowler hat perched on his shaggy, dark brown hair. The other man was taller and slimmer, dressed in a long grey suitcoat, black vest and tie.

"Good sir," Harris said, "could you possibly give me the time?"

"Time to get lost," said the man in black.

"You first," Jackson snapped and threw his overcoat over the man's head.

Harris grabbed the other man's long coat and pulled it up and over his head.

In moments, Jackson had the man in black on the ground, out cold. Harris wrestled a bit longer with the taller man, but together, he and Jackson dropped him, too.

"All right then," said Harris, brushing dust off his pants. "I'll watch our friends and this door. Go find Ophelia. And save her."

Jackson rushed to the door and threw it open. Bounded up the dark staircase and into the hotel lobby.

Jackson pounded up the dark redwood stairs of Port Townsend's Peninsula Hotel, frantic to save the woman he loved. Gaslights pooled pallid yellow along Water Street, the dark winter night eerily quiet. Scent of sulfur and wood smoke hung above the scent of orange oil as he pulled in a hurried breath.

Wood floors creaked with every slick step, top floor painfully quiet except for the steady clack and tick of the dark oak grandfather clock against the hallway's ivory walls. It lamented seven o'clock's arrival with seven mournful notes, a requiem that rose in layers through the empty hallway as he reached the top step.

His stomach dropped, heart beating faster. The door to her hotel suite was wide open and dark, lit only by the gas lamps on Water Street below.

"Ophelia!" he shouted, fear turning his hands to ice.

His heart pounded in his ears, stomach burning as he brushed past the polished redwood balustrade, tails of his black tuxedo jacket whipping against the baluster.

"Ophelia, where are you?"

He couldn't be too late! He couldn't! She meant everything to him.

"Please," he called, "Tell me you're still here. Ophelia!"

He rushed into Ophelia's suite.

As the last moan of the grandfather clock faded to steady ticking, heavy sounds of something fluttering overpowered the painful quiet.

Horrified, Jackson turned toward the sound, toward the picture windows that lined the south wall overlooking Port Townsend Bay and Water Street.

A surge of cold air stung his face, his gasping breaths fogging the air as his brain began processing details. His heart beat a wild staccato against his rib cage.

February's chilly wind fluttered against white muslin curtains. Like topsails on a sloop. At last, he realized it.

The window was open!

His heart dropped like a stone and for a moment, he couldn't breathe. "Ophelia, no…" he said with a gasp.

He rushed over to the open window, rain misting Port Townsend's dark, cast-iron skies, the bay a black, turbulent mirror. And looked down through the gaslights' yellow haze to the street below as shouts and commotion rang out. Rising above the clock's steady ticking and the rustle-clomp of horse-drawn carriages.

A shrill police whistle cut through his pain, dispersing the crowd.

At last, he saw the hazy dark figure in the street. His eyes filled with tears as he sucked in a breath and turned away.

"Oh, God no, Ophelia," he said through gritted teeth. "No!"

His knees buckled, his body aching all over. Desperate to feel her soft, calming presence, to hear her gentle, lyric voice telling him she was all right.

The heaviness of her growing absence broke him with every step away from the window. She was gone.

He smashed his stinging eyes closed, shaking his head. No! He couldn't look at her lifeless body lying in the misty yellow darkness, not one moment longer. He wouldn't allow his last image of Ophelia Swann to be her dead and broken in the street below.

Defeated, he dropped to his knees, shuddering as he wrapped his arms around himself. He had never loved anyone like he loved Ophelia Swann. Ever.

He felt sick inside. He'd failed her.

Something glowed purple to his right. The blue flower pot sat on a small drum table, daffodils in full bloom, glowing purple. The hand mirror beside the pot caught the purple light and cast it back at him. He plucked one glowing blossom off the plant, resisting the urge to crush it. He never even got to use it.

The newsprint page covering the bulb lay on the damp floor. Face up, mocking him with its February 29, 1896 date. And its headline that read: *International Opera Star Leaps to Her Death.*

The same warning he'd seen two days ago. He tried so hard to save her, but he'd failed. Miserably. Tears slid down the sides of his face and he balled his hands into fists.

He ached to hear Ophelia's clear, melodic soprano voice, part songbird and part angel. Her touch had always softened the painful loneliness he'd hidden from the rest of the world. Especially his friends. Even Ava.

He sank to the slick hardwood floor, wet with cold rain misting through the open window. Shadows danced along the suite's ivory walls as he played everything back in his head, his heart crumbling.

Where had it all gone wrong? Why couldn't he save her?

From somewhere behind him, footsteps clamored up the stairs. His heart shattered into a million shards. It was Harris, coming to help.

He turned his head toward the doorway.

"Harris, it's too late," he said with a moan, hanging his head. "I failed her."

"Master Jackson, no!"

Footsteps pounded across the floor, someone dropping down in front of him. Soft hands cradled his face.

He looked up. Into the most beautiful pale green eyes he'd ever seen.

"Ophelia?" he cried, his eyes filling with tears as he rose up on his knees. "Oh, God—Ophelia! I thought you were gone forever."

"Jackson!" she cried. "The paper said you were dead! Your face! What happened?"

He clasped her to his chest, terrified this was all a dream, that she was forever lost to him. Her arms wrapped around him, her lips finding his, kissing urgently. He kissed back, quick, desperate kisses.

He held her out at arm's length, taking in her face, her hair, her smile. She was breathtaking. He held out the glowing blossom to her.

"That flower lady told me I'd know what to do with it when the time came," said Jackson with a shrug.

He struggled up from the floor and Ophelia was in his arms again.

"I don't want to let you go," she said. "I'm terrified this is all a cruel joke."

"Who jumped from your window?" he asked.

"Tetrault," she said. "He tried to shove me out the window, but I twisted out of his grasp and he fell out instead. It was his own fault."

"That's the best news I've ever heard," said Jackson, chuckling at the karmic justice, a distant tapping sound behind him in the hallway. He felt a chill rush down his spine.

"Me, too," said Mayfield from the doorway.

Jackson whirled around, putting Ophelia behind him. Mayfield wore a pressed black-caped suit coat and black bowler, his blue eyes filled with malice. Didn't a lot of villains wear black capes?

Mayfield walked into the room, steps slow and meandering. Like a walk in the garden. Like he'd already won.

"This way, I can collect your money from his estate for the untimely death of my son," he continued with a shrug. "Star-crossed lovers. Such a shame you jumped to your death, dear boy. Let's just hope

Arthur and your other brothers are smarter than you've been. I'll have to find room in my study for two new paintings." Mayfield cast a lingering glare at the doorway. "One for my traitorous butler."

Mayfield took two black vials out of his coat pocket and threw one against the floor. A black mist floated up from the hardwood and within it, a strange presence writhed, like a spirit. It surged toward Jackson.

Jackson hit the floor and rolled out of its path.

It came at him again and he ran toward the far wall, colliding with the dresser.

"No, stop!" Ophelia shouted. "Stop!"

Mayfield laughed. "It's impossible to elude, boy. But I do enjoy watching you try. Watching Harris will be the most fun I've in days."

The mist turned into ropey strands of darkness that wrapped around Jackson's legs, swirling around his torso.

"You're a monster!" Harris shouted.

Jackson stared at the glowing purple blossom. What did it do?

That's when he saw the pure white light reflecting back from the bulb—from the hand mirror on the table.

That flower lady told him to reflect on it. That's it!

He grabbed the mirror and held it in front of him with one hand. With the other hand, he held the bloom in front of the mirror.

The black mist began to tighten around his chest, moving up his arms. Toward the mirror.

White light flared from the glowing bulb, turning into bolts of lightning when it hit the black mist. The two energies clashed, bouncing off the mirror, and passing through the bulb's purple gleam.

"What's this? No, that's impossible! Your mother never taught you this!"

In an instant, the charged black mist shot away from the mirror and hit Mayfield in the chest, dropping him to his knees. Beside the painting he'd trapped Ophelia inside.

Jackson walked over to the man as he scrambled to his feet.

"You're as weak as your mother," Mayfield snapped. "Not sure how you survived the accident in the bay, but I won't make that mistake twice."

A cold shiver brushed Jackson's spine. Had Mayfield drowned his youngest son when he was six? This dude was such a monster.

"And lucky for us, you won't get another chance," Jackson said with a growl. "Asshole."

With the glowing bloom and mirror still in his hand, Jackson shoved Mayfield backward, into Ophelia's empty portrait.

"No!" Mayfield screamed as he fell.

He hit the canvas and fell through it. Disappearing as the whole canvas gleamed white.

Harris gasped.

Jackson whirled around. Ophelia was on the floor, encased in that black mist.

"Ophelia, no!" he shouted, rushing to her.

He dropped down beside her as Harris knelt at her feet.

"Master Jackson, it appears that she's still under this black magic spell."

Jackson laid the glowing blossom in her hair and leaned through the mist, kissing her with all his might. The white light sparked from the blossom, enveloping him and Ophelia in the white light as the black mist melted away. Only when every trace of the dark mist had vanished did Ophelia open her eyes.

"Jackson," she said in a hoarse whisper, "I'm—I'm free."

He glanced over at the daffodil bloom, as yellow as a summer sunrise. The purple glow was gone, the magic spent. It began to wither.

"Let's return to Mayfield's lair," said Jackson, sliding his arm around Ophelia's waist. He put the hand mirror in his tuxedo jacket. "One last thing to do."

She nodded and picked up the blue flower pot with its glowing blooms.

"Jennie showed up in the carriage," said Harris. "It is downstairs, master Jackson," said Harris, "I'll take the painting, too." Harris picked up the portrait and rushed out of the suite, down the stairs.

Jackson and Ophelia followed.

It was late when Jackson returned to the manor with Ophelia and Harris. He took Ophelia's hand and they raced to the study. The key was in the lock, so he turned it and opened the door. He flicked on the electric lights that bathed the walnut wood and red curtains in flickering white light.

He glanced up at the five empty portraits. "We'll have to wait until sunrise." He reached out and caressed Ophelia's face. "You must be exhausted."

"I am," she said, taking hold of his hand and pressing it to her lips in a gentle kiss. "But I want to stay with you until sunrise. I have to know if the spell is truly broken."

He had until almost midnight to get back to his own time. A cold shiver surged through him. With Mayfield trapped in Ophelia's painting now, was there even a portal back to his time? Had saving Ophelia trapped him in her time?

Marti's voice echoed in his head. *It closes at midnight on March 1st. If you don't come back through by then, you'll be trapped in the past. Think about that.*

It was all he thought about on the ride back to Mayfield's manor. But Ophelia was alive and it was still Leap Day. That's all he cared about right now.

When they entered the study, Ophelia set the daffodil pot on the desk and followed Jackson to a red leather sofa. He entwined her in his arms and they held each other, talking, kissing, and exploring until the first rays of sunlight touched the broken window.

Ophelia rose to her feet, reaching out to the sunlight.

"The sun is rising!" she cried, her pale green eyes misting with tears. "It's been so long."

Jackson pulled her closer, taking in the delicate corals, yellows, and pinks reflecting across the grass as the twilight turned warm, the sun as yellow as a daffodil on a crisp spring morning.

Tears slid down her cheeks as she laughed. "It's over, Jackson. It's finally over." She turned to him. "I'm free at last, thanks to you."

He kissed her gently, softly, until her tears stopped falling. "One last thing to do," he said, letting her go.

He moved to the desk and plucked one of the blooms from the

flower pot. It glowed purple as he glanced up at the paintings. All five were grim portraits again. He stepped toward the paintings and studied Abigail Mayfield's face. Her blonde hair and dark blue eyes stared back at him in a white pin-striped blouse and black skirt.

He sighed. The flower lady he'd seen in the mist that night. Who'd given him the keys to free Ophelia. And her from her own portrait.

He slid the mirror out of his pocket and turned it toward the paintings. The blossom's purple glow pulsed as black mist seeped out of the paintings. Drawn toward the daffodil blossom. As the black mists joined and touched the bloom, white bolts of magic shot toward the mist like lightning. Sparks flew.

The paintings shook against the wall until an explosion threw Jackson backward. Knocking all five portraits off the wall.

As Jackson got to his feet, the flower lady stepped out of her portrait and moved stiffly toward him. Four other women stepped out of the other portraits: two redheads, a brunette, and a black-haired woman. All young. And furious!

They all crowded around Jackson, thanking him and crying. Abigail, the blonde flower lady, pushed past them and hugged Jackson.

"Thank you for saving me! You knew I was the flower lady, didn't you?"

He shook his head. "Didn't figure it out until just now. You said love made the magic work. You had access to the magic, but you couldn't release yourself."

She nodded. "Only Arthur or his descendants could release me. Or Jackson, but he drowned at six."

Jackson laughed. "Guess Mayfield never dreamed someone would come through the very painting he'd trapped Ophelia in and break everything, did he?"

"Or that he'd meet the one woman with the magic to undo all of his black magic at a Port Townsend flower stand," Abigail said with a smile.

Ophelia took his hands in hers as Harris carried the portrait of Orson Mayfield into the room and leaned it against the wall. The other women crowded around the butler who knew them all.

"Looks good, Harris," said Jackson, giving the smiling butler a thumbs up.

"Thank you, Master Jackson," he replied, bowing. He turned toward Mayfield's five wives. "Ladies, if you will follow me, I'll find suitable sleeping arrangements for you."

They all filed out, leaving Jackson and Ophelia alone in the study. Jackson moved toward Mayfield's frozen portrait, staring. Had he sacrificed everything to save Ophelia?

With a shaking hand, he reached out to Mayfield's portrait. Touching canvas and dried paint. Fear bloomed cold through his chest at the realization.

The portal was gone. He couldn't go back.

He felt her arms slide around his waist, her face against his back. "I can't even describe what freedom feels like after all this time, Jackson. You saved me." Her voice was bright and airy. Relieved. Content.

He turned around, taking her in his arms, but she saw the fear in his eyes. The pain. She reached out and touched his cheek.

"What is it, Jackson?" she asked, stroking his face, her hand so soft and warm, her touch burning through him.

The ache filled him. "Almost two days ago, I came through this painting to save you," he said in a shaky voice. "Now that Mayfield's trapped in there…" He sighed, bowing his head. "And Leap Day's burning daylight. I—may be trapped, too."

Her eyes widened with fear as she stared at him with watery eyes. "Oh, my God! Jackson…I never even considered that."

He tried to smile through the pain. The indecision. Scott was right. He hadn't thought through any of this. He'd just charged ahead into the dark with a flashlight and a GoPro, not thinking past what would happen after he'd found the portal in Ophelia's portrait. Not even a thought about an exit strategy.

What happened now? She loved him. And she was all he'd ever wanted. But not here. Not in 1896.

He turned away, slapping his hand against the painting. It shuddered, rigid, immobile against his palm. The magic that trapped Mayfield had closed the portal.

There was no way home again.

He struck the painting with his fist. Mayfield was probably laughing his ass off at him now, knowing now that he'd managed to trap himself 124 years in the past.

Ophelia threw her arms around him. "Jackson, don't," she said in a soothing voice, stroking his hair. "Please don't leave me now. I love you."

He whirled around, gripping her hands in his. "Enough to follow me into the future?" he asked.

"What? Follow you?"

Her face turned pale and she stared at him, those light green eyes looking like a deer caught in headlights now.

He winced, studying her face, wondering how much time she had left in her time. Had he given her a long, full life back or did fate have other nasty tricks up its sleeve?

"Yes, follow me! To a new age. A new life. With me."

He smiled, running his fingers through the coal-black wisps of Gibson Girl hair that hung in ringlets around her hairline now. From rain and heat.

He kissed her hard on the lips and took her by the shoulders. "I love you, Ophelia Swann and I don't know if the portal I came through still exists or not now. But if it does, will you come through it to my world?"

She let go of him, a pensive shadow darkening her face as she turned away.

"Leave my own time?" She let out a hiss of breath, her fingers tangling together as she stared at them. "And the most renowned opera career of my day?" She spun around. "Jackson, what would I do there?"

He grinned at her. "Sing opera. Go to college. Marry me? All of the above?"

She gasped as he took her hands in his again. "Marry you?"

He nodded, dropping to one knee. "Here. There. No matter where we land. Marry me, Ophelia Swann. Please?"

Ophelia fell into his arms as his mouth found hers, kissing her with a long, frantic kiss that sparked like desert fireworks, like southern heat lightning, like the Vegas strip in July.

Just then, it didn't matter to Jackson whether it was the 19th or 21st century. As long as Ophelia was beside him, he'd land on his feet. Maybe he'd get rich playing the stock market and sell it all before 1929? And invent things a little early. Like the refrigerator. Or the internet.

Maybe someday he'd get used to 1896, he told himself.

"Jackson!" Ophelia cried, staring behind him. "Look!"

He turned around.

Seeing a hand reach out through Mayfield's portrait.

"Get back, Ophelia!" he cried, getting in front of her. "Mayfield's found a way out of the painting!"

He felt Ophelia shaking as the hand flexed and reached toward him.

"Jackson! Can you hear me?"

It was Scott Branson's voice!

"Scott!" he shouted, moving closer. "Scott, it's Jackson! I hear you!"

"Finally!" Scott shouted. "We've all be calling to you for days. You okay? You need to come through before this thing closes again. See, Marti was wrong. Only years divisible by 400 are leap years."

Jackson shook his head as he slid his arm around Ophelia, pulling her close.

"So? What's that mean?"

"Dude, it means," Scott said, his voice booming through the study, "that the next leap year isn't 1900. It's 1904. That's eight years from now. You don't come through before midnight and you're trapped there for eight freakin' years."

"Doesn't matter," Jackson snapped. "I broke the portrait's magic and freed Ophelia. But doing that closed the portal. I can't come back through again."

Scott's infectious laugh filled the study. "It only closed on your side. When the painting changed and the other portraits emptied, Marti and I figured out how to reopen the portal on our side."

Jackson sighed, seeing the fear in Ophelia's eyes deepen. She wouldn't come with him. He felt sick inside.

"Doesn't help me," he snapped.

"You can't walk through it, that's true," said Scott, "but we can pull you back through."

"How?" Jackson demanded, frowning.

"Your cousin, Dylan, ya goof ball." Scott laughed again. "He's connected to the dude in the portrait just like you, so he can open the portal and bring you across."

Jackson cupped Ophelia's face in his hands. "Ophelia? Come back with me? See the future? Marry me?"

She rose on her tiptoes and kissed him gently. Softly. Her touched burned through him.

"I'll follow you anywhere, Jackson Mayfield," she said, brushing blond hair out of his pale blue eyes. "Yes, of course, I'll marry you."

Grinning, he wrapped his arms around her, holding her against his heart.

"Okay!" Jackson grinned. "Dylan, we're ready. Bring us through."

He held his breath, the sun rising higher as Leap Day 1896 burned away.

At last, two hands reached through the painting, fingers splayed. "Bro, we're ready to bring you and the opera singer through. Take my hand and hold on with everything you've got, okay?

"Got it!" Jackson's arms tightened around Ophelia, holding on with an iron clad grip. "On the count of three, Ophelia," he said in a quiet voice, "we'll both grip one of Dylan's hands. Got it?"

Ophelia nodded, smiling at him.

"Raise your right hand, "said Jackson. "I'll raise my left. On three, grab and hold on for your life."

"Ready," she answered, lifting her right hand toward the portrait.

Jackson positioned her under Dylan's right hand and he leaned left, holding up his left hand. He kept an arm around Ophelia's waist and she held onto him with her other arm.

Waiting for Dylan to count to three.

"Okay, Dylan. On three."

"Got it, bro!" Dylan's voice echoed through the painting, its surface rippling like water around his forearms.

"One. Two. Three."

He waited a beat for Ophelia to reach for Dylan's hand. He grabbed hold of Dylan's other hand as Ophelia grabbed hold of his cousin's hand.

Like a slingshot, Jackson's body lurched forward, toward the painting. Away from Ophelia. The hard surface shimmered, undulating as he shot through it. Into darkness.

⸺

It seemed like ages until the dark dissipated, falling away to bright white camera lights and flashlights in his eyes. The dull roar of voices made his head ache as Scott and Nancy and Marti yelled at him. Reprimanding him. Shouting at him. Berating him.

"Damn, that was dumb, dude!" Scott shouted. "When you disappeared, I wanted to reach through that painting and throttle the shit out of you for being so stupid!"

"Knew you were gonna do it!" Stan snarled.

"And you didn't listen to a single word I said, Jackson!" Marti yelled, her voice shrill and loud. Grating. Jackson scrunched his eyes closed. "You could have been trapped there for eight freakin' years! Eight! Before we could even TRY and rescue you, you dolt! So dangerous and stupid! Can't believe you, Jackson!"

Nancy shook her finger at him as he struggled to sit up, every muscle and nerve objecting to any movement at all.

"So dangerous! We almost lost you forever, you know that? And your poor cousin had to go to the owners and plead for extra time for our investigation, on account of you disappearing." She slapped her arms against her side, motioning at Dylan kneeling beside him. "Of course, he couldn't tell them that you'd disappeared through a portal in an enchanted painting. You scared the living hell out of all of us!"

Jackson glanced around the dark, barren room, all six paintings uncovered now. Five of them were just empty frames with blue backgrounds. The last one, that had contained Ophelia, had Orson Mayfield staring back in his black coat cape and suit. Glaring, Jackson realized.

But cold fear shot through him. Where was Ophelia?

He snapped up from the floor, the room violently tilting. "Ophelia? Ophelia!"

He grabbed his head in both hands as the room rose around him. And he was sinking. The dusty, broken hardwoods rushed up to greet him and his chin slammed hard against it, head ringing, a shooting pain down his neck, into his shoulder.

"Dude, chill," Scott said in a soothing voice as Stan took him by the shoulders, easing him against the wall with its peeling ivory paint and blackened, crumbling wallpaper.

"Take it easy, cousin," said Dylan, holding him against the wall.

"No!" Jackson shouted, fighting against their restraints. "I have to go back through. Ophelia's not with me!"

"Easy, Jackson," said Stan.

Stan helped Dylan immobilize him and he still fought. Hard.

"Stop it, Jackson," Dylan growled. "Stop it!"

"No! Ophelia? Ophelia!"

Nancy grabbed his face and held it, forcing him to look at her. "Jackson! Listen."

His face contorted and his shook his head. "Nancy, please…I've got to find her. I love her."

She pressed her fingers against his mouth, silencing him. "She's over there. With Marti. She's still out cold, but she made it through, too."

Scott rolled his eyes. "Something about love changing the enchantment," he said in a mocking tone. "Let you bring her through or something. Ya big weirdo."

"I asked her to marry me," Jackson said, grinning now.

"Dude? Seriously?" Scott shook his head.

"I said yes."

He couldn't help but grin at the sound of that familiar, lyrical, crystalline voice. Every soprano note was an aria that ached through him. He loved her more than anything.

"Ophelia!"

Marti helped her over to him and she fell into his arms. He kissed her urgently.

"Jackson, I'm really here with you? In the future?" She touched his face. "The only one I have is with you, wherever that is."

"Have you seen his apartment?" Scott snickered. "Tiny."

Jackson laughed. "It's not Mayfield Manor, but we'll look for a new place."

She handed him a worn piece of paper.

He stared at it, shaking his head. "What's this?"

"The deed to the opera house I renovated in 1896," she said, running her fingers through his hair. "The one I bought and still own."

"Looks like we're moving, guys," said Jackson, holding Ophelia close.

Ophelia shook her head. "No, we're opening a theatre."

"Looks like a new generation will hear Ophelia Swann sing," said Nancy as she slid her arm around Scott's waist.

"That's Ophelia Swann Mayfield," said Jackson as Ophelia kissed him hard.

He'd commission a new portrait of her to hang in the opera house when it finally reopened. Without a portal—they had enough with portals already. And he'd hang ol' Orson Mayfield beside it. It was only fitting that ol' Vlad see her content for the rest of her life. Beside his distant relative, Jackson Mayfield. Now, that was a happy portrait worthy of framing.

Duet in the Key of Time

The old Victorian house had seen better days, like the overgrown bluff overlooking the Salish Sea, but Perry Hart was determined to rescue it. And save the house's history. He was good at fixing things. Everything but his own life.

Scent of sweet grass and sawdust tanged the sea salt air as Perry walked past the blue sold sign nestled in the tall grass and stared at the long-neglected San Juan Island home that he'd been renovating since December. He winced. Since Amanda left him.

Wind scoured the bluff framed by Parrish blue skies and fleecy clouds straight out of a John Constable painting. Sunlight glittered off the gunmetal blue sea framed by the Olympic Mountains' snowy peaks to the west, a large trawler cutting across the water's mirror calm as the mournful call of seagulls rose above the whisper of brisk, cool May winds.

In 1913, when the house was built, this place must have felt like heaven. Wind ruffled his dark hair as he imagined how the once robin egg blue Victorian might have charmed the island's west side. With its soaring cupola, ornate spandrels dotting the white wraparound porch, it must have looked like a gingerbread house with fish scale shingles adorning the gabled rooftops and sun-drenched windows facing the sea.

He never dreamed it would be the perfect summer escape from all his friends getting married. Avoiding all the looks, everyone wondering why the guy voted most likely to live happily ever after in high school was still alone at twenty-nine and renovating houses by himself.

His grip tightened around the old glass doorknob on the house's weathered front door. Every time he touched it, he felt a strange connection to the house. A comfort he only felt when he was inside the dilapidated old Victorian.

And only when he heard the music.

Maybe Amanda could explain it to his friends? After she walked out on him six months ago, keeping the ring and losing the fiancé. Canceling the wedding that would have been this next weekend in May.

With tool belt hugging his lean waist, grey Seahawks hoodie fluttering in the wind, faded Levi's already dusty, Perry tugged again on the glass doorknob. The door groaned, rasping against the rotted door jamb until it finally gave way. He needed to put replacing the door jambs higher on his To-Do List.

He opened the door and stepped into the old house that had been empty since the 1990s. And that empty state had done a lot of damage to the place. Especially to the original parts of the house that hadn't been renovated.

Like the floors.

Staring down at the rotted walnut hardwood, Perry crept through the formerly grand gallery with its once graceful staircase, rotting away now. Replaced by a ladder propped against the wall, so he could get up to the second floor. To his left was the sitting room where he had a mattress on the floor. To the right, a parlor. Plumbing and electricity had been updated before he bought the place, so he at least had lights and a working bathroom while he repaired the bones of the house. Starting with these floors.

Already, the house was filling with sunlight. The air was musty and covered in dust, a hint of brine and sweet grass wafting through a broken window as he moved across the dusty, broken marble-floored foyer into the sitting room.

His white sneakers squeaked against the room's original mahogany floors that revealed the rough subfloor underneath as he moved into the huge sitting room. He winced at the handful of dark holes in the floor that meant a long drop into the basement.

But the massive palladium windows that faced the Salish Sea were breathtaking, gathering the light like a bouquet of wildflowers. He turned toward the scrollwork marble hearth across the space, blackened and dusty with time and use. He stared at the dark firebox inside, smelling the stale scent of wood smoke and ash that clung to it.

His life felt as empty as this old house.

An aching soprano note resonated through the house like a bird trill.

Perry froze. This was the first time he'd heard the music during the day.

He'd heard her voice so many times in the night and it had comforted him, kept him from blowing his brains out when the night got too dark and too long. He longed to find the woman behind the voice, but by morning, he'd convinced himself it was just a dream.

Like crystal, the fragile melody lilted like a whisper, carrying through the house in a delicate, soulful echo. Rolling over him like the sound of angels. He ached to meet this woman.

For a moment, he couldn't breathe.

At night, the melody floated like an apparition around him. Kept him safe in the long, lonely hours before dawn. Where his failures with Amanda tortured him the most.

But this angelic voice had eased the pain and every time, he thought he'd imagined it.

Until today. It was resonating in the daylight. And he wasn't dreaming.

This time, he'd find where the music was coming from. This time, he'd find her.

His footsteps thumped across the marble floor, ticking toward the parlor. In the direction of the melody.

He stopped when the door creaked open, revealing its high

ceilings, built in mahogany bookshelves along the walls, and old, peeling teal and gold wallpaper that reminded him of peacock feathers. All covered in a thick grey blanket of dust that smelled musty and old, like a century old book. Or a vintage car.

Again, the soprano notes rolled through the house like a siren song, making his chest tighten and his heart ache.

A chill danced across his skin. The melody was coming from the parlor, a room he hadn't even touched yet.

In the thin light struggling through the dust-laden windows that faced east, Perry made sure the mahogany wood floor was intact first before he entered the room. And moved toward the sound.

But he only got two steps inside it before the floor collapsed underneath him and he plummeted into darkness.

When the light returned, someone was helping him up from the floor.

"Your name, sir?" a man's voice asked.

Where was he? He'd been alone here.

He glanced up at the man standing beside him. Black pinstriped trousers and black dress boots with buttons.

Perry craned his neck, looking up at the man dressed in a black waistcoat and crisp white shirt, dark ascot draped around a tall starched white collar. He was older. Forties maybe? Thinning ash brown hair.

Butler? Phantom from 1913? Or…a chill rushed along his spine… had he somehow traveled back to 1913?

But that was impossible. Right?

Perry stared down at his own clothes. Tool belt was missing, but he was still dressed in Levi's, white sneakers, and grey Seahawks hoodie. He glanced down at the ruined hundred-year-old hardwood floor he'd just fallen through.

Because he had fallen through the floor. Hadn't he?

Waxed, rich mahogany the color of cinnamon glistened beneath the glow of gas lamps dotting the pristine gold and peacock blue wallpaper. A pale blue Persian rug filled the space beneath a blue velvet couch and matching settee. End tables glittered with crystal lamps and ashtrays.

A hint of sulfur mixed with the burn of pipe tobacco as a grandfather clock ticked mercilessly between two bookshelves crammed full of leather-bound books. A fire crackled in the hearth, marble mantle filled with stern-faced black and white photos. Thick sapphire blue velvet curtains covered the east window, giving the room a heavy, forbidding feel that made Perry uncomfortable.

Like he wanted to bolt out of the room.

"Perry," he answered finally. "Perry Hart."

But the other man in the room kept his back to Perry, dressed in a grey tweed boxy suit jacket, tapered trousers, and black short boots that buttoned.

"Please show Mister Hart out, Walter," said the man, his voice gruff and contemptuous.

Perry had no idea what he'd walked into the middle of, but at the sound of the angelic soprano voice that floated through the house, Perry pulled away from this butler. He wasn't leaving until he'd found the source of this music that had lodged itself in his soul and refused to leave.

He had to know where it came from…he had to.

"I'm here because of the music," he snapped and crossed his arms.

The man still had his back to Perry, smoke rising in lazy coils and floating like spirits above his head.

"That's what all of you say," the man snapped. "That it's about her music. About curing her. But it's always about money. I'll not fund another charlatan's phony lifestyle. See him out, Walter."

"Yes, Mr. Barlowe," said the butler, reaching toward Perry.

Perry stepped backward as the lilting soprano voice rolled through the room in a haunting aria that made his eyes tear up. It gave him chills. Moved him in ways he didn't even understand.

"Her music," he said in almost a whisper. "It's like a flight of angels. It's the most moving sound I've ever heard. It puts a siren's song to shame."

At last the man turned around, dark hair pomaded into a slick sheen, mustache framing his upper lip, brown eyes shining with a mixture of annoyance and pain. He wore a white pinstriped shirt, a tall starched collar with short grey tie that looked more like a scarf crossed and tucked into his waistcoat draped with a gold watch chain. A sweet almost bay-leaf like scent mixed with the husky tobacco smoke as the man glared at him.

"All true, Mr. Hart," said the man, but he pointed toward a tall cherry wood cabinet by the window.

A gramophone. Those old record players that conducted the sound through an umbrella-like horn.

Perry's heart dropped. The music was an old record.

"But as you can see, Clara Barlowe has sung her last aria."

"No, I can't see, Mr. Barlowe," said Perry, using the man's name. "She has the voice of an angel. Why has she been silenced?"

Mr. Barlowe grabbed him by his hoodie and shook him. "Don't you read the damned papers, Mr. Hart? Everyone knows about Clara's triumphant return from her European tour!" The man let go of him, pacing as he picked up his pipe from an ashtray on the end table. "She sang in opera houses from London to Rome. From Paris to Vienna. Alongside renowned tenor Louis Everett, her betrothed."

"Sounds like a fantasy," Perry replied.

A bitter smile curled across Mr. Barlowe's lips as he puffed on his pipe and dropped it back into the ashtray.

"Oh, but it was, Mr. Hart," he said, pacing again. "It was. Until their return home. She and Louis booked their voyages back to the States. Their preferred crossing only had one ticket available and Louis had a new show about to open in San Francisco. He purchased the last ticket and she took another ocean liner home."

A chill brushed across Perry, knowing how this story ended. "His ticket was for the Titanic, wasn't it?"

The man nodded.

"Clara hasn't sung a note since last April," he said. "Or spoken for that matter."

Perry understood a little of Clara Barlowe's pain. His fiancée walked out on him for richer prospects. But Clara's fiancé died in the worst accident in the country's living memory and it would haunt her for the rest of her life. He wasn't a therapist or a doctor, but he was good at fixing things.

Maybe he could help her discover her love of music again?

"I can understand why," said Perry.

Mr. Barlowe shoved his hands in his pants pockets and stood in front of Perry now.

"Listen, Mr. Hart. I don't know which opera house or medical facility you represent, but I'll be frank. If Clara doesn't find her voice soon, I will have no choice but to find another suitable suitor for her. Before her twenty-fifth birthday in June."

"What?" Perry felt his anger begin a slow burn. "Your daughter is traumatized from the worst tragedy of her life, lost the man she loves, and may never be the same again. And, if she's not singing like a sparrow after a year of mourning, you're just going to marry her off like she's damaged goods? Part of some fire sale."

He'd expected Barlowe to shout back at him or argue, but he stood stoic, hands in his pockets, an unaffected expression on his angular face.

"Spinsters end up alone, Mr. Hart," said Barlowe in a quiet voice. "I can't let my daughter struggle for the remainder of her life. I'm only thinking about her future."

Perry motioned toward the gramophone and the angelic melody still filling the room.

"Any woman with the voice of an angel deserves the chance to find that voice again. And return to the life she loves. The life she chose. As an opera singer."

The rustle of fabric whispered behind him. He turned to see a wheaten haired woman dressed in a blue pinstriped suit with a long skirt, a white frilly blouse underneath the waist-length jacket. Her hair was twisted and rolled into some sort of fancy bun.

"Husband," the woman called from the doorway. "I don't know anything about Mr. Hart's credentials, but his passion and support of Clara's dreams comforts me. He may be just what's needed here."

Barlowe began to pace again. He grabbed his pipe and puffed on it, rings of smoke drifting up to join the rest of the smoky haze. Finally, he turned to stare at the butler.

"Walter?"

The hint of a smile rose and fell on the butler's face as he glanced at

Perry. "No one else has called for weeks to offer their services. For Miss Clara's sake, we must not give up like the others."

"And arranged marriages have rarely made anyone happy, Arthur," said Mrs. Barlowe, crossing her arms as she leaned against the door jamb. "If Clara could speak, she would have railed at you for even suggesting it."

Mr. Barlowe sighed. "I did suggest it, Bess," he said and set his pipe in the ashtray. "Hoping for just such a reaction. She gave no response. None at all. That's why her situation is so dire. Even arranging a marriage could be difficult." He turned to Perry. "All right, Mr. Hart, Mrs. Barlowe and I give you permission to help Clara find her voice again. You may stay in one of our guest rooms."

Bess Barlowe smiled at her husband. "Thank you, Arthur," she said and left the room.

Somehow, Clara's song had brought him across time to 1913. He had no idea how to get back to his own time. Regardless, he felt compelled to help her.

"I accept," said Perry.

Mr. Barlowe took him by the shoulder and led him out of the parlor and into the foyer's grand gallery. Polished mahogany molding and trim framed the scrollwork banisters and glistening wood of the staircase that curved gracefully upward, delicate and lacy like a climbing rosebush, to the upstairs. Overhead, crystals dripped like raindrops from the massive chandelier that crowned the top of the gallery. Scent of orange oil mixed with traces of tobacco smoke and earthy scent of fresh-cut cedar logs that set by the sitting room hearth.

From the foyer, Perry saw two ivory Victorian couches in front of the fireplace and— Perry's breath caught.

Through the picture window, Clara Barlowe leaned on the wraparound porch railing, staring out toward the sea. White silky layers of fabric draped around her like a Greek goddess, the summer dress as delicate as dandelion fluff on a windy day. Her wavy blond hair fell in ringlets around her face, the rest curled and wrapped into a graceful twist on top of her head. She was radiant. Big blue eyes, pale skin untouched by the sun, looking like she'd just stepped out of a Maxfield Parrish painting.

Mrs. Barlowe sat on one of the sofas, a book in hand. She smiled at Perry and glanced at her husband.

"I see Mr. Hart has met Clara," she said with a chuckle.

Clara Barlowe was the most beautiful woman he'd ever seen and her distant expression made his chest ache. Like she'd lost all connection with the world. Like she felt nothing in that moment. Numb to even the pain she'd carried around for over a year at her fiancé's death.

"She…takes my breath away," he said in almost a whisper.

"Right this way, Mr. Hart," said Mr. Barlowe, dragging him out the front door and around the wraparound porch.

Clara didn't even turn to look when he approached alongside her father. As the sea breeze brushed across the porch, salt and sweet grass hung in the air, carrying a whiff of carnations and roses.

He smiled. From her perfume, he realized.

Mr. Barlowe pulled him in front of Clara. "Clara, I'd like you to meet Mr. Perry Hart."

Those beautiful powder blue eyes narrowed and she swiveled her body around, turning away from him.

Mr. Barlowe winced, his gaze snapping to Perry.

Perry laughed.

That pained look turned to surprise.

Perry shrugged. "What? I like her spunk. That means she's still fighting back. Even though the grief is winning right now."

In an instant, she turned back around, staring at him, a quizzical look in those incredible fairy-like eyes. She was barefoot, cheeks blushed by the wind, full bow lips the palest pink, like the last flush of sunset glimmering for only a heartbeat on the waves.

She shook her head.

"Don't think I know anything about grief?" he said, a hand against his chest.

Her gaze narrowed and she nodded at him.

"Challenge accepted, Clara Barlowe," he said to her. "Everybody grieves in their own way. In their own time."

"But only until your twenty-fifth birthday, Clara," said her father. "Then we must move on."

Perry smirked, pointing at the man. "We?" He fixed Clara with his gaze and shrugged. "He must be French. Or have a mouse in his pocket."

One corner of her mouth lifted almost out of the frown.

"What?" Mr. Barlowe asked with a grumble, looking annoyed.

"We'll let him move on with his own arranged marriage," said Perry. "Although, I doubt Mrs. Barlowe would appreciate him marrying another Mrs. Barlowe. Might get awkward."

"Now, see here Mr. Hart, I—"

But the words died on Barlowe's lips as he stared at his daughter.

Who had a slight smile on her face.

Barlowe looked shocked as he glanced from Clara to Perry.

She watched him through a thick, long fringe of dark lashes and then turned away again. Back toward the sea.

And so began Perry's attempt to save Clara Barlowe from an arranged marriage.

For over a week, Perry sat with Clara on the porch, delivering a monologue that got little if any reaction from her. He talked about safe things. The weather. The sea. The house.

She seemed content to let him ramble on, but she was off in her own world. Her own thoughts.

Perry couldn't imagine what horrors might roam through her head. The thought of the person you planned to marry aboard the Titanic, unable to board a lifeboat, cold Atlantic waters sucking the ship beneath its dark waves. And as the stories began to emerge, each one must have twisted Clara's heart into knots and broken it with every article and account.

He wouldn't want to sing after learning what had happened to the one he loved on that ship, either. With the added pain of knowing that her whole life would change as a result. It would be seven years before women even got to vote. They had to marry to survive.

Finally, he decided to just get real with her. See if he could get through her grief that way.

He glanced down at the clothes he wore, an old pair of grey work pants and blue striped shirt he found in the closet of the guest room.

But he wore the white sneakers he'd arrived in because apparently shoes in 1913 didn't come in his size. Or width.

The sea air was crisp, insects chirring above the hush of the wind blowing the tall seagrass that covered the bluff. Crisp blue sky was pervasive, not a cloud marring the Parrish blue canvas that met the steely blue waves fluttering across the waves. Sunlight glittered off the water, bathing the overlook in warmth as the scent of carnations and roses wafted toward him.

Whitewashed porch smelled like fresh paint as Clara shifted in one of the white wooden chairs covered in afternoon shade, a touch of brine on the breeze.

Perry rose from the other chair and paced alongside the railing that overlooked the sea below. Only the sound of the wind rustling tree limbs and soft buzz of passing dragonflies as they darted past filled the silence. Punctuated by the lament of seagulls. No car motors rumbled. No airplanes buzzed overhead. Everything was a crisp, serene quiet.

That he was about to break.

"So, I'm sure you're wondering why your father stuck you with me. Wondering why he thought that maybe some schmuck like me could ever help you find your voice again."

He glanced over at her as he moved to the railing and leaned against it.

She was watching him despite looking disinterested. He had her attention.

"See, I understand a little bit about what you're going through, except I can't sing like an angel." Perry laughed. "Can't really sing at all—even in the shower. But I understand grief. Probably more than you realize."

Again, he flicked a glance at her. Disengaged, but her head was at least turned in his direction. Was that progress? He had no clue.

"I was supposed to get married this weekend." He chuckled, staring at his hands.

Should have had a ring on his hand. But Amanda didn't want him anymore. He never learned why, either. Only found out when he came home sweaty and dusty from renovating the Craftsman bungalow he'd planned to surprise her with as a wedding gift. And found the apartment half empty. She'd even taken his couch that he'd had since he was nineteen at his first apartment.

Deep down, he knew it had been his fault. He'd never been exciting to her. Or adventurous. He hated arguments after growing up with divorced parents who fought like it was a blood sport. He ended up negotiating everything to avoid shots fired. Amanda had hated that about him. She loved to argue. Thought he was weak and didn't stand up for himself when all he wanted was a little peace and quiet.

"Only she didn't die," he said with sigh. "No, she just disappeared from my life. Took most of the furniture and vanished like a ghost."

Like he hadn't been important enough to even inform that she was leaving. Resentment was a bitter taste in the back of his throat. He swallowed hard, staring out at the sea.

"See, all of my friends are getting married this summer," Perry continued as wood scraped against wood behind him. "Guess I feel like I don't belong anymore. I won't pretend to understand how losing your boyfriend on the Titanic must be giving you nightmares. Hell, probably even daymares."

Scrape of wood against wood again. Had she risen from her chair?

"It's probably turned your whole life upside down, too. But I understand. We have dreams of what we think our life will be like. And when those dreams get set on fire and burned to the ground, we just curl into a ball and want to give up."

The whisper of footsteps echoed on the wind. And he kept talking as he felt her presence behind him.

Was he talking about her or him now, he wondered.

"I laid on the floor a long time after Amanda left," he said, continuing. "But when I heard you singing like a siren, I chose to get up from that floor. And face that loss. That pain."

The first time he'd heard that angelic voice in his time made him forget his pain. Forget Amanda dumping him for a little while. He kept trying to find the source of the music. Until he fell through the parlor floor. And landed here—a hundred and ten years in the past.

Fabric brushed against his arm. He glanced to his right.

Clara stood beside him now, diaphanous drape of a pastel blue silk dress soft against her powder blue eyes, blond hair in a loose, gently waved roll of hair at her nape. She was breathtaking, like the angelic sound of her voice that had sung to him inside the ruins of this house.

She reached out to him and laid her hand on his, her skin as soft as cotton. Her touch sent sparks through him. Burned right down his arm to his chest and for a moment, he couldn't breathe.

Finally, when he got his voice back, he turned to her. "You are the most beautiful woman I have ever met," he said and laid his other hand on hers.

She bowed her head, blue eyes turning glassy. That's when he realized that her pain went deeper than just grief. There was something that ate at her about her loss, but somehow, he had to traverse her chasm of silence to find it. Unearth it. And lay it to rest.

He squeezed her hand. "Clara, I promise you, someday, it won't hurt so much. We never get over this kind of loss. We just learn how to live with the absence."

She turned away now, tears falling onto the porch.

He couldn't help himself. Gently, he slid his arms around her and held her close.

A shame he didn't know how to take his own advice.

"Helps release it. Like a wren from its cage. That only sings when it feels safe."

Or free. Bet Amanda told everyone how dumping him was like a lodestone off her back. Would he ever be free of this pain that had become his cage?

Her arms tightened around him.

"You'll sing again, Clara," he whispered against her ear. "I know it."

"Thank you," she said in a crystalline soprano voice, the sound aching through him. "But you don't understand."

He smiled, softly stroking her hair. "I want to understand. And I want to help."

She pulled away from him, tears running down her cheeks. "It's much more than grief," she said, her voice growing hoarse as she backed away toward the steps leading down into the grass. "Don't you see?" Her face scrunched into a look of despair. "It was my fault."

Her fault? He frowned. What was her fault?

Turning, she ran down the porch steps and into the tall grasses, bare feet thumping against the path that wound downward toward the cove.

Perry ran after her.

Sun warmed the air, wind buffeting the seagrass along the path that sloped into a shaded hollow, opening out onto a sheltered, rock-strewn cove. Bleached driftwood littered the beach, along with twisted spring green tangles of seaweed drying in the sand. The smell of brine was strong, the air cooler in the shade.

Clara sat on a large fallen log, shoulders heaving.

As he drew closer, her soft sobs echoed against the rocky cliffs that wrapped around the island's edge.

"Clara," he called, crossing the hard-packed sand, waves lapping at the edges of the cove.

Red-faced, she looked up at him.

He bent toward her, his hand against her cheek. "Talk to me. What do you mean it was your fault."

She was trembling, breaths coming in gasps.

"Louis," she said. "It was my fault."

He sat down beside her on the long and gripped her hand. "Louis was your fiancé, right?"

She nodded.

"What was your fault?"

"The ticket for Titanic…was—was mine."

The cause of her pain began to sink into his brain. She felt guilty that she'd traded tickets with him.

He stroked her hair. "You had no idea what would happen to that ship when you switched tickets with Louis."

"No," she said, wincing. "You don't understand." She bowed her head. "I ended things with Louis in London. Furious, he stole my ticket and boarded the ship to get as far away as possible."

"You broke up with him?"

She nodded.

"I thought you two—"

"Loved each other?" she said, finishing his sentence. "We met at the Seattle opera house. We courted for a while. Since we started together onstage, everyone assumed we were a match made in Heaven." She shook her head. "Including my father who arranged the marriage."

Stunned, Perry rose from the log, his thoughts swirling into a maelstrom of confusion.

If it had been arranged, why was she grieving so much? It was guilt, he reminded himself.

"So, Louis was just another arranged marriage?" he asked as she flitted across the sand toward him.

"Yes, but I feel terrible that he died aboard the Titanic." She bowed her head. "It should have been me. Not him. I didn't love him, but he didn't deserve that."

Perry gripped her shoulders, her powder blue eyes glistening with tears. She was so beautiful. She just took his breath away.

"But it wasn't your fault, Clara," he insisted. "It wasn't."

Reaching up, she took hold of his hands and nuzzled them against her face. He closed his eyes a moment, the heat of her skin sizzling through him.

"No more than Amanda leaving you was your fault, Perry, but you've been blaming yourself for months."

He'd told her about Amanda, but how did she know he'd been blaming himself?

He frowned. "I never mentioned—"

"Perry, I know you traveled back over a hundred years when you heard my voice."

Stunned, he stared at her. How could she know that?

"I know because I brought you here."

His eyes widened. "You brought *me* here?"

She nodded. "With my music. I know you think you're here to save me, but Perry, I brought you here."

"Why?" He demanded, bristling as he moved away from her. "Was all of this a joke to you? Bored ghosts taunting humans! I'll bet your fiancé Louis doesn't even exist!"

He turned to walk away from the cove. But Clara blocked his path.

A pained expression shadowed her delicate features. "Of course, he exists, Perry. And I feel terrible that he died after taking my ticket home aboard the Titanic. For over a year, I've struggled with the guilt and regret. I'm not a ghost. But I brought you here for a reason."

"Why?"

"To save you," she cried, clutching his forearms.

He felt a chill rush over him. "To save me?"

She nodded. "I've watched you from my time since you moved into the house, Perry. At first, I tried to comfort you by singing to you, but it never lasted long. So, I brought you through to my time. Hoping that you'd face your own pain by trying to heal mine." She slid her arms around his waist, pulling him close. "Perry, you didn't do anything wrong. Amanda wasn't the right woman for you."

He couldn't deny that with in Clara's arms, he felt comfort. He felt safe. And it felt like home, something he hadn't felt for a long time. Only when he'd heard her voice singing to him. But holding her made him feel like he was home somehow.

Gazing into her eyes, he wanted to kiss her, to feel his body against hers. He'd come all this way through time to save her and here she was saving him.

"And Perry," she said in that clear soprano voice that ached through his chest. "I've loved you since you first stood on this porch. Months in your time. Years in mine."

He felt a chill dance across his skin. She loved him?

"I fell in love with your voice, Clara," he said. "Because your music comforted me." He cupped her face in his hands. "I never dreamed loving you would save me." He smiled. "Or release me—like a caged wren."

"But Perry, wrens don't sing because they're safe. They sing because they're in love."

"In love?" he asked, giving her a confused look.

She nodded. "They sing because they're in love. They mate for life and sing a song only their mate can hear."

Perry wrapped her in his arms and as the waves caressed the beach, he kissed Clara with an urgency that startled him. She kissed him back hard, her body pressed against his as the sun reached through the treetops and enveloped the beach path in warm gold light.

Three months later, Perry and Clara stood on the porch of their newly remodeled Victorian dream home, decorated for a wedding. Painted a fresh robin-egg blue, the Victorian crowned the island's west side like a glittering aquamarine with its soaring cupola, ornate spandrels dotting the white wraparound porch, and fish scale shingles adorning the gabled rooftops and sun-drenched windows facing the sea.

Rose petals littered the porch like confetti, the soft perfumed scent mixing with the salt air and sweet grass, the Parrish blue skies dusted with clouds as sunlight sparkled across the Salish Sea. Diaphanous organza fabric garlands draped the porch with purple satin bows anchoring it to the posts.

Wooden chairs wrapped in organza draped the five rows of chairs facing the porch. Perry's family sat on one side, Clara's family on the other. Watching them get married. He never dreamed that falling in love across time allowed the two of them to move between his world and hers. And back again.

Giving them all the time in the world to love each other.

Perry stood in a black tuxedo beside Clara Barlowe who was dressed in 1913 white wedding gown. Its diaphanous silk layers draped her lithe body, soft blond hair in a French roll, and crowned with pale pink roses. As the minister stood in front of them, Perry reached out and clasped Clara's hands.

As the ceremony started, Clara began to sing to him, that same aching soprano aria he'd fallen in love with—and the woman who sang it.

But only Perry could hear the haunting, loving melody meant only for him.

Abide

Playing around with online writing AIs had been a lark, something to do while Astoria Easton waited for her coffee at the Powell's Books café—not an event that would change her life forever.

When she'd asked the AI to rewrite her work biography, it returned a fantastical account of her software engineering career without a shred of truth in it. But the results gave her chills. It was the life she'd dreamed of, a life she'd ached for—and longed to live.

Especially a chance meeting with the love of her life, a hot, bestselling novelist hell-bent on changing the world.

A moment in time that had never happened.

Her tawny hair had worked its way out of the purple scrunchie into a mess of curls as she glanced outside, the grey sky dark and forbidding, unusual for December in Portland. Phone in hand, she swiped the winter storm watch off her screen and returned to the open WriteItAI chat window. It was only an advisory and for Sunday when she'd be home. She tapped out a response, asking the AI bot to explain all these factual errors, as the rasp of steamed milk filled the café.

The scent of brewing coffee mixing with hazelnuts and vanilla was intoxicating as she huddled near the brightly lit counter, waiting for some hot caffeine to make her day off bearable. Holiday music was serene in the background, only ten days until Christmas Eve.

In a moment, the AI returned a single line of text, repeating it every time she questioned the errors.

The book, Peregrinity will explain everything.

Her fanciful AI-generated biography hadn't given her future husband's name, but the book title intrigued her.

Peregrinity. A fancy term for wandering.

After snagging her tall, steaming holiday to-go cup of chai latte, coat over her arm, Stori roamed the crowded floors of Powell's and browsed the myriad colorful racks of used books for a novel she'd never heard of before. Today, she'd traded in her expensive suit skirts for skinny jeans and a soft purple sweater, black pumps for Navy blue sneakers that softly squeaked against the tile floor instead of ticking like time bombs. Like the march of time, her life getting further away from her as every step had become a compromise, every event mediocre instead of things that she craved.

Like the ones in this crazy fantasy biography.

After nine years as a software engineer, Stori became a director, swapping business casual khakis and polos for suits. Hating the meetings and revenue forecasting and missing the days when she got to create useful tools.

Stori re-anchored her scrunchie, scent of hot chai and old books heady above soft strains of *O Holy Night* as she searched for the strange book. Determined to challenge this AI's enticing biography. It was pure fantasy. Like her last relationship—and ex, Vince Tully's fidelity.

When she didn't find the book on the shelves, she sat down in a hard wooden chair tucked against the wall between two tables of paperback books marked half off and pulled out her phone.

Googling the title.

What she found stunned her.

Author Finn Hutton's picture took her breath away.

Sad blue eyes as clear as glass. Thick shaggy dark hair like sable. Haunted smile hinting at loss and heartache.

She discovered a flood of articles about Hutton and the book. In January 2010 (she'd been a college freshman), all the major news sites had featured articles with the cover of *Peregrinity*, a stylized blue and gold falcon soaring. The talk show circuit had lit up with Hutton's charming demeanor, devastating good looks, and amazing new novel. Even Hollywood had fallen for the young author and gone into a bidding war over the film rights.

The book had been everywhere, topping all the bestseller charts for months. But by December 2010, very different articles permeated the web. Alarming reports that Finn Hutton had disappeared during a stressful book signing tour.

And all the news stopped after that.

Stori searched for recent news articles on Finn Hutton's status but turned up nothing.

Finn Hutton had been barely twenty years old at the time. Had he walked away from his life? Missing by choice? Had he been kidnapped? Or was he dead?

By now, the world had moved on, *Peregrinity*—and Finn Hutton— lost in the mists of time and deluge of new books.

Stori sighed. Just her luck. The love of her life in her fantasy biography was either missing or dead. Being held captive where she'd never find him.

Merry Christmas!

"Can I help you find anything?"

Glancing up from her phone, Stori saw a willowy middle-aged woman with a long black French braid, jeans, a faded black Powell's T-shirt that looked grey, and a long-sleeved black T-shirt underneath it.

Might as well ask. She was already in a city block of books and only a short walk back to her loft. They had to have a copy of a thirteen-year-old New York Times bestseller by a vanished author.

"I'm looking for a copy of Peregrinity," said Stori, sliding her phone into her jeans pocket.

The employee's eyes widened, her lips pursing.

"That's a hard book to get hold of," she said in a half-whisper.

Stori stared at her. "Why? It was a huge bestseller. And surrounded by a big, unsolved mystery."

"After he disappeared," said the woman. "Some people held onto their copies. Others thought the book was bad luck—and got rid of it."

"Is the book considered valuable?" Stori asked. "Because Hutton disappeared, I mean?"

Okay, now she was intrigued. Finn Hutton had been devastatingly handsome and this novel got rave reviews. Was his first and only novel that valuable after he went missing thirteen years ago?

The woman shrugged. "Collectors are hoping so, anyway."

"Do you have a copy of the book?" Stori asked again in a quiet voice.

The woman lowered her voice. "Just got one in, but are you sure you want it?"

"Why wouldn't I want it," Stori said, frowning.

"People say it's bad luck," said the woman. "Things happen to people that buy it, apparently."

Stori leaned toward the woman. Fine. She'd play along.

"Things? Like what?"

The employee looked away, glancing around the area for a moment, and then leaned closer, her voice falling to a sharp whisper again.

"Magic things."

Magic things? And that was bad?

Stori held in a laugh. First, the writing AI was a fortune-teller and now, this book was supposedly magic?

She didn't believe in magic or fairy tales, but some small sliver of hope made her believe in love, in happily ever afters. Even after Vince cheated on her. After Patrick left to take that job in Texas. Even before Jon, who after eight months, just ghosted her.

"What kind of magic?" Stori asked. "Since when has magic been a bad thing?"

The woman smiled. "They say it's different for everyone. Some say it's romantic. Some say it's painful."

"Why painful?"

"Sometimes getting what you want can be a bad thing," said the employee with a shrug.

Getting what you want? Stori could use a little of that kind of bad thing in her life.

What did she have to lose? A weekend reading a novel and hoping for magic to spark? It beat washing clothes and getting snowed into downtown Portland.

"I'll take it," said Stori.

"Okay, I hope you're not sorry," said the employee, braid swinging off her shoulders as she motioned down the stairs. "I'll get it and ring you up."

Stori followed the woman into the sea of rainbow-colored spines filling pale wooden bookshelves, down the stairs, and into the line of checkout stations by the wall of glass windows that faced Burnside. It had been draped with garland and Christmas lights. And a bunch of those clingy gel Christmas decorations: snowflakes, Christmas trees, and reindeer. The woman bagged the hardcover book and Stori used her phone to pay.

With a brown paper sack rustling underneath her coat's Navy wool sleeve, Stori rushed out of Powell's and hurried on foot north to her eighth-floor loft. A shotgun-style loft with pale grey walls, grey hardwood, and a south-facing window. A gas fireplace with driftwood inserts stood opposite the large flat screen television, a teal couch and love seat in front of the window—glass coffee table between them.

After tossing her coat on the sofa, she sat down, and laid the hardcover book beside her. Morning light was grey but crisp, warm vanilla room spray soft throughout the space.

With a deep breath, she opened the cover.

Gently worn cream-colored pages, a little dark around the edges, were crisp as she turned past a blurb, past review quotes. And turned a blank page to the title page.

Something was written in black felt tip marker.

She squinted. It was out of focus.

The world began to spin around her like an out-of-control Merry-go-round.

Stori grabbed hold of the sofa but pitched forward into swirling darkness.

When she opened her eyes, she was back at the bookstore, standing near the front of a long, winding line beside a big sign that read, *Finn Hutton Talks Story today only.*

Confused, she glanced past the sign. Past the foreboding grey sky.

At a table stacked with books. Behind it sat a young, dark-haired man with glass-blue eyes and a smile that could melt steel. He wore jeans, dark desert boots, and a blue T-shirt under a grey wool sports coat. She glanced down at her torn faded jeans and dark green Portland State hoodie, thirteen-year-old copy of *Peregrinity* that she'd just bought in hand.

Wait a minute! She hadn't been wearing these clothes moments ago.

The book looked brand new now, not a hint of wear on it. And Finn Hutton was right here. Right now!

She reached into her jeans' pocket and pulled out her phone.

What? An iPhone 4? But that phone came out in—

A cold chill danced across her skin.

In 2010.

She swiped another winter storm warning off her phone's screen and gazed at the date.

December 17, 2010.

She'd just traveled thirteen years into the past. How? In 2010, she'd been a freshman at Portland State.

She glanced down at her still-new Portland State hoodie.

Guess this was the magic that woman mentioned.

"Next, please," said a wiry man with coarse grey hair.

Dressed in a grey Powell's T-shirt and jeans, the man motioned her toward the signing table.

She moved toward the table. Where twenty-year-old Finn Hutton sat a foot away from her. Smiling, black Sharpie poised in his fist.

Alive and well. On top of his game.

And she was a mess, red-tinted tawny curls time-blown and her brain scrambled by that strange trip she'd taken, holding his book. Had she fallen asleep on the couch? Or in the chair here in the bookstore?

Was she dreaming this?

"Hello there," said Finn Hutton in a warm but shy voice, his intense gaze enveloping her and she wanted to swim in its pale blue depths.

He was much more attractive in person. He looked shy. Vulnerable.

"Hi, Mr. Hutton," Stori mumbled, feeling confused and off-kilter, but the steady, patient glow of his glass-blue eyes melted away everything around her, everything but his eyes.

He smiled. "Mr. Hutton is my dad and he's back in Seattle. I'm just Finn."

Stori chuckled. "Well, just Finn," she said. "You wrote a painfully romantic book that's moved and inspired the country. I'd say you earned that mister in front of your name."

He laughed, the sound infectious, comforting like the feel of worn velvet across her fingertips. It was musical and filled her with…magic.

Dammit, she didn't believe in magic! But those glass-blue eyes, that sexy smirk, and that mane of sable hair made her believe every word of her fantasy biography.

And hope it came true.

But in his gaze, restlessness and pain pooled beneath his public persona. Like he was searching for something. Trying to escape something. As she stared into his eyes, she felt a strange attraction between them. And his anxiety, churning like ocean waves, began to calm.

He leaned toward her, the Sharpie's pungent scent drifting. "And you just earned a front seat at my book talk tonight," he said, a twinkle in his eyes. "After the book signing."

His voice had a wistful, ballad-like quality to it, warm and inviting. And she wanted to hear more. Much, much more.

"I hope you'll be reading from your book," she said.

"My painfully romantic book?" he asked, one corner of his mouth lifting into a smile and she blushed. "Haven't heard it described quite like that before."

"I'd love to hear the words in your dreamy voice," she said, her cheeks burning. "Voice, I mean!" she cried. "In your voice, the voice that wrote it."

Oh, God. Could she be more awkward? How many shades of red had her face turned? As red as her hair? She'd stopped wearing it this red when she graduated from college and joined stuffy, unimaginative corporate America. Putting her personality—and her personal life—on the shelf for a six-figure salary.

She was afraid to look at him now, but when she finally did, he was grinning, the sadness in those limpid blue eyes retreating.

"I'll see if there'll be time for a dreamy reading," he said and held out his hand for her book.

Stori extended the book to him and his fingers brushed against hers. God, the sparks! They danced along her heart like lightning striking sand.

"Who do I make this out to?" Finn Hutton asked, his voice sounding bright but distracted.

"To Stori," she said. "With an i."

He gave her a quizzical look. "Story?"

Another shade of embarrassment reddened her cheeks. "It's short for Astoria."

His gaze returned to the book, squeak of the Sharpie looping across the title page in fluid strokes.

"Astoria? That's beautiful. What's your full name?" he asked, quickly adding, "For the book."

"Astoria Easton," she said.

"Story's my life," he said in a quiet voice and she felt a rush of electricity flutter along her spine. Like she'd just felt time and eternity whisper in her ear.

Like she'd just met the love of her life.

"I hope so," she whispered, bringing another smile to his lips as he handed the book back to her.

"See you at six, Stori with an i."

Nodding, Stori floated away from the table, intent to find something to distract her until she got to see Finn Hutton again.

And like he'd promised, of the fifty-some chairs in front of the podium where Finn Hutton leaned toward a microphone surrounded by bookshelves, one seat had a reserved for Stori Easton sign on it. Written in black Sharpie. She smiled. In his clear and fluid handwriting.

She hurried between the rows, sneakers squeaking, and plopped into the wooden chair. She took the sign off the back and tucked it into her book. When she turned around, Finn was staring past her.

Stori turned to look.

A menacing man with fierce brown eyes, stubbled square jaw, and lips curled into a snarl loomed behind the last row of chairs in a dark coat. Glaring at Finn. Arms crossed.

In an instant, Finn's demeanor changed.

His face turned pale. Taut. Jaw tense. Mouth pressed into a hard line.

She couldn't tell if it was anger or fear.

He looked away from the man in the gathering audience that waited to hear him talk about his book. He was stiff, unfocused. Angry. And definitely not enjoying himself.

Stori turned over the book she held, reading his biography on the back. It said that Finn was born in Portland but now lived in Seattle. He was a local!

Finally, when the moderator, an older fortysomething woman with short sandy hair and big brown eyes, moved to the podium, Finn glared at the man as he whispered something to her. The moderator took out her phone and texted something.

In a few minutes, two male employees walked up to the man and led him away from the area.

"You think this is over, Finn?" the man shouted as they led him toward the exit. "I saw your SUV parked outside. This is far from over! Mark my words!"

When Stori glanced back at Finn, he was visibly shaken.

He only talked for a few minutes about the book, not about story, and then took questions. Lots of questions. Until it was over. No reading. As the crowd wandered out, Finn still looked angry and disturbed as he started away from the podium.

Stori stepped in front of him.

"Finn," she said. "Mr. Hutton."

"Excuse me, please," he said, glancing around the bookstore.

His gaze was unsettled. Pain and anger burned in his eyes.

The moderator stepped between us.

"Let Mr. Hutton pass, please," she said, keeping Stori back.

He was leaving. Would this moment be the last time anyone ever saw Finn Hutton again?

She couldn't let him walk away.

"Is Peregrinity more about wandering or taking flight?" she called to him. "Or happy endings?"

He stopped in the aisle and turned around, looking puzzled. "Happy endings?"

"Yes, happy endings," she said, watching his expression soften. "Leaving behind asshats who interrupt your talk about story."

He took a step toward her. "Is that the painful or romantic part of the book?"

"Oh, definitely romantic," she said with a smirk. "Everyone loves to read about the villain getting his ass kicked. Besides, you're successful and he's a loser, so you've already won."

He stopped inches away from her, the beginning of a smile at the corners of his mouth.

"I love a good romance, Stori," he said, his gaze enveloping her.

"Me too," she said.

His glass-blue eyes glowed with heat. But he hesitated a moment.

"Would you…" He nodded at the moderator, who stepped away from him. "I'm only in town until Sunday and then home to Seattle, last stop on my book tour, but would you have dinner with me?"

Every breath in her body wanted to force out a shout *yes*. And maybe if she spent time with him, she could change the outcome of his book tour? Get him home safely to Seattle instead of forever lost in time?

"We can talk story," he teased. "With an i and a y."

His words sizzled across her skin.

"How could I say no," she said.

"Sir, you can't go in there," a muffled voice replied.

Stori glanced up to see that menacing man shove his way through the crowd and rush at Finn.

His fist connected with Finn's jaw, staggering him. The man lunged at Finn again.

Stori swung a chair into his path.

He crumpled as Finn launched himself at the taller, heftier man. He returned the punch as three bookstore employees grabbed hold of the man. Pulling him away from Finn.

Finn cradled his right hand against his chest, lip swelling.

"I told you this wasn't over," the man said with a growl.

Finn pointed his finger at the man. "This was over when I laid you out in the floor two years ago for hitting my mother. She and I haven't had your last name since I was eighteen and I don't owe you a dime. Leave. Now! Or I'm calling the cops."

Stori pulled out her phone. "Dialing 9-1-1 in three, two—"

The man held up his hands and slithered back from Finn as the employees again led the man to the exit.

"Mr. Hutton," said the moderator, looking horrified. "I am so sorry. I'll call PPB—"

"No!" Finn's voice was filled with rage, but he took a deep breath, shaking his head. "No need to call the police. That guy won't be back because I'm leaving. I'm so sorry for the scene and I thank you for allowing me to meet my fans and sign books here."

He was ready to bolt. Stori saw the deer caught in headlights look in his eyes. He wanted out of here. Now.

At the last moment, he turned and slid his arm in hers.

"Let's get out of here."

With a nod, Stori followed him through the bookstore and out the back. It was cold and dark as they hurried down Burnside and up Twelfth Street. Several blocks to a red pearly Forester. With Washington plates and pale blue vinyl letters on the back window that read, peregrinity.

In that moment, Stori understood that Finn's first novel was much more than a work of fiction. It was an escape from an abusive stepfather. It was saving himself from a situation he couldn't control.

Finn thrust the key in the lock that clicked. And glanced around. Streetlamps washed gold against damp pavement as he climbed into the SUV. Stori climbed into the passenger side. He locked the doors and started the vehicle, rushing into traffic. Only then did he stop white-knuckling the steering wheel and settle back against the grey leather seat.

"I'm sorry you had to see that," he said, his gaze narrowing in the glow of blue dash lights.

"Stepfather?" Stori asked.

He glanced over at her, eyebrow raised. "Guess it was pretty obvious."

"I get it," she replied. "I have an evil stepmother who has to be reimbursed for every penny. Except when it's for my half-sister, Kayla."

Finn chewed his lip, teeth grinding. "My stepfather beat my mother and me since she married him. I was nine. Said he'd kill her—and me—if she ever left him. When I turned eighteen, I knocked him on his ass and we left Portland. She divorced him. Haven't been back until today. Didn't stop his constant calls and texts demanding money for raising her bastard son, as he calls me."

Stori couldn't help it. She reached over and rubbed his shoulder.

"I'm so sorry you went through that."

A haunted look touched his face. "Good material for a novel," he said and drove up Eleventh Street until he found a parking spot.

"And a nervous breakdown," said Stori and gripped his arm. "Let's do something unconventional."

His eyes brightened. "Unconventional?"

"No stuffy restaurants or standard experiences."

The corners of his mouth lifted for a moment. "What did you have in mind?"

"Food from my favorite deli at the waterfront park near here," said Stori.

"Tom McCall Park?" he asked.

When she nodded, he leaned back in his seat, a faraway look in his eyes until excitement burned in his gaze. He turned to her and brushed red curls out of her eyes.

"That's a wonderful idea, Stori. Let's do it."

After a stop for Reubens at Kornblatt's and another for a bottle of Merlot and some cups, Finn drove southeast to the waterfront park. After eating, they huddled together under a couple of wool blankets Finn had in his car and drank wine as the city lights flickered across the Willamette River. She still carried his book, nestled in her lap.

No sign of the winter storm that kept alerting her phone. Like it had in the present. Had she brought the bad weather with her across time? Had this little detour changed Finn's fate?

"I didn't know I missed Portland until tonight," said Finn, leaning closer to her.

He smelled like soap and Merlot, a hint of wood smoke warming the chilly night as he slid his hand in hers, caressing her fingers.

"I'll bet it was hard to return here," said Stori, snuggling closer.

He nodded, watching a boat lit with Christmas lights drift down the river. "When my publisher sent me on this book tour, I knew I couldn't avoid it." He gazed into her eyes and she wanted to lose herself in the heat, like a wildfire washing over her. "But I'm so glad I risked coming back."

Stori laid her other hand on top of his, cradling the bruised and swollen knuckles, knowing they must ache in this chill.

"Facing down that dickhead must have felt amazing," she said, marveling at his strong, tapered fingers that had pounded out a bestselling novel at such a young age.

She loved to read and storytelling fascinated her—like Finn did—but she also felt a sense of protectiveness. Wanting to keep him safe from this dark fate that loomed ahead. Where he was lost forever, never to be seen again.

It made her heart hurt.

She wanted to wrap him in her arms and keep him safe until the danger had passed. But she had no idea what happened to him.

Had his stepfather ambushed and killed him? Did he get fed up and walk away from his own runaway success—and its overwhelming pain?

"That's not why," he said in a quiet voice and bowed his head, still holding her hand.

"Why then?"

He cupped her face, his fingers so hot they stung her skin.

"Because I met you, Astoria Easton," he said, stroking her cheek.

She wanted to lose herself in his touch, in the velvety timbre of his voice.

"Me?" she said, her voice barely a whisper misting the chilly air.

He nodded. "In the short time I've known you, I haven't felt that constant need to keep moving. To keep searching. Looking for something I don't even recognize anymore."

He sounded so much older than his twenty years. His stepfather had forced him to grow up at nine and he'd never gotten to be that carefree kid. Maybe that was why his book focused on wandering? Escaping.

"To escape?" she asked and gripped his hand.

"I've tried to for so long, but the memories stay with me," he said in a quiet voice. "If I just keep moving, stay ahead of them, I'll—"

"Never have to face them?" she asked.

A haunted look filled his eyes as he nodded. "Not like my mother did."

Stori slid her arms around him and held him close, knowing he carried around some deep-seated pain and a recent raw ache that he struggled to get past.

"Like your mother?" she asked.

He nodded against her neck and sucked in a breath.

"Tried to kill herself a month after my book released. I found her and got her to the hospital. They saved her. This time." His arms tightened around Stori and he heaved a breath. "What if there isn't a next time?"

He'd been through so much for such a young guy. Part of him wanted to run away forever. The other part wanted to save his mother. And the rest was constantly terrified that he couldn't.

So, he'd escaped any way he could. Through stories. Through this novel. And it must have hit a generation of readers right where they lived. Because they understood this compelling need to wander, to travel. To escape.

"Finn, you can't fix her," said Stori.

"I'm all she's got," he said, wincing as he lifted his head from her shoulder, gazing at her again.

"All you can do is love and support her. While you live your life. Your story. I doubt she'd want anything less for you."

For what felt like an eternity, he stared into her eyes as she ran her fingers through his dark hair, trying to soothe the pain and uncertainty within him. That instinct that made him want to bolt like a deer into headlights.

"I'm not saying let go and wash your hands, Finn," she said, stroking his hair. "I'm saying hold on, but not so tight that you lose yourself. Don't be afraid to tell Finn Hutton's story. Not just the ones that live in your head." She pressed her hand against his chest. "The ones here—in your heart."

He leaned across the distance and kissed her, hands against her face, mouth heat and fire and need. Her arms slid around him as she kissed him back. He pressed her against the blankets, his kiss urgent as another boat passed the riverbank in a wash of twinkling lights, the air frosty with breath.

She rolled him deeper into the blankets as her mouth found his again.

Only when it was well after midnight and the park was closed did she and Finn gather the blankets and return to the car.

He held her in his arms again, leaning against the side of his SUV.

"I think I've finally found my own story," he said and kissed her. "And a new one, too. With an i."

Her chest hurt now. She'd found a love story, but it started on the next to the last page. By Sunday, hers would disappear beneath a wave of time and she had no idea if her stepping back thirteen years had changed anything.

"I want mine to be a fairy tale," she said as her voice broke. "With a happily ever after and all the time in the world."

Finn gave her an uncertain look. "A fairy tale it is then," he said and kissed her again.

It made her so sad knowing what could have been. What might have been if she'd understood how this magic worked. If she'd understood how to change things.

She held him so tight, she could feel his heart beating against her chest. Not wanting to let him go.

"Finn, why don't you come back to my loft tonight? Stay there until Monday. There's a winter storm advisory."

He held her out at arm's length, his eyes like molten glass. "I'll be fine. I'll leave before it starts." He smiled. "Not that I don't want to come back to your loft." He stepped closer, his fingers tangling in her red curls. "It's just that I have to be in Olympia by 4 P.M. Sunday for another signing. Tomorrow's a travel day."

Stori felt a cold wind blow across her heart, knowing that somewhere along that drive, Finn Hutton disappeared. And it made her ache all over.

"Can't you reschedule? Because of weather?" She wanted to plead with him, to beg him not to go.

And she couldn't even tell him why. She didn't have any details. Nothing to convince him otherwise.

He shook his head. "Wish I could, but I have two more signings on the way home to Seattle."

She bowed her head. She couldn't stop this. Any of it. Why had that damned AI told her that his book would explain everything? It explained nothing. All it did was break her heart.

"Finn, please," she said. "What if something terrible happens? What if you have an accident?"

Or disappear forever?

That haunted look touched his face again. He gripped her hands. "How about I stay until Sunday morning and see how the weather unfolds?"

She looked at him in surprise. "What made you change your mind?"

"Whenever I touch you," he said, his voice sounding faraway, "I feel like if I don't stay in one place, I'll be wandering forever." His voice fell to a whisper. "Or disappear."

She felt the march of time in his words. Maybe his change of heart would save his life? She swallowed a breath.

And hers.

Finn Hutton stayed at Stori's loft Saturday. With his book in the bag she carried, they explored downtown and Saturday Market together, sharing food and stories. She was shocked when she learned that he hated to travel. It made him anxious and he felt out of place. That evening, they ate Chinese takeout and drank wine as the first snowflakes drifted out of the dark December sky, the temperature below freezing.

In each other's arms, they laid on her couch and watched Christmas movies until she and Finn fell asleep nestled together beneath a tangle of blankets.

But when she awoke the next morning to heavy falling snow, Finn's book was beside her and he was gone, a note on top.

With his contact information. Telling her he'd call when he got to Olympia.

As visibility dropped to zero, she called his number half a dozen times. No answer.

She paced the floor, his book in her arms, waiting for her cell phone to ring. Desperate to hear his voice at the other end, telling her that their story wasn't over yet. That he was still in the world. That there was still time—and pages left in their book.

By five P.M., snow still falling, he hadn't called. And no answer on his cell phone.

Behind her, the phone buzzed.

She whirled around, grabbing for it on the sofa. It wasn't his number.

But the book fell out of her hands.

She tried to shout, to catch it before it hit the floor. It thumped against the hardwood and she was tumbling into blackness.

When the darkness dissipated, she was still in her loft.

Her phone was dark, but she could see that it was much newer than an iPhone 4. She glanced at Finn's book on the floor. It had returned to its 2023 state.

She was back in her own time. Still in her loft. Alone.

Tears rimmed her eyes as she picked up the book from the floor and cradled it against her cheek.

"Oh, Finn," she whispered. "Where are you?"

Maybe she'd managed to change something?

She snatched her phone off the cushion and sat down, book in her lap, and googled Finn Hutton's name.

Shocked, she stared at the results. Breaking news. A red Subaru Forester had been found in a deep ravine off I-5 with Finn's body inside. It had been buried in debris and snow on and off for more than a decade.

Tears threaded down her cheeks, her face screwing up. She couldn't hold in her anguished shout.

No! Why, Finn? Why?

Why had that damned AI dangled him in front of her face and then snatched him away from her like this? Why had that stupid bookstore employee made her believe in magic and happily ever afters again?

Their love story never got a second chapter. And now, he was dead.

But the map that popped up onto her phone screen forced her grief down deep. Exact GPS coordinates to where Finn's Forester had been found.

Coordinates! Could she use them to locate Finn? In time to save him? Phones in 2010 had GPS.

She had to try. She'd only known him two days, but she felt like she'd known him forever. And loved him for lifetimes.

She grabbed a black pen off the glass coffee table and wrote the coordinates on her hand. Memorizing them and where the map had marked the location of his vehicle.

With shaking hands, she picked up Finn's book, heart racing, and opened the front cover. She flipped past the blurb and review quotes. To the title page. Stroking her fingers across Finn's black Sharpie signature and message. He'd be 33 years old now. She winced.

If he'd just stayed with her one more day.

But her heart fluttered when she saw the new note!

Below his signature and the cute message about looking forward to a new Stori. Two words that chilled her blood.

Save me.

Taking a deep breath, Stori turned the page. And the world spun around her, time peeling backward. To 2010 again.

Still in her loft, Stori tucked Finn's now-pristine book under her arm and picked up her old phone. The display read Sunday, December 19, 2010, 5:56 P.M.

Maybe there was still time?

She glanced at her hand. Coordinates were gone.

Tamping down her panic, she opened Google Maps. And typed in the coordinates from memory.

As the map came up, she put the book in her bag along with a heavy teal blanket off the sofa. She shrugged on her coat and draped the bag over her shoulder, grabbing the keys to her old Toyota 4x4, and hurried to the parking garage.

As she pulled onto the street, she reported Finn Hutton missing near those coordinates and set out north as the snow began to taper. It was an hour's drive just past a rest area. With lots of snowy woods and deep ravines near a river along I-5.

After an hour on I-5's deserted, snowy stretches, she pulled off and parked at the rest stop. The roads were empty because of the weather. She walked close to the shoulder, searching for tire tracks that had veered off the road using the flashlight on her phone.

Ahead, several hundred feet in the snowy darkness, the sharp right curve of tire marks cut through the snow, careening off the road. Over the edge of a ravine with a creek below.

"Finn!" she shouted and grabbed hold of tree limbs as she struggled down the snowy hillside.

Her voice echoed in the stillness of new fallen snow, trickle of water crisp in the chilly night. Cold air smelling like gasoline and burning rubber.

"Finn!"

She slid several times and almost plunged headfirst, but she reached the bottom of the ravine.

The tick of cooling metal touched her ears as she turned her flashlight into the thick, cold darkness.

Onto the outline of a crumpled red Forester. Upright but badly damaged. Smoking in the cold and softly falling snow.

"Oh, my God! Finn!"

She glanced at her phone. No bars. Couldn't call for help.

Struggling, she forced open the passenger side door and scrambled inside.

Airbags had blown at the steering wheel and sides. He was lying back against the seat, blood dripping down his face and covering his clothes from a cut above his left eye and a wound on the side of his head. Burn marks from the airbag scuffed his face, his uneven breathing raspy. Wheezing.

She pulled the blanket out of her bag and draped it over him.

He moaned and shifted, still fastened into his seatbelt, and she kept his body covered with the blanket. Keeping him warm until help arrived.

It seemed like forever until a flood of red lights washed over the dark ravine. Her phone had already gone black, the battery charge empty.

Flashlight beams, firemen, and paramedics followed the oscillating red lights.

"See, Finn," she cried, tears rushing down her cheeks. "You're gonna be okay now."

Stori rode in the ambulance with him and sat at his bedside, her book bag draped on the back of her chair. His head and torso were bandaged, a cast on his left arm and right leg.

A nurse in burgundy scrubs entered the dim-lit beige hospital room to take his vitals. Stori sat up.

"How's he doing?" she asked with a yawn. It was almost five A.M.

"He's holding his own," she said. "He's lucky to be alive. Police said someone cut his front tires. Caused a blowout."

Stori gasped. Finn's stepdad must have done that at the bookstore. Would have been easy. Finn's vehicle was parked on the street. How many red Foresters had the word, peregrinity on their back window?

The nurse turned to leave the room and knocked Stori's bag off the chair. Finn's book slid out and hit the floor.

She didn't even have time to shout as the world began to turn and spin around her.

In an instant, she was back at Powell's Books, a dog-eared copy of *Peregrinity* in her lap. When she saw the sleeve of her purple sweater and the skinny jeans, she jumped up from the chair.

The warm scent of a chai latte hung in the air as *O Holy Night* played softly through the bookstore. Her holiday to-go cup sat on the floor beside her.

No! She was back in her time. But here. At the bookstore.

Had it all been a dream? Her heart twisted into a knot. Was Finn Hutton still lost forever?

She pulled her phone out of her jeans' pocket. The latest iPhone. She tapped the screen. Dead. Battery had run down.

Desperate for answers, she rushed down the stairs to the first floor, to ask someone to search Finn Hutton's name.

But she halted in mid-stride. In front of the big sign. Finn Hutton talks Abide. And Stori.

Her heart raced, tears welling in her eyes, as she crept past the sign and threaded her way through the crowd surrounding a table stacked with books.

But it dropped into her feet when she saw the empty chair behind it.

The hand on her arm made her turn.

Finn Hutton stood at her shoulder, more than a decade older now. In a grey blazer, black T-shirt, black boots, and faded jeans. Still devastatingly handsome with shaggy dark hair, glass-blue eyes, and a smile hot enough to melt steel.

He caressed her cheek, a smile lighting his eyes, and handed her a book.

Abide was the title. With a stylized sun setting behind a cottage by the river.

"Open it," he said in a soft voice, the sound comforting like warm velvet against her fingertips.

With shaking hands, she opened the front cover, turned past the book blurb, past the review quotes. To the title page. And held her breath.

The world didn't spin or go dark. But her heart fluttered.

Inside, on the title page, written in crisp black Sharpie were five words.

I love you. Marry me?

She couldn't halt the flood of tears. She'd saved him. That crazy AI's biography had one true fact in it. She met the love of her life and future husband in a chance meeting. But he was no longer hell-bent on changing the world. He was learning to abide. To stay in one place and enjoy it for once.

"Stori Easton, you saved my life once," said Finn as she turned toward him.

Down on one knee, he held out a ring in his shaking fingers.

Gasping, she reached out and laid her hand against his face.

"No one was looking for me that night. Except you. And you rewrote my story forever. Now, it's time for me to rewrite yours. Marry me?"

Nodding, she threw herself into his arms and kissed him. Grinning, he slid the ring on her finger.

It was time for her to tell a new story of her own. Without AIs or settling. One with two viewpoints. Looking toward the future instead of the past. That started with a new job and a new life. With Finn Hutton. Turning the page together.

The Space Between Us

Art history professor Skye Delaney clutched the century-old vial in her fist as midnight loomed on the terrace of *Dawnflight*, the Oregon Coast winds brisk in the chilly December night. Waiting for moonrise and midnight. The winter solstice. Already, the salt-tanged air was electric, thrumming with his energy. His presence.

She ached to reach across the years and hold him in her arms again —like she had that night in 2010.

Reaching his timeline required a special magic that only coincided with a rare full moon on the winter solstice. Including this even rarer sealed, century-old vial of paint.

They called it the Renfield Glow. A rich, almost magical violet-gold radiance that had been the timeless color of love during America's Titanic Era. Even today, no one had ever successfully recreated it. It was the creation of a handsome young artist that produced three of the world's most hauntingly beautiful and romantic paintings. A love story told in three canvases: two lovers bathed in the golden purple sunset of the Renfield Glow. Called *Dawnflight*, *Magic Hour*, and *Eventide*.

And then he disappeared without a trace.

Skye had first used the magic to meet him in his time, at this place, never expecting it to actually work. This time, she'd use it to try and save him. Now that she knew what happened that Christmas Eve night at the seaside town that no longer existed.

She'd waited eleven years for this conjunction of magics. Her last chance to save him.

"Skye, are you sure about this?"

Thea Galanis, proprietor of the inn/museum, *Dawnflight*, stood beside her on the elegant, weathered patio overlooking the ocean and rocky coastline. Artist Renfield Oakes named his enchanting Queen Anne *Dawnflight* after his first painting. *Dawnflight* was closed until the new year, allowing Skye this private moment to harness the gathering magical forces as the moon climbed through the dark clouds. Winter solstice approached.

"Of course, I'm sure," Skye replied, watching the full Cold Moon rise above the Victorian house.

Her long, coppery blond curls fluttered in the wind as she pulled her black coat tighter, ready to peel back time's layers to find him again. It felt like a lifetime ago. Would he even remember her? How much time had passed on his side? Days? Weeks? Minutes?

Thea grabbed her sleeve, the moon an ethereal glow against the delicate blue Queen Anne with its cupola, wraparound front porch, fish scale siding, and gingerbread white trim along its eaves and gabled rooftop.

"What if something goes wrong?" Concern swirled in Thea's sea-green eyes, her gaze flicking toward the sky and back again.

The sound of the surf was a soft, ubiquitous presence as birds winged past the eaves and cedar trees along the grassy overlook.

"It won't!" Skye snapped, pulling away as the rest of her words caught in her throat, the *what ifs* mounting. "It can't."

Thea's brow pressed into a shadowy line, her mouth taut. "Now that you know what happened that night, it may be too dangerous to return."

Tall and willowy, Thea looked about forty not seventy, her short winter-white bob framing her chin. Her lavender dress rustled in the wind.

Last time, Skye only saw sketchy details. A fire along the boardwalk and a storm surge just before midnight on Christmas Day.

And the memory of Renfield Oakes disappearing.

"Still going back," Skye insisted, crossing her arms against her black coat. "Don't you understand? I have to save him." The words came out small and tight.

She glanced at her wristwatch. Almost midnight.

Thea was awash in the full moon's frosty glow and gleam of Christmas lights that draped across the patio between the black cast-iron lamp posts.

Waiting for midnight and the first burst of winter solstice magic.

Like a hurricane, it would propel Skye back to 1912. And return her like an avalanche at midnight on Christmas Day.

"But the magic may be too strong this time!" Thea grabbed her hands and held them tightly. "Not allowing you to change anything, Skye. There's too much that can go wrong this time with a whole town at stake."

Skye winced. Would she have to watch him die a second time? That thought made her ache over, heart twisting in her chest.

This time, she had to change it. And save him. Even if it meant she couldn't be with him.

"I have to try," she insisted, squeezing Thea's hand, her eyes misty. "Don't you understand? I'll be 104 the next time there's a full moon on the winter solstice. It's my last chance…his last chance." She bowed her head, fidgeting, grey leggings swishing against her charcoal grey knee boots and purple tunic. "Besides, I only have one unsealed vial left."

In 1912, Renfield Oakes sealed three small paint samples of his famed Renfield Glow in glass vials. The vial she clutched was the last thing connecting her to him and when the last vial was opened, even the winter solstice's magic couldn't bring them back together again.

Not even if she loved him.

She'd loved him from the first curious glance at his painting, *Dawnflight*. Found in her Nana's attic when she was nine. She'd been captivated by it, sneaking into the forbidden room to catch glimpses of the lovers. Until the night when a strange conjunction of full moon, winter solstice, and a small glass vial of paint she'd discovered in a box beneath a loose floorboard allowed her to step through the painting.

Falling through more than a hundred years.

Until she landed on the dark, moonlit beach below. And gazed into the swirling, frost-blue eyes of the painting's handsome, black-haired artist. He was part dream, part apparition. Stunning, windblown waves of shaggy, coal-black hair tangling around his oval face and softly tapered chin. When he smiled, laugh lines curved down from his sad eyes and around his chiseled cheeks. Like Titian had painted him out of light from the full Cold Moon and Mount Olympus to create an otherworldly violet-gold glow like the painting she'd stepped through.

The sight of him took her breath away.

Until Nana dragged her back through to the attic. And locked the door.

"Skye Delaney, are you listening to me?" Thea demanded.

"Don't you understand?" Skye shouted, pulling away. "For the first time, I know what happened to the town!" Her voice cracked, the sound falling to a hoarse whisper. "And maybe I can save him?"

Sighing, Thea put her arms around Skye and hugged her. "I know," she said as the wind rose, the surf wild below, magic building like static electricity in the air as the tide kept rising. "Ever since you were nine, you've been obsessed with that painting and Renfield Oakes."

"Nana, you knew?" Skye cried, pulling back from her.

Thea smiled, holding her at arm's length. "Of course, I knew. That's why I told you I'd sold the painting. Didn't hang it back in the inn until you went off to college. Was afraid you'd leap through it on winter solstice and disappear forever." She sighed. "Like right now."

Anger spiked through Skye, but it quickly cooled. She knew her grandmother was right. Even at nine, she'd have done anything to go back to that beach again. For another glimpse of Renfield Oakes painting on this very terrace. She even wrote her dissertation on him, researching his life alongside the magic that had let her into his world for only moments.

In 1912, Renfield Oakes' three paintings had defined love for a generation, even after he'd disappeared beneath the waves of time like the Titanic. His work remained a runaway success, still reprinted today. Nana never expected her to encounter *Magic Hour* or *Eventide*, both safely housed in Washington, D.C.'s National Art Gallery.

But in 2010, *Magic Hour* traveled, on loan, to her university's art museum when she was an undergrad. Right after she'd discovered an article about Oregon ghost towns that explained how fire and a storm surge had consumed this town. With two old photos showing the town leveled. So, Skye returned to the solstice magic to find out what happened to him.

When she reached 1912 for the second time, she met Ren on the beach behind *Dawnflight*. His frost-blue eyes had burned in the moonlight, staring at her like she'd been a ghost along the shore.

Dressed in a blue pinstriped shirt, sleeves rolled to his elbows, dark blue coat, and baggy tan, paint-spattered trousers, Renfield Oakes had been enchanting. He flirted with her and told her about his work, his handsome oval face paint splattered, flecks across his chiseled nose and cheeks, those luminous light blue eyes melting her into a puddle whenever he smiled.

The memory of his strong, squared hands against hers rushed over her like a summer wind. She was five foot eight, tall and willowy like her Nana, but Ren had been a head taller, his moonlit smile burning right through her—like it had the first time she saw him.

This time, he looked smitten with her.

Lean and tall with shaggy, tousled black hair, longer than she'd expected. He'd smelled like sun-drenched cotton, warm like cedar. His tall, starched white collar framed his face, the baggy brown trousers making him look much younger than his twenty-eight years. His dark blue coat had smelled of walnuts and lavender.

His tousled hair had given him a boyish smile, but those sad, downturned eyes were a piercing frosty blue, burning like a branding iron through her and she'd wanted to melt into his gaze. Into his touch.

They spent a few amazing days together. At his house, *Dawnflight*, where he'd shown her the nearly completed canvas of *Eventide* that hung beside *Magic Hour* and *Dawnflight*.

Until Christmas Eve, when devastation struck the town. A storm had come ashore with high winds and dangerously high surfs. The town caught fire and a twelve-foot storm surge wiped it out.

Dawnflight had been spared, but Renfield Oakes disappeared trying to fight the fire. They never found his body—like many others that night.

Skye shuddered at the memory, remembering him rushing headlong into the flames. As the waves surged over the burning wooden boardwalk and surrounding buildings. She'd tried to save him that night, but suddenly, 1912 had begun to fade.

Fighting the currents of time had been futile. She couldn't stop the years from churning forward like a tsunami until she'd reemerged in 2010. In an empty, beige store room at the university.

Magic Hour was gone. Crated and loaded into a truck bound for the airport.

A mix-up with the transport service had caused them to remove the painting earlier than scheduled, returning it ahead of schedule.

Interrupting the magic.

Skye glared at the dark clouds above the patio.

"I didn't realize it until now," said Nana, shaking her. "But I've been slowly losing you since you were nine years old. To the memory of a man who died more than a century ago."

Skye pulled away. Didn't she understand? Time wasn't a line. And it wasn't a great distance traveled. It was a series of loops and tangles resting side by side and against each other. Like a decade in her time had only been moments in his—it had all been the same day to Renfield Oakes.

Of all people, Nana should understand that. She'd raised her. Skye never knew her parents.

"This is my only chance to change that, Nana," she said in a faraway voice.

Thea squinted, propping one hand on her hip. "Knowing what happened doesn't mean you can change it, Skye. I taught you that! Remember?"

Her eyes turned glassy. "But this time, the magic will be stronger."

"Why?" Thea demanded.

"Because everything is here! The house, the painting…" She turned around beneath the moon glow and Christmas lights, the air sparking with magic. "Even his echo! Don't you feel it, Nana?" She held out her arms. "I feel him all around me. I just need the space between us—the distance—to overlap with the winter solstice."

Thea crossed her arms, frowning. "Then what, Skye?"

"Then I can bring us together," she said. "At last."

Already, Nana shook her head.

The tears brimmed in Skye's eyes as she rushed toward her grandmother, gripping the sleeves of her dress.

"Then tell me how to save him, Nana!"

The glass vial in Skye's fist began to warm, growing hot as the frosty moonlight bathed the patio in ripples of celestial light.

Thea's eyes glistened as she pointed at the distant full moon overhead. Midnight. Winter solstice was here.

"The answer is in the Renfield Glow, Skye," Nana said. "That's the real magic. If you love him, find it."

Already, Skye felt the world around her fluttering, fading as time began to run backward.

Years shifted, the present falling away.

She gripped the vial tighter as it began to glow with unearthly light. The tide went out, crash of the waves against the foamy beach constant until everything went dark.

And then she was falling.

Moments of silence fled as cold seawater surged around her, soaking her leggings, filling her boots, and drenching her clothes. Seaweed tangled across her body, sea foam clinging to her hair as the cold December wind buffeted the beach. That had grown darker.

Skye flailed against the wild surf, trying to drag her waterlogged body out of the pull of the waves and rising tide.

"Take my hand!" shouted a voice from the mist and darkness.

Ren! His voice was a rush of heat against the chilly seawater.

Her heart somersaulted at the sound of his warm, velvety voice. She reached out for a handhold.

And felt the heat of his strong hand burn against hers. It was raw. Electric. Charged as it thrummed against her palm and fingertips, surging across her skin to his and back again.

Renfield Oakes pulled her out of the rising tide and pounding waves.

Exhausted, she crawled away from the chilly water, onto the dry, wintry sand below *Dawnflight*, and collapsed. His footfalls hissed across the sand as he dropped down beside her. The air smelled of sea salt, linen, and ozone.

He dropped to his knees and wrapped her in a soft grey blanket, brushing her damp, coppery blond curls away from her mouth and nose. His blue pinstriped shirt sleeve brushed against her face, smelling of walnuts and cedar.

"What luck to find my muse amongst the driftwood and sea foam again! A solstice blessing before Christmas, when the veil thins and spirits abound."

"Spirits?" What did he mean by that? She'd read about the Victorians telling ghost stories as part of their Christmas celebration.

He cupped her face in his hands. "I'm not sure if you're flesh or spirit…woman or Nereid…magic or a mirage, my beautiful muse." He brushed his fingers across her cheek. "My Skye of the golden dawn… returning to me on the next wave. Like a dream I once had. Stepping out of the surf like a vision."

On the next wave? Had the eleven years she'd endured, waiting to return to him, been that fast for him? Or did he think all of it a dream?

"Ren…" She laid her hand against his shaggy black hair, damp and windblown, fluttering around his collar. "I—am so happy to be with you again."

She wanted to tell him that she loved him, but she didn't know how he felt yet.

His frost-blue gaze enveloped her with a connection she'd ached for—for more than a decade. They lit with amusement, corners of his mouth quirking into a smile.

"Again?" he asked with a quizzical look.

First, she'd been a starry-eyed child and later, a college sophomore, chasing her sense of wonder. Falling hard for him. Never dreaming she could ever return to his time and place. This time, she would fight for him as the woman who loved him.

And she needed to tell him that.

"After all this time, I've found you again," said Skye, touching his hand.

He frowned. "All this time? It's been only minutes."

How could she get him to understand?

"Look at me," she said, pushing coppery blond curls away from her face as she turned toward him. "Use your artist's eye. I'm—older now."

She'd aged. At thirty-one, she wasn't that fresh-faced twenty-year-old—much less nine years old. He'd been enchanted by her more than a decade ago. She was much older than the face he remembered. Would his feelings cool after seeing that decade around her eyes? Shadowing her face?

"Right before my eyes." He shook his head, wonder in his expression. "Like a climbing rose in full bloom at last," he said, brushing his fingers across her cheek. "Finally reaching her beautiful zenith."

Her breath caught. He didn't mind.

"But I confess," he continued. "I don't quite understand it all." He cupped her face in his hand. "It was only minutes you were gone, but I swear, it felt like a century."

She gripped his hand. Needing to try and explain it to him. But not here, with the roar of the waves and the whistle of the wind. In the warm quiet of *Dawnflight*.

"The solstice brings magic and spirits for Christmas," he said in a soft, wistful voice as a crooked smile lit his face, laugh lines curving around his cheeks. "Some that are flesh and blood, my muse. And 'tho it all feels like a tangled ball of string to me, I remember holding you in my arms on this terrace. For three beautiful days until..."

Sadness returned to his eyes, his hand falling away from her cheek as he gazed into the surf. Pain glistened in those frost-blue eyes.

She squeezed his hand, letting him know she wasn't an apparition. That she was still here.

"I...think something happened to me," he said, squinting, his voice an intense whisper above the surf. "I remember little beyond the tree lighting." His gaze shifted back to her face. "But now that I'm with you, I feel like I'm home."

"So do I, Ren," she said, cradling his hand.

Pain and concentration shadowed his brow, flattening his mouth into a grimace as he held her close.

"And I confess—I feel the whisper of time in the surf," he said in an intense voice. "Swirling around you like a dark spirit and I can't help but wonder if I'll die soon."

Skye couldn't stop the tears from threading down her face. She'd been forced to watch him die last time.

He brushed away her tears. "But time isn't really like a ruler, is it?" he said, shaking his head. "It's more like a tangle of loops and purls—string. Touching and overlapping. Allowing my muse to find me in those rare moments when they line up to create a…a corridor."

"Yes, Ren," she replied, nodding. "I don't know how you know that, but the magic of the solstice full moon in my time created this strange magic that allowed me here. In yours."

"I was fascinated by Wells' Time Machine as a child," he said, holding both her hands. "Read it over and over, always believing in the possibility, but having doubts. Until I saw you stand in this wild surf and in a series of moments, face me as a child, a young lady, and now, a woman. In such strange clothes."

She struggled to stand up, her soaked tunic, boots, and leggings like ice in the chilly wind. Her teeth began to chatter.

"You recognized me?" she asked. "Each time?"

He nodded, using his body to block the wind. "Those moments became the inspiration for my paintings," he said.

Somehow, he understood some of what was happening, acknowledging that those eleven-year spans had been only moments. Like she'd never left. And he had a distant memory of dying.

This time, she had to tell him everything. Make him understand what she was and where she'd come from. And when.

He caught her when she began to sink. "Let's get you out of the cold night air and by the fire, my enchanting Skye with an e."

Gently, Ren Oakes picked her up in his arms, his warm breath misting the air. She laid her head against his shoulder. Back in his arms at last.

She inhaled his clean linen and cedar scent and the hints of walnut oil from flecks of paint on his cheeks and down his neck and collarbone. The gentle *tick, tick* of his pocket watch was steady against the thrum of his heart against her ribs. She lost herself in the feel and smell of him, so warm and familiar. Like his charming Victorian, *Dawnflight,* ahead through the trees.

He carried her along the short, winding beach trail toward the Queen Anne's delicate blue gingerbread façade. Globe-shaped Christmas lights twinkled like fairy lights along the concrete patio and stretched from lamp post to lamp post.

His easel stood beneath the flicker of colored lights, facing the ocean, with *Eventide,* the third panting in his Victorian love story, covered with a waxed cloth.

Her heart ached as he stepped onto the patio, moving toward the door.

"You'll be the angel for my tree lighting party on the eve of spirits and ghosts," he said, opening the back door.

She squinted at him. "Spirits and ghosts?"

Was he talking about Christmas Eve?

He nodded. "Wouldn't be a proper Christmas without the traditional ghost stories and spirit readings. When the veil is thin and the spirits are close." He smiled. "They've already brought me back my muse."

She couldn't help herself. She reached up and ran her fingers through his thick, coal-black mop of wavy hair flecked with paint that hung just past his collar. He looked like a romantic-era poet.

"And mine," said Skye, but already, the words felt hollow.

In the uneven glow of electric lights, warm cherry hardwood floors creaked as he carried her into the high-ceiling sitting room with its elaborate, columned fireplace in rich, dark cherry wood. Marbled blue tiles framed the firebox where flames danced.

Ren set her down on an over-stuffed blue sofa that flanked the hearth. Smell of wood smoke mixed with the fresh pine scent of a six-foot tall bare, unlit Douglas Fir standing in the bay window that overlooked the patio. Ready to be decorated and lit on Christmas Eve, as was tradition in his time.

He disappeared into the nearby white kitchen for a moment, firelight flickering against the cream and gold-leafed wallpaper and warm glow of electric lights. Ornate, wide wooden casings and medallions framed the open doorway into a dark parlor and the bright white kitchen as he returned with two delicate white cups of hot tea. He sat beside her and handed her a cup. She cradled it, warming her hands.

"My muse returns home to Dawnflight," he said, sipping from the white teacup. "For the unveiling of Eventide."

Home. Hearing him say that made her ache all over. She'd always felt an emptiness within this old Victorian where she grew up.

Now that Ren was finally beside her again, *Dawnflight* felt like home.

She snuggled against him, sipping hot tea and honey as wind whipped around the house eaves with a shrill, banshee-like warning.

She had four days to love him before the magic subsided and sent her back to her time forever. Four days to save him.

What had Nana been trying to tell her about saving Ren? And the Renfield Glow.

The next morning, she awoke on the sofa, embers glowing in the hearth. Her coat hung on a hook beside the back door and her boots leaned against the wall. In grey leggings and purple tunic, she rose from the couch, floor creaking as sunrise's fragile gold light washed over the room like watercolors.

From the bay window, she saw Ren on the patio.

Her heart raced. He sat on a stool, easel partially draped, his brush in motion across Eventide's canvas. She opened the door and stepped out into the soft morning light beside him.

Nutty scent of walnuts mixed with linseed and lavender. He wore an old white shirt rumpled across his lean body, splattered with paint, like his baggy dark pants. His thick black hair looked windblown, sleepy blue eyes concentrating on the lovers' faces.

She gasped at the flutter of coppery blond curls taking shape as she stared at her own face.

In those few, precious hours since she had returned to him, she'd already changed the face of one of his most famous paintings. With her own. This one hung in the National Gallery of Art and now, it bore her face. Painted by his hand. From memory. His work had pre-Raphaelite style and Parrish luminance.

"Ren…it's beautiful," she said in awe at his skill.

"Your visage will inspire artists and poets for generations," he said with a crooked smile and picked up a small glass jar at his feet with four glass vials. "With this aura of color. Like the golden hour and sunset—what's left of the paint, that is."

The vials! The paint gleamed like molten gold sunlight and sugared plums. Against the canvas, it became a stunning, otherworldly glow when applied by his deft hand.

"The Renfield Glow," she said in a reverent tone.

"The what?" he said with a laugh. "It's a series of layers and brushstrokes. It took more than a decade of practice, solstice magic, a certain ocean treasure, sea glass—and my muse—to create the aura paint formula."

He looked amused.

"And no one knows the formula but you?" she asked.

For more than a century, artists and scholars had tried and failed to recreate the Renfield Glow in oils.

He rose from the easel and held out his left arm, motioning her across the patio to another door into the cupola.

His studio.

It was all windows to gather the light. The concrete floor was spattered with paint, a driftwood table in the center beside another easel and stool. Driftwood shelves stood against one wall, filled with dozens of glass tubes, jars, and bottles of dry pigments.

Turpentine, varnish, walnut oil, linseed oil, beeswax, rolls of canvas, and unassembled wooden frames crowded together on the rest of the shelves. The room smelled like turpentine and walnuts and fresh-cut wood.

From studying his work, Skye knew his color palette. He mixed his cobalt and cerulean blues from crushed glass, including sea glass. Ultramarine from lapis lazuli. His yellows, oranges, and reds came from cadmium metal pigments and he preferred viridian green, manganese violet, and zinc oxide white, a colder, cleaner white to the lead whites of the time.

But even from the doorway, she saw it.

A wide mouth canning jar on the bottom shelf that shimmered lavender even in the shadows.

Ren bent down and plucked the shimmery jar off the shelf, holding it out to her. It looked like a short, thin strip of translucent kelp the color of pale violet. Incandescent. Magical.

"What is that?" Skye asked, taking the jar as he wrapped his arms around her, holding her close.

She'd seen this before. But where?

"The secret to the Renfield Glow, as you call it."

She examined it closer. Where had she seen this before?

"I dry it, grind it into powder, and mix it with other dry pigments," he explained, motioning to the jars of pigments on the shelves. "I add walnut oil and a little lavender oil to thin it."

Something about this luminous, glimmering strip was familiar. Fabric? A plant? What was it? Nana said this glow was the key to saving him. She had to figure out how. Before Christmas Eve erupted in a firestorm and the town got hit with a massive storm surge.

"It looks magical," she said, brushing a wave of black hair out of his eyes. "Like you and your work."

"It's almost gone," he said with a groan, setting the jar back on the shelf.

Beside it stood another jar with more glass vials of the paint he called aura paint, sealed with wax. They gleamed with a faint resonance like this strange substance.

"I found it on the beach one morning. Like a mermaid's ribbon or part of a sea goddess' veil. Odysseus' cloak. But I've never seen another one."

It came from the sea! But what was it?

"Mr. Oakes?" a timid voice called from the patio door.

"Hilda, come in, please!"

Ren motioned her inside. A stocky woman in a long, blue-and-white striped skirt, white blouse, and frilly white smock stepped into the studio. Ren's housekeeper. Her warm, curly brown hair was pinned up in a bun in back and her face was a mix of embarrassment and annoyance. At the public display? A huge no-no in 1912, unless he meant to marry her. Skye's heart raced.

Hilda's gaze shot to Skye and she thrust a hand to her mouth. "Sir!" she cried with a gasp. "It's…it's her!"

Skye frowned. What did that mean?

Ren's expression brightened as he rested his face against Skye's hair. Making Hilda's eyes widen and her cheeks blush.

"Your paintings…" Hilda said, pulling in a breath, and pointed at Skye. "She was more than your model, wasn't she?"

Ren nodded vigorously. "She's my muse."

At last, Hilda smiled and folded her hands against her smock. "No, sir," she said. "She's your beloved."

Beloved?

Ren's face flushed as he moved in front of Skye, gazing into her eyes as he held her hands.

"Must be no accident that the male lover has your face in all three paintings, sir," said the housekeeper with a wink.

Ren nodded. "Yes, Hilda, my…my beloved." He brushed a coppery blond curl off Skye's cheek. "I've tried to paint her face a million times." His voice got soft and quiet. "Always from memory until now."

She wanted to kiss him, but it might just break his housekeeper's 1912 mind.

He gave her hand a gentle squeeze. "Eventide is from my heart to yours, Skye Delaney."

The housekeeper backed out of the door. "I'll start baking for the party now, sir."

"Party?" Skye asked.

"The tree lighting party on the eve of Christmas," he said, a twinkle in those frost-blue eyes. "When I'll unveil Eventide and turn on the brand-new Mazda tree lights that came all the way from New York. While we drink mulled wine and tell ghost stories with good friends and spirits."

Skye slid her arms around his neck as the sparks of attraction ignited like Fourth of July sparklers between them.

"My beloved," he whispered, brushing his lips against hers, teasing with the whisper of a kiss. "From dawn's flight to eventide."

In his final painting, the lovers entwined together forever of his ethereal love story, alight with that Renfield Glow.

But the memory of that night from a decade ago made her ache all over. When she lost him.

"Perhaps this eventide," he said, a soberness filling his playful gaze. "Time will be on our side?"

"I've waited eleven years to take back what it stole from me," she said, her voice catching in her throat. "You."

He smashed his mouth against hers and she returned his kiss with an urgency that stung her eyes and made her heart ache.

Somehow, she had to decode the Renfield Glow. Bend the clock hands to her will.

For her and Ren.

***

Christmas Eve brought storm clouds and high surfs that pounded the coast. She and Ren had been inseparable. She'd sat for him yesterday as he put the final touches on Eventide, placing it on a covered easel beside the dark Christmas tree. Together, they laughed and talked about H.G. Wells while they wired stiff strands of multicolored globe lights onto the branches as afternoon fled.

Skye helped Hilda cover the dining table with a white tablecloth and array it with little minced pies, chocolates, roasted nuts, dried fruits, and plum pudding beside a large, white soup tureen of warm mulled wine. Cinnamon and cardamom warmed the air as the first knock echoed through the house, wind whipping around the gables.

Ren put a record on the Victrola that stood in a tall walnut cabinet between the Christmas tree and the covered easel. A tinny, brassy choir rendition of *The First Noel* filled the dim-lit sitting room as Ren's guests began to arrive.

Six people in all. Two women and four men, all of them at least a decade older than Ren. The men wore loose-fitting wool suits in greys and browns. The two women wore long, silky chiffon dresses in pale cream and blush adorned with lace and embroidery. They stared at Skye with an assortment of looks, eyes widening when Ren put his arms around her. But he seemed to enjoy their shocked and concerned looks.

He bowed, dressed in baggy grey pants, suspenders pressed against his lean frame and crisp white shirt, sleeves rolled to the elbows, shaggy black hair in wavy but sexy disarray—like he'd just walked along the beach.

"I present my lady fair, Skye Delaney," he said, making a grand sweep of his arm.

Still dressed in her grey leggings, boots, and purple tunic, they must have thought she was either a stage performer or a jockey.

"Why, Renfield Oakes!" exclaimed a tawny-haired woman with a hawkish face and a sleek, blush pink dress when Ren held Skye's hand. "This is the woman whose face graces your paintings."

Ren nodded. "Yes, Millie," he said and caressed Skye's cheek. "And so much more. She is my timeless muse that I met on the beach."

His gaze was encompassing, that cheeky smile burning through her with such heat that her face flushed.

"You met her on the beach?" a lanky, balding, scarecrow-of-a-man crowed.

"Yes, Philip," he said, his gaze not leaving Skye's face. "The discovery of a lifetime. As you'll see tonight when I unveil the final act of the lovers' story," he said and motioned toward the covered easel beside the Christmas tree. "Eventide is complete and in a week, I must ship it off to New York."

Philip held up a glass of mulled wine. "To Ren, his muse, and Eventide."

Millie and the other guests lifted their glasses of mulled wine and drank. But Ren stayed Skye's hand as she raised her glass and gently shook his head.

"No," he said, staring into her eyes as he held up his glass. "To Skye Delaney and Eventide."

She grinned and put her glass to her lips, sipping it gingerly.

"To Renfield Oakes and his incredible glow," she said, leaning toward him until her lips brushed against his, tasting warm Merlot, cinnamon, and oranges. "The most amazing man I've ever met."

Those laugh lines curved around his cheeks as his smile became a grin. He returned her kiss. Until the Victrola needle bumping against the end of the record interrupted it.

He left her to change the record as wind moaned like a banshee around the eaves, shaking the house.

"Wind's been howling off the ocean since sunset," said Millie, casting an uneasy glance at the other guests as the lights flickered.

"Storm's coming," said Philip, refilling his glass with mulled wine. "Don't care what anybody says. I saw the red sky this morning. Gonna be a storm for Christmas."

Skye's stomach twisted into knots as the others scoffed at him. She knew what was coming, but she still didn't know how to save Renfield Oakes and it made her eyes well with tears.

What had Nana meant by telling her to find the real magic in the Renfield Glow? And it all connected to that odd glowing strip of lavender translucence.

How could that save him tonight?

Again, the lights flickered as Ren played a popping, scratchy quartet singing *Hark! The Herald Angels Sing!*

"Gather around, everyone," he called, motioning them toward the tree.

She'd spent hours helping him light that tree, but she'd have done anything to spend so much time that close to him.

"I now present this year's Christmas tree with authentic Mazda lights all the way from New York," said Ren, plugging in the lights.

His guests cheered and clapped as the tree gleamed with fairy lights bathed in the warm glow of the crackling hearth. Again, the wind moaned like the dead around the windows.

"The spirits speak!" Ren cried, turning toward the window, a hand to his ear.

"What do they say?" Millie asked, her face pale as she white-knuckled her glass of mulled wine.

That cheeky grin widened across his face, laugh lines curving deeper across his cheeks, frost-blue eyes sparkling.

"They say, behold!" He snapped the cloth off the easel, revealing *Eventide*. "The lovers, together at last."

Skye gasped and rushed toward it. Marveling at the fine, crisp details reminiscent of the pre-Raphaelite brotherhood works by Waterhouse, Rossetti, and Millais. But the Renfield Glow gave the painting an ethereal, otherworldly feel. The lovers embraced like it was their first and last time together. And their faces! She was staring at her own reflection. The woman's face was hers. And the man had Ren's handsome face, tousled black hair, and stunning frost-blue eyes.

Like he'd drawn the space between them, the time and the distance, and wrapped it tightly around them. Bringing them together at last. Like she yearned to do.

"Ren...it's like you've opened a door into Heaven," she said, kissing him.

His face lit with delight as his other guests crowded around the painting, but in that moment, she was the only one in the room. He caressed her hands.

"Only if you're behind it, Skye Delaney," he said in the flicker of the lights as the wind moaned around the gabled rooftop.

And the first rush of rain pounded against the windows and thumped against the roof. It was beginning. The storm was coming ashore.

She glanced at the clock on the wall. Steady, rhythmic tick, like everything was all right with the world. That Christmas Eve was still a night full of magic and wonder. But she knew what lurked behind the ten o'clock knell. The death of an entire town began, including the only man she'd ever loved.

Unless she found a way to stop it.

"Dance with me?" he whispered against her ear with a brush of his lips.

Shivering, she nodded, fighting to control the anguish she felt bubbling up as she gripped his hand, letting him lead her into an embrace as they slowly waltzed in front of the tree and *Eventide*.

She held him close, comforted by the steady rise and fall of his chest, the gentle beat of his heart. As the beginning of the end began.

Lights dimmed and with a sharp snap, went out.

By the light of the hearth, they danced to the Victrola that spun out *Adeste Fidelis.*

Candles glowed around them and she held him tighter, her heart breaking as that second hand ticked closer to ten o'clock. And it would bring a knock on the door.

"Ren," she whispered. "There's going to be a knock on the door soon."

His face turned pale. "How do you know that?"

She fought to keep her voice steady and not break. "Something terrible is about to happen to the town."

"What?" he cried, stopping the dance. "Skye, what are you talking about?"

"Ren, listen," she snapped, shaking him. "There's nothing you can do to stop it. And if you leave Dawnflight, you'll die."

"I'll die?" His eyes were wide with a mixture of fear and shock.

She nodded as the words hung in her throat. She gasped for a breath, her voice barely above a whisper now.

"I've waited more than a decade for this alignment. To travel the space between us and stop you from dying tonight. This is my last chance to save you." She threw her arms around him. "Ren, please don't go. You can't save the town."

His eyes narrowed. "You want me to stay here? Safe? While the town dies?" He shook his head. "Skye, I can't do that."

Tears flooded her cheeks. "Ren—don't you understand? This is the night that you die! And the town still gets wiped out."

The knock at the door came ten minutes early this time, the space between them growing wider as he turned toward the hallway.

Skye grabbed his arm.

"Ren, please!"

He stroked his fingers along her cheek, his warm touch sizzling against her skin.

"Everything's going to be okay, my Nereid muse," he said and leaned down and kissed her.

She couldn't halt the tears as he opened the door, the words ringing in her ears. Stabbing her heart with every line.

"High winds have knocked out power," said the deep voice at the door. "Fires are burning along the promenade. A twelve-foot storm surge at high tide is imminent. We're trying to evacuate everyone we can."

She mouthed his last words as they chilled her skin, breaking her heart with every warm, velvety syllable.

"I'll get my coat," said Ren to the voice at the door.

Like he was going out for a stroll. Shortly after kissing her, he disappeared in the storm surge. And she got pulled back across the chasm of time, more than a century in the future. Leaving her to wait a decade to try again.

He returned to the sitting room, looking unnerved. "Everyone, there are fires burning along the promenade."

His guests gasped and whispered to each other, looking to Ren for direction.

"And a storm is about to make landfall, bringing a twelve-foot storm surge at high tide." Ren slid on his blue wool coat. "If you stay at Dawnflight, you'll be safe. I'm going to go help evacuate people from the boardwalk."

Skye launched herself at him. "Ren, I'm going with you!"

He shook his head. "Skye, no—it's too dangerous."

"I don't care," she said, holding onto his arms. "I'm going with you."

He leaned down and kissed her hard on the lips. With a nod toward his guests, he turned toward the hallway.

Skye moved toward him, but felt arms wrap around her, pulling her backward. Toward the Christmas tree.

"No, don't!" she shouted, struggling as Ren moved toward the front door. "Ren! REN!"

Was Nana right? Was it impossible for her to save him?

Dammit! She had to try.

She dropped to the floor and rolled underneath the two men holding her back.

"Miss Delaney, no! Wait!"

She launched herself toward the patio door and threw it open, into the wind and rain, emerging onto the patio. She fought through the gale force winds to reach the cupola door. Into Ren's studio.

To grab the jar with that strange translucent remnant of cloth or seaweed or whatever it was that gleamed with otherworldly brilliance.

In the darkness, it lit the entire studio with light. And life.

She remembered Ren calling it a mermaid's ribbon or a sea goddess' veil. Odysseus' cloak.

Wait! Her undergrad mythology and art history courses rushed back to her. Homer's *Odyssey*. A sea goddess saved him with her veil. A chill danced along her spine. Leucothea.

She pulled in a breath. Thea. Was her Nana that sea goddess?

Who'd always been so cagey about her past. Never really explained how Skye had managed to walk through a painting at nine with an old vial of paint. And traveled back to 1912.

Unless there'd been more powerful magic at work, even during a rare winter solstice full moon.

Like the scrap of veil that a sea goddess had given Homer's hero so long ago.

Would this remnant of powerful magic, that just happened to wash up on an Oregon beach around 1912, save the man she loved?

She'd plunge headfirst into that storm surge to find out.

Clutching the jar, Skye rushed out into the storm, running along a path toward the wooden promenade and the beach hotel. Where the love of her life perished eleven years ago.

Fire bells clanged above shouts and the surf as a distant, smoky red glow burned along the coast. Embers danced like fireflies, winds casting them in all directions as Skye rushed through the gritty, acrid smoke. She covered her nose and mouth and ran toward the bucket brigade forming on the boardwalk and ahead, in front of the hotel. Men and women handed off buckets of water, dousing flames along the promenade as the sea roared behind them.

Her heart raced, stomach dropping. Ahead was the Harmony Hotel. The last place she'd held Renfield Oakes in her arms.

Already, she felt the pull of her own time tugging at her body as the town clock lamented eleven o'clock.

One hour left to save him.

Skye pushed away the sensations and hurried along the promenade.

"Get out of the street!" she shouted at anyone who would listen, wind whipping her hair in her face. "A huge storm surge is coming! Run toward high ground or you'll be swept away!"

Some of them listened, dropping buckets, and running east through the cold, smoky haze, toward the forested rise above the boardwalk.

She rushed ahead, warning people.

"Let it burn!" she screamed, waving her arms. "Get out while you can!"

More people ran as waves crashed closer to the wooden promenade, scattering foam and spray.

It took forever to reach The Harmony Hotel. She ran toward the six-story, wooden salt-box building, one side on fire.

Clutching the glowing jar, Skye warned the bucket brigade there and ran inside the dark hotel.

Why hadn't Nana told her she was a sea goddess! She had the magic to save this man that Skye loved so desperately. Even at nine years old, she knew that she'd never love anyone but Renfield Oakes.

Skye called his name as the fire rumbled, smoke hanging above the red glow as the ocean swept closer and midnight approached.

Tears rushed down her face. Ren only had minutes to live.

"Ren!" she shouted, moving toward the stairs.

Right here, by the banister. She'd held him in her arms. Moments before the first wave hit the hotel.

Already, the storm surge was like a freight train behind her. Building. Rising.

Skye rushed past the empty front desk as Ren careened down the stairs, wavy black locks windblown. He stopped, turning toward her.

"REN!"

"Skye, go back! It's on fire!"

He waved her away, but she threw her arms around him.

"Storm surge!" she screamed above the fire's churn and the swelling ocean's roar.

She felt the first wave careening across the beach toward the hotel and took the shred of shimmery cloth from the jar. The essence of the Renfield Glow. A scrap of sea goddess veil that had once saved Homer's hero long, long ago.

Could it save hers right now?

The first terrible wave splintered wood and shattered windows. Plowing into the hotel as the clock's mournful requiem announced the first stroke of midnight.

Already, the solstice magic began to expire, deteriorating as the pull back to her time began.

The wave slammed them against the stair railing.

She shoved him up the stairs, knowing the next wave would rip him from her arms. Just as it had eleven years ago.

She held onto him with every ounce of strength she had and kissed him hard on the lips.

"I love you, Renfield Oakes," she said, her voice aching as the town clock counted down the remaining strokes of the hour, breaking her heart with every mournful tone.

Five.

"I've always loved you," he said, the ghost of a smile on his face. "That glow was never just paint. It was always how I painted my love for you, so it would never fade from my canvas."

Four.

His words stunned her. He hadn't said that last time. Had she changed his fate?

"What is that?" he cried.

Three.

The lavender glow startled her and him, expanding. Unfolding, she realized.

Two.

The scrap of sea goddess veil began to unfurl after the seawater hit it. It floated in the air around Ren.

One.

The second wave slammed into the hotel like a steam roller, ripping Ren from her arms as Skye was pulled from the hotel when it collapsed into the surge.

She careened forward in time as the darkness and layers stretched. Sending her forward. Toward 2021 with a jolt.

Leaving 1912 and Renfield Oakes behind.

—————

Skye materialized on the patio of *Dawnflight*. As the sea calmed and the world shifted into the present.

Nana Thea caught her as she collapsed.

"Skye!" she cried. "Are you all right?"

She shook her head, tears flooding her face. No. She wasn't all right. She was miserable. For the second time, she'd watched the man she loved die.

And it had broken her into little pieces.

The distance had been too vast. Telling him what was to come and loving him more hadn't saved him. Why hadn't Nana told her about that veil? Or just given her the magic that would have saved him? Magic that Nana knew how to use!

She snapped out of Nana's embrace.

"You could have saved him!" she shouted, pointing a finger. "Why didn't you? Thea. Leucothea. Or whatever you are!"

Nana's face turned pale, her sea-green eyes filled with pain. "Skye, listen to me."

"You're a damned sea goddess! Why didn't you give me the magic to save him?"

Nana Thea grabbed her by the shoulders, forcing her to look at her. "Skye...I couldn't give you the magic. And I couldn't use the solstice magic—only you could do that."

"Why only me?" she demanded.

"Because I didn't love him—that connection let you go back. The one you forged when you fell through my magic and the painting."

Tears tracked down her cheeks. "Then why couldn't you give me the magic?" she asked in a soft, defeated voice.

Nana stroked her hair. "Because, my beautiful granddaughter, the magic had to exist in his time. So, I let it wash ashore on the tides from Ogygia. That's why I told you it was in the Renfield Glow."

"The scrap of your veil," said Skye as Nana nodded. "That saved Odysseus. A scene painted by several masters."

A smile touched Nana's face. "A scene I knew my art history professor granddaughter would know. Did you—"

"The tiny scrap unfurled in the seawater, but—" Her breath caught at the memory of Ren ripped out of her arms again.

"But what?" Nana asked.

Skye hung her head. "But I still couldn't save him."

Nana pulled out her phone and looked up Renfield Oakes. Skye's heart sank. It still said that he disappeared in 1912.

"See, I've lost him forever," she said with a moan. "The space between us was too great."

A shimmer of lavender rippled at the edge of her vision.

"It was in 1912," said a familiar voice from the door into the cupola.

Skye whirled around at the warm, velvety sound of Renfield Oakes' voice.

He leaned against the door frame, smiling, that windblown mop of black hair dripping, suspenders taut against his drenched white shirt as they held up his baggy, sea-soaked grey pants. And those frost-blue eyes burned against the lavender glow of Nana's veil, wrapped like a cloak around his shoulders.

Skye crossed the distance between them, running across the patio. And threw her arms around him, kissing him with an urgency that left her and him breathless. He held her against him, his clothes cold and sodden with seawater.

"Math problem finally solved," said Ren with that cheeky grin.

"Welcome home," said Nana. "Both of you."

Skye held Ren tighter. Home at last. Just in time for Christmas.

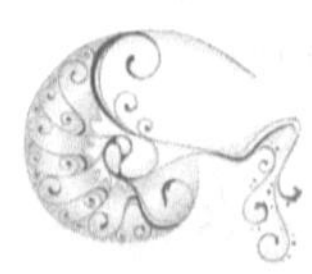

The End of Timeless: 8 Time Travel Romance Stories

CHAPTER 1

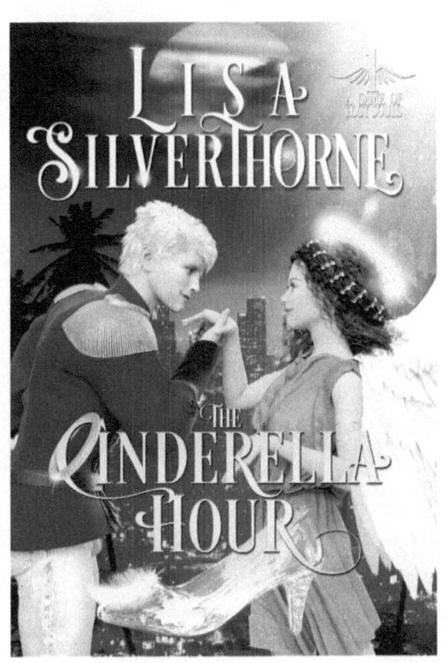

The Cinderella Hour

CHAPTER 1: A GAME OF LOST SOULS (BOOK 1)

Why did humans always insist on doing stupid things that got them killed? In terrible, terrible ways…in dark alleys. Forcing angels of death to sort it out and clean up the mess.

And Talia was tired of it. Of them.

Everything in the Creation had a rhythm. Pure. Rich with a sound all its own. Cicadas buzzing in August twilight. Chicago streetlights thrumming at three A.M. Steady *dub dub* of a human heart's final beats against moon-washed pavement. She'd heard that sound way too many times. And when it stopped, the silence was infuriating.

Talia shook her head, stepping over one of two dead humans, light grey shift rustling as she left the dark red-brick alley that smelled like urine and death. Rush of Chicago traffic was steady as she moved toward the busy sidewalk, people passing by on all sides.

But they couldn't see her or her two colleagues waiting beside her, dove grey wings flexed, gold halos spinning. She sighed. There was nothing more she could do here. She was an angel of death after all, not a guardian angel. She didn't even have a chance to cross them over.

Humans! She didn't understand any of them!

She offered one of her angel colleagues a supportive shrug as the smell of rain touched the air, ready to wash this carnage clean. First light was a couple of hours away.

"One of yours, Talia?" Muriel asked as she slipped past with soft footfalls.

Muriel's flowing, dark chestnut hair framed her face and soft grey eyes, wings twitching at her shoulders, the wind billowing her light grey robes. Talia's hair had darkened to the color of night since she'd become part of Azrael, Archangel of Death's guard. She didn't get out much.

But she was done trying to save humans. They didn't want to be helped—even when an archangel like Azrael sent her.

She pointed at the thin, dark-haired woman's body, spread eagle on the wet, pocked pavement in torn jeans and a dirty blue tank top. And the brown-haired, bearded man slumped beside her in a grey striped shirt and worn cargo shorts.

She nodded. "Azrael wanted me to save the crackhead. Stupid human didn't want to be saved though."

Muriel shook her head and then nodded at the man. "Neither did mine."

"Guess Azrael has them both now," said Talia.

"The shock of what these humans do to each other must make Azrael weep every single day," Muriel replied, wincing as she squinted at the rain tapping softly against the pavement and the two bodies.

Or he raged when he collected their souls. *You did what? What do you mean, challenge accepted?* Idiots! Talia could almost hear his voice thundering at them.

"Two more clueless wonders at the pearly gates to be retrained," Talia replied. "And so lucky to be there instead of below. With Lucifer and the other fallen angels."

Maybe they'd be retrained? She didn't know where they would land. Their problem, not hers.

She brushed the dust off her pale grey shift. How many more would follow before the day was out? The sun hadn't even risen yet.

Muriel nodded.

"I'm off to report in," said Talia. She tossed her thick, black hair off her shoulders. "Azrael's not going to be pleased."

Talia knew that displeasure well and when he saw her, he'd be even angrier. The last four humans he'd sent her to protect had slipped through her fingers. Not something she was proud of either, but they were impossible!

"See you soon," said Muriel.

Muriel's dove grey wings furled a moment then stretched as she took flight, muttering to herself above the hush of wind. Above the rushing paramedics and police officers. Above the sirens' wails and sooty grey clouds spitting rain on the sidewalks.

Those human rhythms were once intended as poetry and beauty, sounds that made an angel weep, knowing all she could ever be was death's servant to God's Chosen.

Right now, she wanted to spit on two of God's Chosen: a crackhead and a rapist sharing a few cherished hollow points before splattering the alley walls with Chicago's newest graffiti.

No amount of gentle guidance and golden rays of light clued these fools into the reality of their situations. Talia was tired of the kid gloves. She was tired of the whole guardian arrangement. It was just easier to be an angel of death and carry their souls away. Sometimes, she couldn't even do that.

Why should she fight for these ungrateful, hard-headed, whiny humans? Insisting on destroying their lives. Maybe the Maker was better off without them?

Every day, hundreds of them broke His heart. And every day, He forgave them. She knew she'd be better off without them. Just thinking about some of them gave her wing rash.

I swear, if I hear one more, "Hey y'all, watch this?" I'm going to go on a rampage.

Not that Lucifer had it right or anything: looks nine, presentation two. Sure, he was the most beautiful of angels, but his arrogance got him where he was today: a two-bit hood, nickel-and-diming souls on street corners and in bars. Making pathetic deals like a multi-level marketing shill. As if he'd keep any of those souls on technicalities. There was always an angel of death ready and willing to void one of his contracts. Angels were much nobler than these malleable humans.

Like worn out silly putty.

Most of them ignored magic when they saw it. The ones that noticed a little magic, didn't understand it and they either screamed about Satan and/or crossed themselves, convinced that some wind brushing across their shoulder was a demon. When it was really her—not Lucifer—saving their miserable hides from being crushed by a speeding car.

Being a guardian to humans shouldn't feel like owning pets. No, it was worse than that.

Talia walked through the crowd of people gathering at the mouth of the alley and moved toward the half-deserted streets, her dove grey wings pressed tight against her back.

Even if they could see me, they don't, Talia thought. I could let them all see me in a fiery burst of white light, descending from the clouds with my burnished sword raised, halo spinning. They'd just think it was a Marvel Comics stunt or something.

Her eyes stung and she balled her hands into fists. This wondrous world had lost all its magic and wonder. These humans were too busy stepping on and killing each other to see it anymore. Even when help was offered, they still made bad choices.

Azrael must be pulling out his wing feathers by now. The centuries of senseless deaths had to weigh on him. She'd only been at this death thing for a few centuries now and she was sick of seeing intelligent creatures willingly pour out their lives like this.

It could be worse, she reminded herself. At least she wasn't handling the new angels anymore.

Teaching them to fly and (even worse) land. Teaching them death angel tricks and navigation. Just the thought made her shiver. She'd moved from clueless angels to clueless humans—not sure this was a promotion.

She leaned against a shady ash tree, its bark feathering onto the sidewalks, and closed her eyes, the shrieking pulse of police sirens grating against her ears. Now, she had to go to Azrael and tell him she'd lost another one.

Well, not lost really. She preferred the phrase, *displaced into other divine hands*. She hadn't done her job. She hadn't kept them in the present. Kind of like going from first grade straight to college.

She felt bad for them sometimes, knowing the hard road they had ahead of them. But right now, she felt bad for herself because Azrael would be furious. She let a deep sigh flutter free.

He'll probably blame me for losing Muriel's human, too. Stupid humans.

Closing her eyes, she unfolded her wings, halo bright in the sharp drizzle, and rose above Chicago's Southside until everything turned into funny little shapes and winking lights.

She'd lost another one. Time to head back to the ethereal and face Azrael's wrath.

Outside the grand white hall of Eolowen, Azrael, an Archangel of Death was murderous.

Sunlight streamed across Parrish blue skies, shadowy Constable clouds flowing like a river above. Thick green grass stretched across the hilly expanse beyond the terrace. The Middling lay beyond it, a hazy grey blot on the horizon. Faint scent of gardenias and honeysuckle from the nearby pergola sweetened the light breeze. The solitude was a song in itself, a hush that was the music of clouds passing overhead. But nothing could ease the turmoil quivering through his shoulders and wings.

With his great, dark wings spread, Azrael paced the carpet of grass stretching around the pocked, white stone dais, awaiting Talia's return. He wore a burnished gold breastplate and pauldrons over billowy, grey silk robes and winged sandals, his halo surging with life as its reddish gold light spun around his head. He brushed aside a thick lock of silver-black hair and leaned against a weathered white pillar, his heart heavy with duty, a hand on the hilt of his sword of Holy fire sheathed at his side.

Once again, she'd failed in her guardianship duties. And her duties as an angel of death.

Assignment after assignment blown. Little regard for her human charges, the other angels had whispered in his ear. When Talia made a disaster out of the novice angel training, Azrael asked that she return to training herself, relearn her duty to His Chosen. Thinking it was just boredom, Azrael instead requested her presence in the most solemn duty given an angel: shepherding a human's moment of death.

But her growing lack of concern for human deaths disturbed him deeply, so he gave her the power to preempt that moment, a position that every angel in service would have given their wings to possess. And so far, she'd wasted it. Again and again.

And today was no different.

Youth and arrogance in an angel were dangerous. Combined with Talia's wintry beauty, Azrael worried. Worried that her path would lead her to Lucifer and his unholy pursuits. He turned as many souls to confusion as he could, sparing no tricks or disguises to get the job done. Lucifer was lost to any good cause, but Azrael wouldn't lose Talia to the same dead end.

Somehow, he had to get through to her. Before it was too late.

"Enjoying the fine weather, Azrael?"

Azrael halted in mid-stride, a cold chill fluttering at the tips of his wings.

That sunlit-warm voice, melodic with British precision, smooth as the finest silk and as beguiling as a desert mirage. Lucifer. The Fallen One.

Azrael turned his lean frame, storm-dark wings spread like a halo around him as he faced God's most beautiful angel. Pale gold curly hair and sky-blue eyes, his long, sculpted face was all smiles and light. Tall and statuesque in his pure white robes, Lucifer stood with head held high, as if he was out for an evening stroll.

Azrael stiffened at the ghost image of wings that had once stretched up into the skies at Lucifer's back. And the thin white scar stretching across his forehead. Where his fallen halo had burned its afterimage, forever scarring his flawless face.

Oh, Lucifer was still beautiful, charming, deceiving. Dangerous to human and angel alike. His wingless frame betrayed him to most angels, but to humans? He drew in a quick breath. He feared for them.

Azrael didn't pretend to know the mind of God, but it puzzled and disturbed him at Lucifer's unfettered access to the corporeal and ethereal realms as if he'd never fallen. No other fallen angel was able to step foot into the Heavens, but somehow, Lucifer gained access again and again.

"What do you want here?" Azrael demanded, unable to disguise the anger in his voice.

"You seem…on edge, Azrael," Lucifer said with a chuckle. He offered a toothy grin and held out his hands. "Can't a former member of the guard come for a friendly visit?"

Azrael crossed his arms against dove grey robes, unable to hold back a steely glare.

"Nothing about you is friendly, Lucifer. Yours is the way of ruin and you're eager to take as many of us with you as possible."

A smug look lit his pale blue eyes, the grin fading to a smirk as he steepled his fingers and walked toward Azrael.

"I don't deny that the offer to join my rebellion is always on the table," he said in dulcet tones. "But that's a much heavier subject than I had intended on this—" He held out his arms to the streaming clouds and bright sunlight. "On this glorious day."

Azrael felt the scowl twist his features when he realized the reason Lucifer had come. To gloat. He'd come to gloat that two souls had fallen into his hands.

"What will get you on your way faster?" Azrael asked, squinting.

"Haven't you heard?" he said in a mocking voice. "I'm considering Talia for my flock. She's doing some fine work for me already." Lucifer ran his index finger across the white scar on his forehead. "Her joining us—it's all just a formality at this point. Wouldn't you say?" He smiled, motioning at Azrael's wingspan. "Just need to discard those silly wings."

Azrael rushed at Lucifer, grabbing hold of his arms. "You stay away from her—and the rest of them! She's young and she's still learning."

Lucifer's sky-blue gaze turned icy, that dangerous stare boring through Azrael. Maybe it was pride, maybe it was duty, but he refused to look away. He was a seasoned soldier, wielding death in one hand and life in the other. He wouldn't be intimated by the likes of Lucifer who chose to give up a place at God's left hand for a misguided campaign to capture the throne. From the one who made him.

Arrogant and impatient to the very end, Lucifer would never stop until he or his creator was destroyed.

But trying to sway lesser angels? A new low even for Lucifer.

Lucifer shoved Azrael backward as the sky darkened, puffy white clouds rising into thunderheads.

"I recognize that reckless youth, Azrael. I lived it. She recognizes the power in her hands. The glory we could all have if we rise against these little godlings and take our rightful place." Lucifer clenched his hands into fists. "The promised place at His side—before He made the others. His *children*."

He nearly spat the word children as he thumped his fist against his chest.

"You're deluded," Azrael said with a growl.

"*We* were His children! And He relegated us to servants. To serve those spoiled, self-serving beasts that will one day command us."

Azrael shook his head. "They're children, Lucifer! Needing our protection and our guidance. All His Hopes rest in them. To fill the void. We aren't their servants—we're their teachers. And we'll walk among them one day. Not beneath them. Beside them."

Lucifer let out a cackle that ruffled Azrael's wing feathers and raked his spine.

"Beside them—you're the one deluded, Azrael! You, of all the angels, must see their unworthiness. Why even your own charge, Talia is sickened by their presence. They're unworthy inheritors."

Azrael glared at him, hands on his hips. Anger trembled through him, into his wings that flapped against the cooling air.

"Talia is tired of their senseless deaths. Her faith is firmly in God and His Chosen."

The darkness lifted from Lucifer's face, the thunderheads rolling into softer shades of grey as the sky quieted.

"Are you ready to prove that statement, Azrael?" Lucifer asked in a soft voice as he propped his hands on his hips.

"My angels are above reproach, including Talia."

"Care to test that statement in a friendly little wager?"

Azrael's eyes narrowed. "What wager?"

Lucifer gestured as he paced the grass, his sandals swishing against the thickness.

"Oh, nothing too taxing for spiteful little Talia—just saving a soul or two." He steepled his fingers again. "In seven days."

Azrael inhaled sharply, his stomach twisting. He'd given Talia twenty-one days to save a drug-addicted woman from an untimely death and it ended in a gun battle and two deaths.

"What's the matter, Azrael?" he said with a grin. "If your master could create the world in seven days, surely your finest angel of death could save two souls in that time?" He laughed, the sound like broken glass. "It's not like she has to save them from dying. Just keep them from me, that's all."

Talia had been unpredictable for some time. Azrael rubbed a hand across his chin. He'd been trying to speak with her for days, but she'd blocked his attempts, avoided him. Talia needed to save herself before she dared meddle in human affairs again.

"So, the rumors are true," Lucifer said, letting out a hiss of breath. "There *is* dissent in the ranks. And you've lost your authority over the guard. Unlike Samael and his guard."

"You're mad, Lucifer! You always have been."

Archangel Samael was incompetent at best, but his death angels' guard was talented in spite of its leader.

"If everything is fine, then my wager shouldn't alarm you."

Azrael shook his head. "Why are you so insistent?"

"Because I'm bored, Azrael." He slid his hands behind his back, white robes fluttering. "And I'd love the bragging rights. A morale boost to my own followers." He laughed. "You're scared. Admit it. Your guard isn't what it once was, Azrael. The younger angels are no longer following." He stood straighter, taller. "They're looking for new leadership."

Azrael felt fire burn at the tips of his fingers. If only he could smite this wretch. But that task was reserved for God's Destroyer, Abaddon.

"What are the conditions, Lucifer?"

That smug look slid onto Lucifer's long face and Azrael fought down the urge to smite him. A waste of fire, he knew, but the childish urge hovered there just the same.

"Terms," said Lucifer, still grinning, his eyes glowing with amusement. "No angelic means. She must save two souls in human form. In human fashion." He chuckled. "I turn them all the time in human form. Surely one of your finest could do no less."

"Seven days in our time?" Azrael asked through gritted teeth. "That's about seven weeks in Earth time."

Lucifer waved a hand at him. "Whatever. Seven of our days then." He laughed again, drowning out the soft sound of wind. "I'll even let you pick the first soul."

"What about the second soul?"

Lucifer grinned. "My pick, dear Azrael. I think you already knew the answer to that question." He turned away. "And you'll say nothing of the wager to Talia or it's forfeit. She'll decide what side she's on by the end of this, I assure you."

"What do you get out of this, you snake?" Azrael shouted.

"Bragging rights, my friend. Bragging rights."

And then he was gone in a rush of smoke and the sweet smell of honeysuckle returned to the air.

Azrael felt rage burn through him, more at himself than Lucifer. He'd let that serpent trick him into a wager for Talia's future. And like a prideful fool, he'd fallen for it. Somehow, he had to outwit Lucifer at his own game.

For Talia's sake, he had to outmaneuver the Prince of Darkness.

The rest of the story continues...
A Game of Lost Souls, Book Two:
THE CINDERELLA HOUR

NOVELS BY LISA SILVERTHORNE

Standalones:
ISABEL'S TEARS
LANDFALL
PACIFIC BLUE TATTOO
BEAUTY: CAPTURED AND FRAMED

A Game of Lost Souls series:
THE CINDERELLA HOUR
THE PRINCE CHARMING HOUR
THE EVER AFTER HOUR
THE FALLEN HEARTS SEASON
THE RISING SPIRITS SEASON
THE ETERNAL SOULS SEASON
THE ROYAL WEDDING HOUR
THE HEAVENLY HONEYMOON HOUR
THE DIVINE NEWLYWEDS SHOW
THE CELESTIAL COUPLES SHOW
THE ENOCHIAN APOCALYPSE SHOW

The Spiral series:
BETWEEN
REPRISE

SHORT STORY COLLECTIONS
THE SOUND OF ANGELS
THE MAGIC OF ORDINARY THINGS
TIMELESS

SCIENCE FICTION WRITING AS **L.S. SILVERTHORNE**

Standalones:

REDISCOVERY

Experiencing True Purple series:

RECOMBINANT, Book 1

HELIX, Book 2

SPLICE, Book 3

COMING SOON!

A Game of Lost Souls series:

The Angelic Anniversary Hour, Book Twelve

The Perdition Picture Show, Book Thirteen

The Spiral series:

A DARK DYSTOPIAN ROMANTIC FANTASY SERIES

Avenge, Book 3 (10/29/23)

Ruin, Book 4

Descent, Book 5

The Resurrectionist Papers:

A ROMANTIC FANTASY MYSTERY SERIES

Grave Reckoning, Book 1

Corpses Delicti, Book 2

Stiffed Again, Book 3

SCIENCE FICTION WRITING AS **L.S. SILVERTHORNE**

Experiencing True Purple series:

A GENETIC ENGINEERING ALIEN INVASION MILITARY **SF** WAR SAGA

Cipher, Book 4

Renascence, Book 5

About the Author

LISA SILVERTHORNE, an award-winning author, has published over 20 novels and 150 short stories and novelettes in many genres. She is the author of *A Game of Lost Souls* series, *Experiencing True Purple* series, *The Spiral*, and the new series, *The Resurrectionist Papers*. She lives in Las Vegas, Nevada.

Before you go, you are invited to please leave a **review of this book**!

Reviews are a wonderful way to help an author. They are also an exciting opportunity to share your honest thoughts with other readers, so **please post yours,** in as many places as possible!

Thanks for reading! We appreciate your support!

f facebook.com / lisa.silverthorne.writer

X x.com / lisasilverthorn

BB bookbub.com / profile / lisa-silverthorne

a amazon.com / stores / author / B08HHZ9D1F#author-footer-B08HHZ9D1F

♪ tiktok.com / @lisasilverthorne